Praise for *Purgatory Chasm*

Named *RT Book Review*'s Best First Myst[ery]

"Conway Sax is a has-been racing driver, an ace auto mechanic, a recovering alcoholic, and a refreshing new character solving hardcore crimes. . . . Non-racing and non-car fans will appreciate [Ulfelder's] hero as well as his crisp plotting, hard-boiled style, and realistic dialogue. In his debut novel, Ulfelder deftly solves a mystery, and explores how family ties are established and what they mean."
—Associated Press

"The redemption that every flawed person tries to find in life enhances the complex plot that percolates in former journalist Steve Ulfelder's exciting mystery fiction debut. And *Purgatory Chasm* is certainly loaded with myriad flawed characters and their avenues to redemption, starting with Conway Sax. . . . *Purgatory Chasm* moves at a brisk clip as Ulfelder smoothly steers his plot from one hairpin twist to the next. . . . Ulfelder brings a gritty, uncompromising view to his hard-boiled debut. At the same time, the author makes Conway both tough and vulnerable, a man who has made too many mistakes in his life and, unfortunately, will make even more. *Purgatory Chasm* is a superb beginning for an author who shows much promise." —*Sun-Sentinel* (South Florida)

"Ulfelder's debut combines elements of the thriller with tales of tangled families. Violence runs through the novel, but Ulfelder tempers it with compassion—and evocative prose. *Purgatory Chasm* may be hard-boiled, but it's heart-wrenching, too."
—*Richmond Times-Dispatch* (Virginia)

"A gritty razor-sharp new voice in crime fiction."
—*The Keene Sentinel* (New Hampshire)

"Working throughout is the edgy, self-effacing voice of a flawed main character, a good guy with plenty of baggage who's just trying [to] stay alive and to get it right this time." —*The Boston Globe*

"A promising debut . . . with one of the funniest, punchiest, most memorable—and for this paper unprintable—first sentences in recent murder mysteries." —*MetroWest Daily News* (Massachusetts)

"A surprising and satifying hard-boiled crime novel, the author's first, and both grimly realistic and exciting . . . If the author can sustain this level of invention and vivid writing, this is a great career a-borning." —*Sullivan County Democrat* (New York)

"Ulfelder couples precise, evocative prose with an original private investigator in his compelling hard-boiled debut. . . . Ulfelder smoothly navigates the many plot twists, and effortlessly introduces wrinkles in his protagonist's backstory that enhance the character. Fans of Michael Koryta's PI crime novels will find a lot to like." —*Publishers Weekly* (starred review)

"Conway is one of those tough but tender, emotionally damaged protagonists that calls out to certain mystery readers. . . . Ulfelder's first novel gets a thumbs up." —*Booklist*

"Steve Ulfelder's debut novel weaves a gritty tale of justice and redemption." —*The Herald News* (Massachusetts)

"This outstanding debut by a former journalist and racing enthusiast is gritty and fast paced, with an intriguing plot and believable characters. Ulfelder has introduced a solid new protagonist, and the many race car anecdotes add to the novel's allure. It will appeal strongly to readers of Loren D. Estleman and Ross Macdonald and those who enjoy hard-boiled detective mysteries." —*Library Journal* (starred review)

A THOMAS DUNNE BOOK FOR MINOTAUR BOOKS.
An imprint of St. Martin's Publishing Group.

PURGATORY CHASM. Copyright © 2011 by Steve Ulfelder. All rights reserved. Printed in the United States of America. For information, address St. Martin's Press, 175 Fifth Avenue, New York, N.Y. 10010.

www.thomasdunnebooks.com
www.minotaurbooks.com

The Library of Congress has cataloged the hardcover edition as follows:

Ulfelder, Steve.
    Purgatory chasm : a mystery / Steve Ulfelder.—1st ed.
        p. cm.
    "A Thomas Dunne book."
    ISBN 978-0-312-67292-8
    1. Automobile mechanics—Fiction. 2. Murder—Investigation—Fiction.
    3. Alcoholics—Fiction. I. Title.
    PS3621.L435P87 2011
    813'.6—dc22

                                                          2011001265

ISBN 978-1-250-00702-5 (trade paperback)

First Minotaur Books Paperback Edition: April 2012

10 9 8 7 6 5 4 3 2 1

For Martha, with love

ACKNOWLEDGMENTS

My family's encouragement never wavered. Peerless agent Janet Reid, like everybody at FinePrint Literary Management, toils on my behalf even when I forget to send whiskey and chocolate. Anne Bensson and the entire editorial, production, and design teams at Thomas Dunne Books made the novel better. So did friends from Mystery Writers of America, Sisters in Crime, and several writers' groups.

Finally, I thank the gang at Flatout Motorsports for giving me the time and space I needed, even if they had an ulterior motive: keeping me away from wrenches is a wise business move.

Purgatory Chasm

CHAPTER ONE

There are drunken assholes, and there are assholes who are drunks. Take a drunken asshole and stick him in AA five or ten years, maybe you come out with a decent guy.

Now take an asshole who's a drunk. Put him in AA as long as you like. Send him to a thousand meetings a year, have him join the Peace Corps for good measure. What you come out with is a sober asshole.

Tander Phigg was a sober asshole.

I was thinking this while he bought me lunch at a diner in Rourke, New Hampshire, just across the Massachusetts border. From the outside, it looked like one of those small-town diners people wish were still around—plate-glass windows, fifties-style brushed-aluminum letters that spelled DOT'S PLACE, turquoise tiles surrounding the door.

But once you got inside you stopped pining. It smelled and felt like fifty years' worth of grease had coated the floor, the walls, the vinyl stools, even the black-and-white pictures of locals and the deer they'd killed. The food was bad, too.

Sitting across from me in a booth, Tander Phigg gave me an eyeful of some of it while he chewed—an egg-salad sandwich. He was pushing seventy-five and getting heavy. His belly pressed Formica through a yellow polo shirt with the collar flipped up. He had a red nose that twenty-plus years of sobriety couldn't get rid of, snow-white hair that was too long for a man his age. He'd always worn it that way. You got the feeling somebody once told him he had a great head of hair, and he believed them.

There were other things: The hair was a little too greasy, and Phigg's eyes had gone greedy when he looked at the menu, and there was a smell to him he hadn't quite masked with Old Spice.

Tander Phigg was desperate.

I'd never liked him, hadn't wanted to drive an hour to meet him. But I shut up and ate my burger and listened anyway.

Tander Phigg was an asshole, but he was also a Barnburner. Barnburners saved my life. I help them when I can. No exceptions.

"So what do you think?" Phigg said. "You going to let these crooks hold your baby hostage?"

"*My* baby?"

"Hey, you were always talking about how she was ahead of her time, all the technology packed inside her."

"Here's what I liked about that car," I said. "The technology you're bragging on was always screwed up. *It* kept me busy, made me money." I hit the *it* extra hard. I hate when people talk about cars like they're women or babies. A street car's a tool. A race car's a weapon. When they break, I fix them. There's not much more to it.

Phigg's baby, his *her,* was a 1980 Mercedes-Benz 450SEL 6.9. Nice car, ahead of its time. It had the first antilock braking system I ever saw, a suspension you could adjust from the driver's seat, and a bunch of other fancy features.

But the fancy stuff broke—all the time. Those 450SELs made techs like me a lot of dough, even when they were brand new. And by '99, when Phigg bought one with 140,000 miles on the clock, it was an ass-dragging smoker. I went through each system at least once. I'd been happy to do it as long as his checks cleared.

Which they didn't always anymore, according to the Barnburner grapevine.

"I *had* to fix her," Phigg said. "With a car like that, a classic, I didn't see myself as the owner. I was more of a caretaker."

I rolled my eyes, wiped my mouth, dropped my napkin on the plate.

Phigg's eyes darted to the plate. He made a lightning grab for three fries, chewed. "How about it?"

Hell. He was a Barnburner. "How long they had it?" I said.

"Going on eighteen months, for chrissake."

That did seem like a long time, unless there was something else Phigg wasn't telling me. "How far have they gotten with the work?"

"I went by last week. They've done *nothing*, Conway. They parked her by a back wall and threw a tarp over her."

"Why'd they say it's taking so long?"

"Blah blah this, blah blah that, parts from Germany, other customers ahead of me."

"That's bullshit," I said. "They ought to've taken it apart by now, put it on a rotisserie. Or given you a good reason why not."

"So you'll take a look?"

"Where's the shop?"

"Two blocks back."

"On Mechanic Street," I said.

"How'd you know?"

"Every town has one."

The waitress came by, coffeepot poised. I flat-handed a *no-thanks*. Phigg ignored her until she left, then leaned in. "I want my car and my money back," he said. "I can drive it around a few more years before I fix the rust. Hell, maybe I'll sell it as is."

"What money back?"

His face went the same color as his nose. "They wanted some dough to get started."

"That was stupid and you know it," I said. "How much?"

"The way the guy explained it, it's like when a contractor gets money up front."

"How much?"

"Thirty-five hundred." Phigg fingered his yellow collar, ran the back of a hand across his mouth.

I took a breath, let it out. "Stupid."

"You'll help me?"

"I'll talk to them. Not today, though. Busy."

He smiled, rapped the table twice, reached to touch my forearm.

I pulled it back.

He wrote the name of the shop and his phone number and address on a corner of his paper place mat, tore it off, handed it to me, said thanks, split. He was in a hurry to get out the door before the waitress made it over with the check.

Asshole.

I wanted a peek at the shop before I headed home. I hadn't lied to Phigg: Every town does have a Mechanic Street, and they're all the same. They run perpendicular to the main drag in whatever part of town was lousy when the town was born. More often than not they dead-end at railroad tracks, as this street did. Before I U-turned at the tracks, I passed an off-brand transmission shop, a generic diesel station with a propane-refill cage, and a place called Santo's Custom Interior where a Mexican and a pit bull chained to the Mexican's chair stared at me.

I cruised past the place that was ripping off Phigg. It had been high-end once. The building was a former barn, thirty feet across and deep. It had two roll-up doors and a simple sign: DAS MOTOREN-WERK.

One of the roll-up doors was open. I saw a two-post lift with an Audi A4 up high, its engine oil draining into a long funnel stuck in a drum.

I'm a grease monkey myself—I've worked at dealerships, run a shop of my own, even been part of the NASCAR traveling circus—so I could see Das Motorenwerk wasn't breaking any records. For starters, there was no little group of customer cars outside. One lousy oil change was the day's workload.

The Dumpster at the side of the barn was overflowing, which meant the shop had saved a few bucks by switching from an every-two-weeks Dumpster service to monthly. Next to the Dumpster stood a triple stack of used tires with weeds growing through. It costs money to get rid of tires, and God help you if you're caught sneaking them into the Dumpster.

I put my F-150 in reverse, backed to the upholstery shop. As I neared, the pit bull went crazy. Without looking at the dog, the Mexican hit its nose with a closed fist. The dog shut up.

I leaned, rolled down the passenger window. "I'm a tech looking for work," I said. "Heard Motorenwerk was a good outfit, but the shop looks pretty tired. Know anything about it?"

He looked at me fifteen seconds and said, "Where the fuck you hear that?"

I'd wanted him to ask. Pretended to hesitate. "The guy who told me, he's been away awhile."

The Mexican smiled, rose, hitched his khakis, came to my window. The pit bull whined. Up close the Mexican looked older. Had a tear tattooed at the outside corner and just below one eye. He said, "State time?"

Another fake pause. "Walpole."

"You on paper?"

"Eleven months to go," I said. "How about the shop? They any good?"

"Used to be. Now . . ." He fluttered a hand, stopped in mid-flutter, narrowed his eyes. "State time down in Mass. Mass. license plate. So why you looking for work up here?"

"I live in Townsend, ten minutes away, so my PO said I can work in New Hampshire." I took off before he could ask more questions. Or unchain the pit bull.

I'd lied. I didn't live in Townsend. Lived in Framingham, Massachusetts. Or Shrewsbury, a couple towns west. Or both. I wasn't sure, and that was a problem.

I headed for Framingham, thought about Tander Phigg while I drove.

He'd been sober forever, was already a Barnburner old-timer when I showed up ten-plus years ago. I'd looked up to him for a while, the way new fish always look up to old-timers. Hell, he'd even been my sponsor for six months.

But the more I hung around, the less I liked him. The stories he told at AA meetings changed as years passed. What had been arguments became bar fights. What had been funny DUI stories that ended with Phigg in the drunk tank became *COPS*-style megachases, half the cruisers in Worcester County hound-dogging Phigg.

Like that.

As I exited Route 495 I set aside my dislike and focused on the interesting development: Tander Phigg smelled broke. Back when I'd worked on his Mercedes, he was a cost-no-object guy—and happy to tell you about it. He'd moved to New Hampshire to escape Taxachusetts and build his timber-frame dream house on a river. For a while, he'd bored us all half to death with artist's renderings and blueprints.

Now he was a man who seemed itchy to get thirty-five hundred bucks out of a car-repair place. And as I thought about it, I realized it'd been a long time since he'd bragged about his big house at the Barnburner meeting-after-the-meeting.

I sobered up a long time ago. I'll never know why: People talk about hitting bottom, but what's the bottom? I'd crashed through a dozen.

Whatever the reason, I woke up one day in the dry-out wing of a Brockton, Massachusetts, VA hospital—a clerk's mistake; I'm not a veteran—and grabbed the tired mattress with both hands and white-knuckled my way through the worst of the DTs. When they figured out I shouldn't be in the VA hospital and bounced me, I wound up in Framingham. Salvation Army cot, day-labor gigs, food-pantry hand-outs.

What you have to learn for yourself is that each AA meeting has its own character. Some groups—in Framingham, a town full of halfway houses and methadone clinics, a *lot* of groups—go through the motions so attendees can get their parole cards signed. Others wheeze along for the benefit of a half dozen old-timers. Some groups give you the hairy eyeball if you bring up drugs. Some are cliquey as hell. All you can do is stick with it, try meetings until you find the right fit.

It took me three months. My knees were bruised from praying. My knuckles were death-grip white. I was tipping, getting set to backslide, feeling ashamed of the next inevitable relapse, when I hitched a ride to a Barnburner meeting.

As soon as I stepped into the basement at Saint Anne's, everything changed. I knew I was in the right place. Didn't know *how* I knew—still don't—but I knew.

Three people shook my hand. A biker with a cobweb tattooed on his neck took one look at me, knew I didn't have a buck for a raffle ticket, and gave me one on the house. When I made my way to the coffee table and started throwing back Dunkin' Munchkins like they were dinner (they were; it was February, a slow month for day labor), people pretended not to notice, and an old-timer who turned out to be Mary Giarusso disappeared into a back room and came out with another box.

As soon as I sat on a folding chair, I figured out the Barnburners' core. The key players sat at the left front, kitty-corner, where they could see the speaker while keeping an eye on the rest of the room.

Charlene wasn't there yet—she came along later—but most of them were. Mary Giarusso took a seat. Butch Feeley, who was seventy then and beefy, sat near the center like the group's Godfather (he was), arms folded, legs stretched, ankles crossed, a lieutenant whispering in each ear. One of the lieutenants was Chester Bagley, who didn't yet wear a toupee but did have a horrendous comb-over. The other was a mean-looking South American dude—Colombian, I found out later—who wouldn't even speak to you until you were sober a year.

Tander Phigg was in that front corner, of course. Hair already white, vinyl jacket with a Porsche logo, Rolex Daytona slopping around on his wrist. He was telling a Commander McBragg story to a shaved-head black guy who looked like he wished he'd picked a different seat.

There they sat, nine or ten altogether, giving off a parole-board vibe I hadn't yet seen in a meeting. The vibe said this was serious AA for serious people. No tools, posers, or dilettantes need apply.

I wanted in. Hung around after the meeting, putting chairs away and checking out the parole board, who were in no hurry to leave. Aware of me, they hemmed and hawed and made small talk. Finally the cobweb-tattoo guy took my arm. "See you next week, pal?"

"Well," I said, glancing at the front of the room.

"That's the meeting-after-the-meeting, pal," he said, gently aiming me at the door. "You're not ready for that. No way, no how."

I hit my house just before twelve and saw Randall Swale in the driveway staring at a pile of decking. The wood delivery was the reason I'd made the Phigg meeting a very early lunch deal: In this neighborhood, anything we didn't screw down today would be stolen tonight.

A friend had left me the house. He'd died badly. I made sure the guys responsible did the same. I was spending a lot of time there, rehabbing the place so I could sell it. Needed the cash: My last job at a Pontiac-GMC dealership hadn't worked out, and I'd sworn off working for anybody but myself. The idea was to flip the house and use the dough to start another shop of my own.

It's an old four-square colonial on a quarter acre, south side of Framingham. For years the neighborhood had been mostly Brazilian, but the Brazilians were moving out because the feds were busting illegals. That was a bad deal for the neighborhood. Brazilians liked to get drunk and fight each other with knives on Saturday night, but otherwise they mostly worked their asses off and minded their own business. And as the houses emptied of Brazilians, they either went to Section 8 tenants or became squats for bums and junkies.

The guy who left me the house, and his mother before him, had lived here sixty years. Everything needed work, especially the in-law apartment on the top floor: I couldn't sell the place until I brought the place up to code. I was nibbling away at the work. Sometimes I slept here. Sometimes I slept at my girlfriend Charlene's place in Shrewsbury.

I stuffed my truck at the foot of the driveway and climbed out. Randall wore work boots, khakis, no shirt. He worked shirtless a lot in this freak mid-June heat wave. His skin had started UPS-brown and had gone purple-black in the sun. He's half a foot shorter than me and has half a pound of fat on him. Earned his muscles in the army, not the gym. His father, Luther, my parole officer, introduced us. Randall had standing offers, some with full-boat academic scholarships, from a half dozen good schools. I didn't know why he was still hanging around with me; the nearest I'd ever been to college was a transmission swap I did for the dean of Framingham State.

Heat wave or no, Randall always wore long pants. He'd lost his right foot to mid-calf in Iraq and wore a prosthetic with a cool ceramic-and-titanium ankle joint. You'd never guess he had a leg and a half—especially if you challenged him to a footrace.

He swept a hand. "What in God's name is this?"

"Lumber for the deck," I said. "Ordered twelve hundred linear feet. Looks about right."

"You call this *lumber*?" He picked up an eight-footer, sighted down it at me. "I'll never claim to be an expert, but this isn't Home Depot decking. This is serious, tight-grained hardwood, and the truck that delivered it had a fancy specialty-shop logo."

My face went red as he spoke. I knew where we were headed. I said, "Ipe."

"Ee-pay?" he said. "Are you speaking Pig Latin now?"

I spelled it, pronounced it again. "It's a Brazilian hardwood. Good stuff, lasts forever."

"Cost?"

I shrugged.

Randall shook his head, bent, picked up more ipe, headed for the back of the house. I scooped ipe and followed. "The plan was bring this place up to code, pretty it up a little, and sell it fast," he said. "Remember?"

We stepped through the skeleton of the new deck we'd built off the kitchen. I said, "In case I wind up renting the place instead of selling, the ipe'll save me money in the long run. No maintenance, no splits."

"You can barely say that with a straight face," he said. "What about blowing out that kitchen wall? What about the fancy tile in the bathroom? What about pulling the perfectly decent vinyl siding?" He finger-ticked as he spoke.

I said nothing.

We went around front for more wood.

"You keep finding excuses not to finish up and sell," Randall said. "And the neighborhood's going downhill fast, so every nickel you spend is a nickel lost."

We stacked a half dozen twelve-footers and each took an end. I walked backward and said, "Nothing wrong with doing a job right."

"Nonsense." Randall's voice was soft now.

I said nothing.

Randall said, "Ask yourself what's really going on, Conway. And be honest, okay?"

"I'll get the chop saw."

Five hours later we stood sweating on ipe. I held a water. Randall held a beer.

"Nice," I said. "Small, but a good selling point. You think?"

"Sure."

"'Preciate the help. You take off. I'll clean up, put a coat of oil on it tomorrow."

He toasted me, finished his beer, set the empty next to the kitchen door, grabbed his T-shirt. On his way past he set a hand on my shoulder. "Ask," Randall said, "and be honest."

My jaw felt tight. I nodded.

I swept, policed up screws we'd dropped, stacked leftover ipe in the one-car detached garage we planned to tear down soon. Although lately I'd been rethinking that: It'd make a nice workshop. For someone.

I brought the chop saw and cordless drills into the kitchen. I didn't dare leave them in the garage, with its rotted door. The way this neighborhood was going, they'd be stolen and traded for meth before the eleven-o'clock news.

I drank another water. Talked to my cats, Dale and Davey. Thought about dinner.

Thought about Charlene. I should call.

I texted instead: *Wrking on deck, will stay here 2nite, xoxo*.

She texted back: *K*.

I stared at the letter.

I'd been pushing Charlene away for a while.

It was working.

Shit.

I looked at Dale. "We like it here," I said. "Right?"

Both cats stared.

CHAPTER TWO

The next morning, a Tuesday, at nine, I parked across from Das Motorenwerk and crossed the street. Out front was parked a BMW 2002tii, one of the last ones they made. It was rotting from the rockers up, the way those cars do.

Through the open roll-up doors I saw two cars on lifts, a newish Mercedes SUV and an Acura Legend. The Acura told me a lot. Snooty German garages don't work on Japanese cars unless they're in deep shit. A few years back, when I had my own shop, I'd been forced to bite that bullet myself. It was Charlene's idea. The move had worked, business had grown. Then a jerk I'd hired out of pity had torched the shop.

I stepped inside the garage, knowing I'd learn more there than in the office, and looked around.

In a back corner I saw what had to be Phigg's car beneath a dust-cover. I started toward it but stopped under the Mercedes SUV. They were doing a soup-to-nuts brake job. On a two-year-old truck? I spotted the old brake pads and rotors on a rolling cart, picked up a pair of front pads. They were only two-thirds gone.

The garage held some expensive restoration tools: an English wheel and metal brake for bodywork and fabrication, a small paint booth, a bead-blasting cabinet. But all that good stuff looked un-used, tucked away, shoved in corners. This used to be a serious auto-motive shop. Now it was doing yawn-city maintenance. Why?

"Help you?" The bathroom door closed and a voice rose. Work boots squeaked toward me. "Sir, please don't stand under the lift!"

I turned. He was a young guy, short, with red wire-brush hair and pale green eyes that were bugging with anger.

I stepped from beneath the SUV, knowing how the kid felt. No tech likes civilians in the shop, let alone dicking around under the lift.

I held up the brake pads. "I'm guessing here," I said. "The cus-tomer's a lady, probably a mom with young kids. She came in and said her brakes felt funny."

The kid folded his arms. From the way his lips thinned I knew I was on to something.

"So your boss looked her in the eye," I said, "and told her brakes aren't something to gamble with. Now you're nicking her for all four corners, rotors and all. I'll say . . . eleven hundred, eleven-fifty?"

His face had gone the same color as his hair. "What the heck do you want, mister?"

"Was I close?"

Long pause. "Fourteen hundred," he finally said. "The parts for these German cars, you wouldn't believe it. Besides, the dealership wanted seventeen hundred. Can I *help* you?"

The way he looked at me made my shoulder blades tense, and I wasn't sure why—if I had to, I could pick him up with one hand and body-slam him. But there was something at work behind his eyes, an ice-cold evaluation, that tweaked me.

I pointed at the office. "Boss in there?"

The kid nodded and wiped his hands as I walked away. I felt his stare. My shoulder blades didn't unclench until I was through the door.

In the office, the boss stood behind a counter and tried to sell

work to a tall thin man. I listened as I eyeballed the usual ASE certi-
fication plaques, photos of the Little League team the shop sponsored, and Chamber of Commerce testimonials. The thin man owned
the 2002 out front and didn't look like anybody's sucker. His frozen
smile told me he wouldn't let this shop touch his car. He was waiting
for a pause so he could leave without being rude.

But the boss knew all this too, and he wasn't giving the thin man
a pause to leave on. On the other hand, he wasn't pitching real hard.
He should've had the prospect out in the shop, showing off the spray
booth and the English wheel. Instead, he was going through the motions.

In four minutes the thin man stopped being polite. He said he'd
take a business card and call later, then walked out.

I stepped to the counter, elbow-leaned, shook my head. "Selling
the job," I said. "It's always the hardest part, huh?"

"Right you are, friend, right you are." He looked past me through
the plate-glass window, wondering what I'd driven up in, whether I
was another prospect. If he stood five-six he was lucky. He was bald
on top with a ring of black-running-gray hair. Above the pocket of
his light-brown work shirt: MOTORENWERK and Ollie.

In maybe three seconds, he figured out the F-150 was mine and
realized I wasn't a potential customer. His eyes shut down. "Help
you?"

"Tander Phigg's 450SEL," I said, nodding toward the shop. "The
one you've got covered in the corner."

The eyes went hard. "What about it?"

"He wants it back."

Ollie reared back, laughed hard, clapped his hands a couple times.
Later I wondered if it was a signal, or maybe a distraction while he
hit a panic button.

Ollie's laugh slowed. He wiped an eye. I said, "Wants his thirty-
five hundred bucks, too."

Ollie loved that. He slapped one hand on the counter, braced himself with the other on his thigh. He was laughing too hard to stand up straight, saying "thirty-five hundred!" over and over like a punch line.

The laughter was contagious: It made me smile even while I wondered what the hell was going on. I watched Ollie, waited for him to catch his breath so I could get the real story.

I felt an air-whoosh as the door behind me opened. Ollie cut his eyes toward the door. I started to turn.

Too late. Something busted my head open. I watched the floor come up at my face. The flooring was antique oak. Good stuff.

I woke up on my left side, scrabbling away from a roar, then finding my back against something hard. I felt a pulsing ache that was like biting down on tinfoil—but in my head.

I creaked an eye open and reached behind me, figuring things out. The roar was a train, a long CSX freight, forty feet dead ahead.

I squinted at my old workhorse Seiko diver's watch. It was going on ten. I'd been out fifteen minutes or less. The hardness behind me was a Dumpster.

Connection: I was at the end of Mechanic Street, a few lots west of Motorenwerk.

I blinked, shook my head to clear it. Saw the Mexican from the upholstery shop. He was maybe ten feet away with his back to me. Had his hands splayed on his hips while he took a piss and watched the train.

His pit bull was licking blood from my head.

The train passed. The Mexican zipped up. I started to put my right hand to my head wound, but the pit bull growled and got low. The Mexican turned. "He like you better when you out cold," he said. "Think I do, too."

I said, "Willya?"

He whistled. The pit bull backed off but stayed low. I sat, got a head rush, closed my eyes, let it pass. "You didn't do this to me," I said.

The Mexican said nothing.

I said, "You see who did it? Who dragged me here?"

He said nothing.

I swiveled left. My neck felt like somebody'd poured sand between the joints. "How bad is it?"

"Pretty bad," he said. "I looked while you out. Nothing busted, I think. Lump like this, though." He made a fist.

I rose, turned, got both hands on the rim of the Dumpster to steady myself. Felt okay for a few seconds. Then the heat-wave trash stench came at me, and I lobbed puke into the Dumpster. Then again.

I took deep breaths and looked at my truck, seventy yards away. I could make that. Took two steps, still holding the Dumpster.

Behind me the Mexican said, "Hey." Then I heard soft sounds in the weeds next to me and looked down. He'd tossed my wallet, phone, and keys. I stooped for them.

As I straightened I said, "You leave my plastic in the wallet?"

"Fuck yes," the Mexican said. "I got no taste for ID theft. 'Sides, you don't look like you got much of a credit limit."

I waved to thank him. Criminal etiquette: He was within his rights to rob me, and we both knew he'd done me a favor by not throwing my stuff over the tracks. It was the only break I'd gotten so far on Mechanic Street.

I wobbled toward the F-150. As I passed Motorenwerk I stared in the plate-glass office window. Ollie was gone. In the garage, the redheaded kid was lowering the Mercedes SUV. He looked at me from the corner of his eye, pretended not to see me. I decided that when I came back, I'd start with the kid—creepy or not, he was the weak link.

And I would come back.

As I neared my truck I saw they'd slashed all four tires and busted out the side and rear windows. "Windshield's good," I said out loud. "My lucky day."

I opened the door, brushed safety glass from the bench seat, climbed in, and fired it while I thought. There were a dozen people I could call for a lift, but any of them would have to piss away their day coming up.

I sighed. Tander Phigg. He lived nearby and deserved to see his day pissed away after what he'd sucked me into.

I called. Voice mail. Like anybody in hock, Phigg was screening his calls. I needed to leave a message that would bring him quick. "Good news on your car," I said. "Get over here to Motorenwerk before Ollie changes his mind." Click.

By the time Phigg rattled up in a shitbox '92 Sentra, I'd talked the redheaded kid into helping me. His name was Josh Whipple. He wouldn't look me in the eye. I didn't ask him who'd cold-cocked me. Gain trust now, ask questions later. We used two floor jacks to trundle my truck to a lift. That way I didn't have to pay for a flatbed to haul it to a tire shop.

Phigg popped from his car with hope on his face. As he looked at me, my truck, and the back corner where his Mercedes sat covered, the hope faded. "I got your message," he said. "Good news on my car?"

I rolled him a tire, faced him full, waited for him to spot the lump on my head. He stopped the tire with his foot. "Put the tire in your car," I said. "Looks like we can fit two in the trunk and two in the backseat. What's with the shitbox? Thought you were driving a Jag."

"It's a loaner. Jag's in the shop. What about my Mercedes?"

I stepped toward him and pointed at the lump.

"What happened?" he said.

I jerked a thumb at Josh, who was lugging tires to Phigg's car. "Somebody who works for this kid's boss clocked me." I did a double take as I said it: Even with all the air gone, those tire-and-wheel units had to weigh sixty pounds apiece, and Josh had one tucked under each arm like beach towels.

Phigg fingered his collar. "So you haven't, ah, liberated my Mercedes?"

"I told Ollie you wanted it back," I said. "He laughed in my face. Then somebody creamed me. We're going to buy me new tires now. While we wait you can tell me the truth."

Ten minutes later, we sat with our backs against the shaded side of an Exxon. I'd bought us each a Gatorade. Red for him, yellow for me. I'd also bought a bag of ice. I pressed it to my head and said, "Cost you almost seven hundred with the mount-and-balance and the disposal fee."

"*Me?*" Head-whip.

"You sent me in there with a bullshit story. You didn't tell me Ollie's some kind of hard case. You've heard stories about me, about what I do for people. You thought I was going to walk in and kick the snot out of Ollie, then drive your car out of there whether he liked it or not. I got that about right?"

A semi blatted past on Route 31, downshifting for the speed zone ahead, full load of tree trunks on its flatbed. I smelled pine and diesel.

When the noise died Phigg said, "About right, yes. But . . . you *do* kick the shit out of people. The stories are true. I've seen the aftermath. All the Barnburners have."

Well, he was right about that. "Point is, my fresh tires are on you," I said. "New glass, too."

"I don't have it." Real quiet.

I sipped. "Say again?"

"I don't have any money," he said. "I'm broke, Conway."

"Finally." I looked at him for the first time since I'd sat. "It's obvious you don't have a pot to piss in or a window to throw it out. I can't help you unless you tell me what's really going on."

"I'm broke." I barely heard him over the air compressor inside.

Phigg's face was pale, his eyes flat as he stared at his shitbox Sentra that wasn't a loaner after all.

"You drinking?" I said.

"*Hell* no."

"Cocaine? Prescription drugs?"

"No!"

I wondered what else could burn through the kind of money everybody thought Tander Phigg had. Needed to get him talking.

"Your dad made paper, do I have that right?" I said. "Did okay for himself."

"Phigg Paper Products, Inc. Biggest employer in Fitchburg for thirty years."

"Left you in good shape?"

Phigg half laughed. "Money to burn," he said. "But good shape?" He tried to shrug and laugh again, but his breath hitched. He put up a hand as if to scratch his forehead—he didn't want me to see him cry.

The Exxon guy leaned out the door, hollered my tires were all set.

I paid with the credit card the Mexican hadn't stolen.

Phigg and I were quiet as we loaded tires in his shitbox, drove back to Motorenwerk, and unloaded.

As Phigg got set to drive off I stepped to his window. "Let's meet at eight tomorrow, that diner again. You can tell me what's going on, we'll try this Ollie again."

"Sure." He rattled away, pale, staring straight ahead.

Five minutes later my F-150 was down on its fresh rubber. While Josh torqued the wheels I said, "Where's your Shop-Vac?"

"I vacuumed the glass out of your interior already."

I looked. He had. "Thanks." I stepped to the right side of the truck, away from the office. Josh was finishing the right front wheel. He straightened. I said, "What are you doing here?"

"Working." He looked me in the eye, and my shoulder blades tensed again.

"You know what I mean," I said. "What are you *doing* here? You're fast, you're good, you're ASE certified. You could be pulling sixty an hour at any dealership. Something stinks about this place. Best case, Ollie's set to go belly-up. I think it's worse than that. I think there's some crooked shit going on. You may think you're not part of it, but you are."

"Why are you even talking to me, after what happened in the office?" Josh said. "Why aren't you either talking to the cops or hightailing it home?"

"I'll answer your questions when you answer mine."

He held my eyes. For a few seconds he looked like a nervous kid, and I thought he might tip and talk to me.

"Yoo-hoo!" The voice came from the office. We turned. A mom, maybe thirty, cute, two little kids hiding behind her jeans. She said, "I'm here to pick up my car? The black Mercedes?"

Josh said, "Right with you, ma'am," and walked away fast.

Shit. Almost had him. I would have to come back later.

I climbed into my truck, backed out, and drove to the mouth of Mechanic Street. Phigg had turned left here. A right would take me south, homebound.

I took a left. Why not? Phigg wasn't telling me everything. Thanks to him I had a gashed head and a big-ass credit-card bill coming. I help Barnburners, no questions asked. But not all Barnburners are created equal.

When they saw I was showing up at every meeting and working hard, Barnburners filled me in on the group's backstory. It was launched by outcast bikers, post-WWII GIs who were into vendettas as much as sobriety. They called themselves the Barnstormers because AA National refused to sanction them, and without the sanction they lacked a regular meeting place. For fifteen years they met every Wednesday in people's homes, fields, warehouses, barns.

Over time, the rowdy regulars aged and the Barnstormers matured, but the core remained a group of hard cases with an Old Testament credo. Barnstormers believed in an eye for an eye, and they never turned the other cheek.

One mid-sixties Wednesday, during a meeting at a dairy farm, some joker flipped his cigarette butt the wrong way and burned the host's barn to a cinder. Twist: The host was the town fire chief. Once they realized the barn was a goner and nobody was hurt, everybody (including the chief) laughed their asses off, and the Barnstormers instantly renamed themselves the Barnburners.

Time passed. AA National sanctioned the group. Saint Anne's became the regular meeting spot. But the take-no-shit mentality hung on, boiling down to a kernel called the meeting-after-the-meeting.

It took me six months to earn my way in. I hit Saint Anne's every Wednesday. Got there early, set up chairs, made coffee, doled out raffle tickets. Spoke a couple times a week, driving to Ashland, Upton, Clinton, Hudson with a carload of Barnburners to tell my story. Got my first steady job in five years, working the muck pit at a Jiffy Lube.

The commitment I showed was half the picture. But you needed skills to get into the meeting-after-the-meeting. As I got to know the old-timers, they realized I had skills. Skills I'd picked up in rail yards, alleys, county jails.

One Wednesday, as I finished stowing the little banners we hang on the walls next to the picture of the pope—ONE DAY AT A TIME; LET GO, LET GOD; like that—Butch Feeley said, "Conway."

I turned. Butch had never spoken to me. I didn't think he even knew my name.

"Why don't you stick around?" Butch said, softly kicking the chair next to his.

I was in.

No shoulder-claps, no "welcome to the group," no initiation. I was just there, one of them. Pretty soon I learned why.

"Rosie Fagundes," said Mary Giarusso, glancing at a reporter's notebook. "Brazilian girl, three months sober, sits in back by the long radiator?" Mary had a hellacious Boston accent: *three months sobah, long radiatah.*

"Why's she still sitting in back if she's got three months?" Butch Feeley said. Serious AA for serious people.

"Be that as it may," Mary said. "She waitresses at the Early Bird over on Fay Court. The owner's all right, but the manager knows she's an illegal. He's been helping himself to half her tips right from the get-go, and now he wants to help himself to some blow jobs, too."

Far as I could tell, I was the only one surprised at how easily this woman, who looked like a retired school principal, said "blow jobs." Lesson: A lot of things got talked about in this room, and none of them were dainty.

"Manager's name?" Butch said.

"Oswaldo. He's Brazilian too, but legal."

Butch turned to me. "Want to take this one, Conway?"

Every head turned. Every eye locked.

"Hell yes," I said.

By dinnertime the next day, Rosie had 100 percent of her tips, retroactive. Oswaldo had a busted nose and a dislocated shoulder.

And I had a purpose.

Phigg had a five-minute head start, but there weren't many roads up here. Hell, there weren't many places for roads to go. Rourke became boonies real quick. I saw the occasional ranch house or trailer, sad little vegetable stands, a state forest to my right. To my left I caught glimpses of the Souhegan River, which paralleled the road.

In ten minutes, I came to a crossroads. Straight would continue northeast, a right would pull me southeast, a left would cut back northwest. On pure gut I took the left. This road was a little wider and a little faster, with occasional slow-vehicle lanes for trucks working their way into the White Mountains.

I was passing a semi when I flashed past a Gulf station, so I damn near missed Phigg. As I cleared the semi I cut a glance over my right shoulder—and saw, around the side of the Gulf, a red car that might be an old Sentra.

It took me another couple miles to find a safe turnaround, so it was ten minutes before I eased to the shoulder a hundred yards north of the Gulf. It was a shitty spot: I couldn't even see most of the gas station's side parking area, and if it was Phigg in there and he pulled my way, he'd spot my truck.

But I didn't want to drive past a second time, and if I pulled any closer, I'd draw attention. So I lit up my hazard lights, left the truck, scrambled uphill to a layer of tall pines that shielded me from the road, and walked toward the Gulf until I nailed a view.

And it was a hell of a view.

Phigg's shitbox had its tail to me. Phigg sat in the driver's seat, elbows resting on the sill of his open window, talking with somebody in the next car.

That car, a silver Jetta, was backed into a parking space, making for easy driver-to-driver chat.

Huh.

I sat in pine needles and watched. The sun on the Jetta's windshield made it hard to see the driver, so I focused on Phigg, reading his body language. He seemed tight: He listened more than he talked, made small nods from time to time, checked his rearview mirror a lot.

After five minutes of this, Phigg gave a final big nod and they started their cars. Phigg reached through his window like he wanted a high five or a handshake, but he got nothing and pulled the hand back in.

I gritted my teeth. If Phigg swung north, he'd see my F-150 at the side of the road and any edge I'd just earned would evaporate.

I got lucky: He took a left and drove south.

The Jetta headed north with its window still down, and I got a good look at the driver. A black woman, youngish, with short hair. Huh.

Ninety minutes later I pulled into Charlene's driveway, my stomach tight. With the truck's windows busted out I hadn't bothered to run the AC, so my shirt was sweat-pasted to my back. I saw nobody was home, and my stomach loosened. I tried not to think about why an empty house relaxed me.

It's a Cape Cod–style place in Shrewsbury—not far from Framingham, just east of Worcester. I've dated Charlene Bollinger on and off. We're both divorced. We both have eighteen-year-olds. That turned into a soap opera a while back when my son, Roy, and Charlene's daughter, Jesse, fell in love. For now, Jesse was in Chicago getting help for anorexia. Roy just finished high school out in western Massachusetts, where his mother raised him. He didn't want to commit to college until Jesse came back and graduated. Their plan: Go to the same school. True Love Always.

As the goddamn world turns.

I keyed my way into the air-conditioned house, took my shirt off, tossed it in the laundry hamper on my way to the kitchen, fixed an ice water, looked at the clock.

I smiled. Just past four. Charlene's other daughter, Sophie, would step off the late bus from middle school any minute. Sophie was going on twelve, smart as a whip, funny, my pal.

I thought about calling Charlene. Decided not to. Instead: made sure I'd left the front door unlocked, headed up to shower.

Ten minutes later I came downstairs, followed sound to the big kitchen–family-room combo where we spend all our time. The sound was a *Hogan's Heroes* rerun. Sophie was sofa-splayed, sunburned nose, spray of freckles. Her tank top and her Popsicle were lime green. I looked at the TV for a few seconds. Sophie and I both laughed at Schultz. I said, "My father loved that show." First time I'd thought about my old man in years.

"Was it on when you were a kid?"

"Yeah, but past my bedtime," I said. "Not sure when your mom's coming home."

"By seven. She texted me."

"We should make dinner, have it on the table when she gets here."

"Oh . . . oh my!" Sophie had finally peeled her eyes from the set, had spotted the bump on my head. She sprang up and bounced on the sectional, beckoning me over. "What happened?" she said. "Jeez, it's near your good eye. Can you see all right?"

A few years back, someone tried to put my left eye out. Didn't, but wrecked it. The eye tracks okay, so people don't realize it's useless.

"I'm fine," I said. "How about I tell my story over dinner, so I only have to say it once?"

"Conway Sax, always tight with the words." She smiled as she said it.

When Charlene came home she got to watch Sophie and I finish grilling chicken, peppers, and onions. She kissed Sophie and asked about school. She didn't make eye contact with me.

Not even over dinner, while I told them the whole thing. Charlene was interested—she was a Barnburner and she knew Tander Phigg— but cool. Mad at me.

Sophie was too smart not to notice all this. She filled conversation-space, kept everything smooth. It was her default role, always had been. I felt bad for her. I wanted to say *Knock it off; let your mother be mad at me,* but that would make everything worse.

I was bad at families.

Later, as the dishwasher ran, Charlene and I drank seltzer on the deck. She watched me scrape clean the grill. The day's heat faded quickly; we switched off the AC, opened the sliding-glass doors.

"You're mad because I slept in Framingham last night," I said.

Charlene sipped, looked over her small backyard. Everything was full-throttle green, the chain-link fence to the back neighbor's yard barely visible. She said, "It's a symptom."

"Symptom." I scraped.

"A symptom of your inability to commit." She set her glass on the deck railing. "You said you wanted to spruce up the Framingham house and flip it. But you're taking your sweet time, and you're pumping in money you'll never get back. You sleep there at least half the time. When you do, you don't even have the guts to call and tell me. You text me instead."

My throat felt tight. I scraped, said nothing.

"Conway, if you're unhappy here, just say so and go. Batch it up. Live by yourself in your shitty neighborhood in Framingham."

I scraped like hell.

"Sit there all alone watching TV every night," Charlene said. "Watching TV and wondering why you feel like a clenched fist all the time."

I whipped the grill brush to the deck, slammed shut the grill cover, spun. "Don't call me that. You know I hate that."

Charlene looked at me over her seltzer, held out a hand, made a fist, tightened until the hand was white and shaking. Then she opened it like a magician showing me my quarter. "Unclench," she said.

I wanted to tell her I knew she was right. I wanted to tell her it was hard. I wanted to ask how to do it.

Instead, I wiped my hands on my pants. I stepped into the house. I closed the screen door quietly, precisely. I walked through the hall and out the front door. I climbed into my truck and drove to Framingham.

The next morning at eight, I sat outside Dot's Place in Rourke. My stomach felt lousy—had since I left Charlene's—and I didn't want to face the grease-and-burned-toast smell until I had to.

I was in the handicap-equipped Dodge van my friend left me along with the house. It was barely roadworthy anymore, but I'd left my F-150 in a glass-shop parking lot with a note taped to the steering wheel.

No sun today—thick gray mugginess instead, the kind where you hope it'll rain soon but it doesn't. I watched townies go in and out of Dot's.

At ten past, I called Phigg's cell. I got no answer, left voice mail.

At twenty past I dug through my wallet and found the scrap of place mat Phigg had given me. For an address he'd written only *Jut Rd.*, no house number. He'd said it was on a river. The river had to be the Souhegan. It defined Rourke and all the nearby towns; you couldn't miss it.

I fired up the van and tracked the same road I'd used yesterday to follow Phigg, looking to my left more carefully this time. Finally came to a dirt road I hadn't noticed before. There was no street sign, but it seemed a little too wide and a little too tamped to be a driveway, so I turned and eased down a steep hill, hearing the river before I saw it. I cut hard right, felt scrub oaks scraping both sides of the van, and popped into a clearing.

Phigg's car and the beginnings of a big timber-frame house told me I'd found Jut Road.

As I parked next to an outbuilding, I checked out the dream-house-in-progress. Or formerly-in-progress. I'm no contractor, but the skeleton told a story.

First, I saw it wasn't genuine timber-frame construction. It was a hybrid: impressive old rough-cut timbers at its center, where they'd be visible in the house's public spaces, but conventional two-by-four framing for the outside walls. When finished, the house would seem like a genuine timber-frame job, unless you knew what to look for. But deep down, it'd be a dime-a-dozen stick-built house.

I half smiled: That suited Phigg perfectly.

It would have been a cool home, I thought, turning to look at the

Souhegan. The outbuilding in front of me would be knocked down, I assumed, to clear the view. And it was a damn good view, especially this time of year, with White Mountains runoff rushing and forest as far as you could see.

The thing was, though, this house never would be finished; the framing and the site had "ran out of dough" written all over them. The two-by and the presswood flooring were warped and grayed by weather. The electricians had started their rough-in but had up and quit, disgusted one day, leaving a spool of cable. To my right, at the edge of the woods, a three-foot-tall stack of additional presswood— probably for second-story flooring that never got installed—sat water- logged, a blue tarpaulin having blown off months ago.

It was easy to see why Tander Phigg had stopped bragging about his dream house.

I called his name, quieting bugs and frogs for a few seconds.

Called again, with a question mark at the end this time.

Then I turned to the shack, thinking this *couldn't* be where he lived. He'd said he was living at the construction site in a guest- house, but this was more like an outbuilding. Twelve feet by twenty, built over the bank of the Souhegan. There were no windows on the narrow side I was looking at, and the two good-size windows on the front were boarded up. The door, a rough-cut plank job with a Z brace, sagged open.

I called Phigg's name again.

Nothing.

Over the years, the woods had closed in too much for any river breeze to chase bugs away. Mosquitoes sniffed me out and strafed me.

Underfoot it was dank clay, not like most New England soil. I stooped, picked up a handful, looked at the river, figured things out. I bet there had been a house here, years before. A nice home, a river house like the one Phigg had begun. But the original house was built too close to the Souhegan. It wouldn't take much rain to push the riverbank up there. After a couple hundred years, whoever owned the house got tired of cleaning up after floods and abandoned the place. If I walked ten yards past the stack of presswood, I'd probably find the remains of that house. The outbuilding had to be a mill or storage shed. It survived because it was built on brick piers high enough to stand clear of most floods.

If Tander Phigg lived here he had fallen further, faster, than any of us knew—and was too proud to tell anybody, to ask for help.

I stepped toward the shack and spotted something odd on the downriver side. I checked it out and saw a couple of toothed wheels, cast iron, the bigger one as large as a hula hoop. Click: Back when the original house stood, they likely used the river for power, making their own electricity. The outbuilding was a primitive generator. Good idea.

I shoved open the sagging door, called Phigg's name again. Nothing.

I stepped in. Felt the floor sag—not creak, but sag—beneath me, and thought how easy it'd be to drop straight through into the river.

Inside, it was dark as hell. I paused, let my eyes adjust. I wrinkled my nose at the smell—your grandfather's basement multiplied by ten. It seemed you could reach for anything in this room, tear off a chunk, and ball it up like a sponge.

I thought all this for maybe twenty seconds, slowly turning clockwise, finally looking past the door to the north side.

Tander Phigg was hanging from a stub of cast-iron pipe that came through the wall.

He'd dressed up, then hung himself by his necktie. One of those preppy striped ones, orange and black.

His khaki pants were stained with piss.

He'd kicked over a double stack of milk crates. Not far from the crates was a green sleeping bag on an old door supported by a cinder block at each corner.

Home sweet home.

Atop the sleeping bag was a blue hard-shell Samsonite suitcase. It was open. Both halves were filled with folded clothes. Topping the stack was the yellow polo shirt he'd worn Monday, a thin black wallet, a wristwatch, the key to his shitbox Sentra. I looked at Phigg's blue-black face. "Oh hell," I said.

CHAPTER THREE

I stepped outside. Realized I'd stopped breathing when I saw Phigg, gulped air. I squatted at the riverbank, splashed double handfuls of cold water on my face. It felt good. Helped me think.

My gut said vamoose. My head said that would be a bad move. I rose, looked around the back of the van. Sure enough, I'd left strong tire tracks in the clay. Plus the locals had seen me and Phigg in Dot's Place Monday. Plus me and Phigg were all over each other's cell phones. Plus the guy at the Exxon would remember us, would remember my truck.

If I split now, the cops would pick me up before dinner.

I sighed, pulled my cell, started to punch 911.

Then a stray thought hit me and I stopped dialing. What if Phigg's body just went away? That might stir things up, might put pressure on whoever drove him to hang himself.

It would be interesting to make Phigg disappear, then keep an eye on Ollie.

But as I played with the idea I saw how stupid it was. Start with logistics. Even if I could get Phigg down from that pipe stub and clear all signs of him from the outbuilding, what would I do with his car? I'd wind up with his DNA inside the van. When somebody wondered where he was—and somebody would—Dot's Place and the Exxon guy would point back to me.

I shook my head. Dumb. Always looking for ways to outsmart myself. I punched 911 fast, before I could think of any other ideas.

A lot of the little towns up here don't have their own police departments, so I was probably waiting for a state trooper. Figured I had a few minutes—the troopers have a lot of ground to cover.

Phigg's car was unlocked. Its interior stank. A quick search found nothing good: a damp beach towel with a surfer on it, random magazines, cereal and cracker boxes, a jug of generic laundry detergent, half a twelve-pack of Sam's Club Diet Cola.

In the trunk, yard-sale crap: a box of old *Gourmet* magazines, a snorkel, three mismatched golf clubs, a Hefty bag half full of aluminum cans, a pair of wading boots. Tander Phigg, sole heir of Phigg Paper Products, Incorporated, had been prowling roadside ditches for returnables to earn a nickel a pop.

I shook my head at that, slammed the trunk, went into the shack. Breathed through my mouth while I did a light search on Phigg's suitcase. I went through his wallet first and found a ten-spot, three singles, a driver's license that expired last year, and a dozen coupons. That was it.

Didn't want to mess up the suitcase, so I probed with gentle hands around the sides. I found something right away, slid it out. An address book, worn black leather. That made sense for a guy Phigg's age—you could convince him to use a cell phone, but you'd never get him to part with the hard copy.

I slipped the book in my pocket, then thought about the cops coming. I untied my right work boot, slipped the book into it, retied.

The address book made me think of Phigg's cell. I spotted a bulge in his left front pants pocket, patted. It was his phone all right.

I stared at the body. Getting the phone wasn't going to be easy.

Phigg was hanging too high for me to get a hand up to the pocket, then down for the phone. I'd need to climb on something, and it'd have to be one of the milk crates.

While I balanced the info against the risk, I thought I heard something over the river-burble. I stilled, focused, definitely heard it—wide tires on a dirt road. The cops were here. I was glad I wasn't standing on a milk crate with one hand in Phigg's pocket.

As I stepped outside I tried to look horrified, then tried to look surprised at the copper-over-green Dodge Charger the New Hampshire Staties had been buying lately. I noticed the Charger was parked in the only spot where it blocked both Phigg's car and my van. Smart cop.

I started toward the Charger. A deep voice said, "Stay right there, please."

I stopped.

The door opened. A man unfolded, putting on a tan Smokey the Bear hat as he rose.

And rose. He was huge. Half a head taller than me, and I'm six-one. His shoulders were half again as broad as mine, and mine aren't small. His forest-green shirt tapered to a waist two inches smaller than mine, and I'm not fat.

He had deep-set eyes, blue. High cheekbones, acne scars from teen years I bet he wanted to forget. Take Abe Lincoln, shave the beard, add thirty pounds of chest and shoulders—you'd have this trooper.

He looked at me maybe five seconds. I wasn't sure how, but he made me feel small in every way.

He said, "You the caller?"

I nodded.

"What happened to your head?"

I fingered the purple lump I'd forgotten about. "Banged it on a Dumpster yesterday." I turned my head to let him see it wasn't a fresh wound.

He keyed a lapel mic on his shirt, talked code on his radio. Then he said, "Show me." As he passed I read the name board pinned to his shirt: MCCORD.

Inside, McCord looked around with that unsurprisable nonexpression cops have. He faced the body. "You make sure he's dead?" he said.

"He's dead."

McCord turned and looked at me with a little more interest. He turned back to Phigg, pulled on a pair of purple rubber gloves, and ran a hand up Phigg's pant leg. Looking for a pulse at the back of the knee, I guessed.

McCord said, "He's dead," took notebook and pen from his shirt pocket, wrote. He stepped back and cocked his head the same way Phigg's was twisted. "Huh."

"What?"

"The necktie," McCord said. "Dress up to kill yourself, okay. More likely with women than men, but I'll buy it. Once he had his necktie all done up"—McCord pointed—"he didn't have much tie left to work with, uh? But he made a sturdy knot that's held up for a bunch of hours. Hard to do."

"Probably made the knot before he slipped it over that pipe," I said. "Made it right in front of his chest, looking at it, then slipped it over."

"Still. You're getting set to kill yourself, you're balancing on milk crates. You've got to make a nice tight knot, a slipknot or a square knot, can't tell from here. Then you've got to reach back over your head, tippy-toe on the crates, find the pipe, slip it over, snug it. Hard to do, uh?"

"Sure."

McCord wrote in his notebook again. Without looking up he said, "Did you kill this man, sir?"

"No."

"Know him?"

"His name was Tander Phigg."

"Your name?"

"Conway Sax."

"Did you kill him, sir?"

"No."

"Did you touch anything in here?"

"No."

"Touch *anything*?" Swept a long arm. "Go through his wallet, maybe?"

"No."

"Did you kill him?"

"No."

McCord pointed at the door. As we stepped from the shack he asked for my ID. I passed him my license. "I'm on parole in Mass.," I said.

"What for?"

"Manslaughter."

"You don't say."

McCord didn't seem to rush, but in a half second he had my left wrist behind my back and was working his cuffs off his belt.

I said, "My mistake. Should've told you first thing you pulled up."

"*My* mistake," he said. "I should've done this right away." As he spoke, McCord bent me over the Charger's deck lid, kicked my feet out wide, started to feel around my pockets. He said, "So you're on parole down there but messing around with dead bodies up here. Not good, uh?" He was businesslike, almost gentle. A man his size probably had to be: He could hurt you without trying.

"My PO knows I'm outside the state," I said. "I'm trying to get a job up here. He says as long as I live in Mass., I'm okay."

I could tell McCord was looking through my wallet. He said, "Shrewsbury to Rourke? Long commute, friend." He tugged at the handcuffs, let me straighten. Told me to stay still, took my license, sat in the Charger, worked his radio and laptop awhile.

I hoped they couldn't get in touch right away with Luther Swale, my parole officer. He and Randall and I worked together a while back to help some people out. Luther and I have an arrangement where I get a longer leash than most parolees as long as I stay clean and invisible. If he got cold-called by a New Hampshire Statie, our deal would expire on the spot. For the most part, Luther's a by-the-book grinder. He reluctantly gave me the long leash out of gratitude—his son had a hard time adjusting to post-Iraq life, and I guess I gave him a way to feel useful.

I was lucky. After ten minutes McCord unfolded from the Charger, unhooked me, pointed at my stuff on the deck lid. "Okay," he said. "I'll move my car so you can clear out."

"Just like that?"

"ISB won't be here for three hours. They'll call you when they need you." He saw the question on my face. "Investigative Services Bureau."

"Detectives, in other words."

The left corner of his mouth moved an eighth of an inch. It might have been a smile. "People do like fancy titles, uh?" He folded into his car as I walked toward the van.

I thought of something, stopped, turned. "How do you like the Charger?"

"I prefer the Crown Vic. Almost as fast, rides better, more head-room."

"How about the other guys?"

"Most of 'em like the Charger because it's badass."

"You, you don't need a car to make you feel badass."

McCord gave me the eighth-inch smile again and lit the Charger's Hemi. "Have a nice day."

Southbound, I called Luther Swale's office number. Got voice mail, left a message. I called Randall. "Where the hell are you?" he said.

"Headed for Framingham. You?"

"I'm standing beside the new deck. You were supposed to oil this fancy ipe yesterday. I came by to see how it looked. Nada. Decided to do it myself. I just finished the second coat. It looks great."

"Thanks," I said. "Got something important you can help me with. I'll be there in forty-five minutes."

"Bring lunch." Click.

I looked at my watch. Jesus, it was past noon already. I'd been at Phigg's shack a long time. I hit the gas.

The oil on the deck did look great. It was dry to the touch, but we didn't want to scuff it up before it cured, so Randall and I sat at a card table in the kitchen and ate meatball subs.

The kitchen had been our first project. We'd blown out a wall to make the whole first floor seem bigger, stripped three layers of linoleum, redone the hardwood, painted the cabinets, and finished it all off with granite countertops the color of jade.

I split a meatball, gave half to each cat, filled Randall in. I started with the night Phigg buttonholed me at a Barnburner meeting and told me he needed help.

Randall was a good listener. Hungry, too. He worked through his sub, chips, and Snapple, nodded once in a while, kept quiet until I finished. Then he said, "Don't think too long, just give me your gut feeling. Did Tander Phigg kill himself?"

I ate a salt-and-vinegar chip. "No."

"Are you saying that because the state cop pointed out the awkwardness of the necktie?"

"Partly," I said, and ate another chip while I asked myself why it felt wrong. "Phigg was all front." I explained the not-really-timber-frame house. Randall looked a question at me.

"Point is, he worked hard to fake it," I said. "Hung on to his cell phone when he was broke, kept a suitcase full of preppy clothes even when he was picking up cans in ditches. Faked it pretty good for a long time. A lot of Barnburners were whispering he was low on dough, but nobody had any idea how bad it'd gotten."

"So?"

"It doesn't fit with the way I found him," I said. "That miserable little shack, you should've seen it. Two milk crates and a sleeping bag. A three-hundred-dollar car full of saltines and Price Chopper coupons."

Randall helped himself to a couple of chips. "And you think if Phigg decided to kill himself, he wouldn't draw attention to his situation."

"He would've done the opposite," I said. "Would've ditched the car, saved pennies until he could check into a nice hotel, something like that." I shoved him the rest of my chips, balled up the sub wrappers, rose, threw them away.

"Pretty thin gruel," Randall said.

"There's more." I told him about following Phigg, watching his meeting with the woman in the silver Jetta.

"Well," he said, "that ought to give the cops something to chase down." Long pause. "You told them, right?"

Longer pause.

"*Con*way," Randall said. "For crying out loud. Why would you hold back on something like that?"

I said nothing.

"So you could nose around, that's why," he said, pinching the bridge of his nose. "What now?"

"I need to call some Barnburners, get the telephone chain going for the memorial."

"What about me?"

I leaned on the countertop. "You going to help me out with this?"

Long pause.

"It's either that or start another expensive project around here," he finally said. "Either way, your money burns while I have fun."

I leaned over, pulled Phigg's address book from my boot, tossed it on the card table. "Have some fun with that."

Randall set my laptop on the card table and began working his way through the address book. I didn't know why he needed the PC—it'd be easier just to thumb through. But I'd learned that when you gave him a task, he was going to by God do it his way. If you tried to point him in a direction, he muled up.

I stepped to the front porch. My first call was to Mary Giarusso, the Barnburners' nerve center. She lives a couple blocks north of me, feeds my cats when I'm gone. She's a gossip hound—folks call her Switchboard Mary behind her back. Her head just about hit her kitchen ceiling when I broke the news. I asked if she could call a few Barnburners to spread the word and set up a memorial. *Could* she? I asked if she would do a little digging, see if Phigg ever talked about his family. *Would* she? I told her not to sprain her finger dialing. She didn't hear, had clicked off already.

I squinted at the sky. Storm clouds. I hoped the rain wouldn't hurt the deck's fresh oil.

Inside, Randall had set up a spreadsheet on my laptop and was entering info. I stood behind him, saw the address book open to the Bs.

"You AA types are a pain in the ass," Randall said. "It's mostly first names and last initials. Ed A., Ginny B."

"You start with the Ps? Family?"

He said nothing, but clicked on the spreadsheet's P tab. The only name was *Trey*. Next to the name was a weird phone number, must be outside the U.S., and a Gmail address.

I said, "Trey was under the Ps?"

"Yup. A son, I'm guessing."

"Why?"

Randall pointed at the e-mail address: tp3_72@gmail.com. He

said, "Tander Phigg the Third? Born in 'seventy-two, maybe? Known as 'Trey'?"

"That's either a good guess or a pile of horseshit."

"That narrows it down," he said. "Also, your pal Phigg isn't—wasn't—a big Internet guy. This is the only e-mail address I saw when I skimmed the book."

"So?"

"So this Trey was pretty special to Tander."

"Before you enter any more names and numbers, you want to Google him?"

Randall's shoulders tightened. "I'll enter everything first," he said. "Then I'll Google."

His task, his way.

I said, "I'm headed back to Rourke. Want to talk to the guy at Motorenwerk."

"The garage where you got cold-cocked? Are you nuts?"

For starters, I was supposed to be the cold-cock*er*, not the cold-cock*ee*. Pride. But I couldn't tell Randall that. He's Mister Pragmatic. "I need to figure this deal out," I said. "What's going on with Phigg's car, whether he's entitled to money back, all that."

"Then let me come along," he said, and waved at the address book. "We can do this later."

"I'll go alone."

Long look. "Is that smart?"

"I'll bring my tire iron."

"Somewhat smarter."

CHAPTER FOUR

I parked across from Motorenwerk at 5:15 as the rain, which had been trying like hell all day, finally started. Thunder closed from the southeast as I looked at the shop. The garage doors were closed. Through the office's plate-glass window I saw Josh. He was counter-leaning, finger-drumming. An Audi A6 Avant sat outside the office. It looked like Ollie had left for the day, and Josh was stuck waiting for the Audi's owner to show.

For me, it was a good setup. I wanted to talk to Josh without Ollie around. Wanted to surprise him, fluster him. I decided to wait for the Audi owner, then bust in.

I looked around the interior of my F-150, which I'd picked up on the way. The glass-shop guy had said the glue for the new windows was set up already, rain wouldn't be a problem. So far, there were no leaks.

I eased the truck backward twenty yards, moving out of Josh's sight line. Rain picked up, thunder waded in. I ran the AC to keep the windows clear, waited, thought. What was Josh doing here? He could be earning more anywhere else, and it had to be killing Ollie to keep him on the payroll.

At quarter of six, the thunder and lightning peaked. At the end of Mechanic Street, a bolt hit not twenty yards from the Dumpster I'd puked in yesterday. I half jumped in my seat, smelled ozone, felt neck hairs rise.

A minivan pulled up. The man who hopped from the passenger side wore a suit, had a briefcase but no raincoat. He hunched, waved thanks to the minivan's driver as it turned and left, ducked inside.

I stepped from my truck and stood in pouring rain next to the office door. After two minutes the customer stepped out. I startled him. He recovered, nodded, hopped in his car. I waited near the door where Josh couldn't see me. I was trying to time my entry—wanted him relaxed, but didn't want to give him a chance to lock up. I was ready to push my way in if I heard keys jingle.

In maybe three minutes I stepped into the office, hoping to intimidate the hell out of Josh.

He wasn't behind the counter.

Shit.

I stepped into the garage. Heard noise near the back, walked along the wall. Tried to keep it quiet, but my shoes squished.

Josh stepped around a corner, walking with purpose. He held a good-size rubber mallet, raised and ready. His eyes were narrowed, his mouth open a little. His teeth were slightly apart, and I saw the pink of his tongue-tip between them. If I hadn't known better I would've thought he was looking forward to beating the bejesus out of an intruder.

This wasn't working out the way I'd pictured it.

Josh saw it was me. I made a *whoa-now* gesture with both hands. He stood four feet away, mallet poised.

"Really coming down out there," I said.

"The hell'd you come from?" He breathed hard through his nostrils. Did I read disappointment in his eyes? Had he *hoped* I was some meth-head burglar he could cream?

"Got some paper towels?"

He nodded at a roll of blue shop towels on the bench beside me. I snapped off a half dozen and toweled my hair.

Josh said, "Where'd you come from?"

"Ollie live nearby?" I said.

"Why do you want to know?"

"*Je*sus, kid!" I fist-thumped the bench as I said it. "I don't know what Ollie is to you. He's more than your boss, isn't he?"

Josh said nothing.

"I'm going to talk with Ollie," I said. "Soon. Here. What I need from you is his last name, how close he lives to this place, his phone number. This is going to happen, with your help or without."

"Maybe it is, maybe it isn't," he said, twirling the mallet in his hands. "Maybe you're going to get your head busted in again."

Jesus, had I ever misread this kid. "It wasn't you who nailed me yesterday. Was it?"

Josh said nothing. He didn't drop his gaze, didn't stop twirling the mallet.

Something clicked. I smiled slow and big and edged past Josh, putting my hands up when he cocked the mallet. I cleared the corner and saw what I'd anticipated: One corner of the car cover on Phigg's Mercedes had been lifted.

"What the hell is it about this car?" I said.

"I think you ought to leave."

"Tander Phigg hanged himself this morning," I said.

"I heard."

"What is it about this car?"

Josh said nothing.

"Look," I said, sighing. "I need to talk with Ollie. Here, tonight. Let's work it like this: You give me his number. I'll bust a window around back, tell him I climbed in after you left. I'm guessing he used to pay for a security service, but not anymore. That sound right?"

Josh nodded.

"Must be twenty ways I could find his name and number without your help," I said. "You're just my shortcut." I took a Sharpie from the bench, slid it and a dry shop towel toward Josh.

He stared at me for twenty seconds. Then he wrote a number on the towel. "When you talk with Ollie, you won't mention this," he said, nodding toward Phigg's car. "In fact, you'll forget all about it now that Phigg's dead."

I said nothing. It was easier than lying. Instead I tore off another paper towel and wrote my name, cell, and e-mail on it, shoved it to him.

He eyeballed it. "What's that for?"

"This place is going to change, fast and soon," I said. "It's probably going to go away. Maybe you'll need help finding your next job. I know a lot of guys in the business."

As his fingertips touched the paper towel, I put one of my own on it. "Or maybe you'll just want to tell me more about Ollie," I said. "About what the hell's going on here. You thought it was a high-end restoration shop. Thought it'd be more fun than doing oil changes at the local Toyota store, huh? But it was something else."

Josh wanted to tell me. I could feel him tipping, the same way he nearly had in the garage yesterday. But he just reached a hooded Windbreaker from a hook and unclipped a huge key ring from his belt loop. "I'll need to lock you out," he said, flipping through keys. He looked at me. "Second window in on the back side is so sticky we can't close it to lock it. Be easy to open it with a pry bar. Ollie would think you just got lucky and found the right window."

Two minutes later I fired the F-150, watched Josh drive away in a rough old Audi 4000. It was a cult car, an all-wheel-drive sedan that came out back when that was rare. They were hard cars to keep running right, especially now that they were a quarter-century old.

I sat in the truck and figured out how to work what I wanted to do next. The weak link was going to be a missing cop car. I needed to pressure Ollie, rush him, to get him to overlook that.

I was going to get wet as hell, no way to avoid it. The thunder and lightning had moved past, but the rain was hard and steady. The upside was with the sky gray to begin with, it'd get dark earlier.

I called Charlene at home. She was brisk, chopping something while we spoke. Sophie was fine. Work was fine. She hadn't heard from Jesse. I wouldn't make it for dinner tonight? Fine. Click.

By eight o'clock it was dark enough. The rain wasn't dramatic anymore, but it wasn't letting up either. I cleared my throat, hit *67 to block Caller ID, and dialed the number Josh had written.

Ollie took his time answering. I heard a TV as he said, "Yeah."

"Mr. Dufresne?" Said it Doo-FREZ-nee on purpose.

He sighed. "Doo-FRAYNE. What?"

"Sorry. Rourke PD, sir. We got a report of a lightning strike here at your shop. Looks like it holed your roof. Helluva lot of water coming in."

It worked. The TV clicked off. Ollie said, "Office or garage?"

"Garage."

"*Fuck* me. I'll be there in ten minutes."

I was set to click off when he said, "Who is this? Scharf?"

"Giarusso."

"You new?"

"Been here almost eight months." I tried to sound offended.

"How come you show up as 'Unknown Caller'?"

"They've got us using our personal cells for calls like this. Budget, you know?"

"Do I ever. Ten minutes."

I worked fast. Parked my truck down the street, alongside the upholstery place, while the pit bull barked.

I rain-sprinted back to Motorenwerk, tire iron in one hand, stout flashlight in the other. It's the kind cops use—knurled aluminum barrel, eighteen inches long, packed with four D batteries. It's as much a club as it is a flashlight. Comes in handy.

I ran around back, found the unlocked window Josh had described, levered it with the tire iron, climbed into the garage.

Dark as hell in here. I flashlighted my way to the front, killed the light, rested it on my shoulder.

Waited.

Not long. I saw headlights. I heard a heavy splash out front, then a key-scrabble as the office door opened.

But the office lights didn't come on.

Dufresne wasn't stupid.

I heard the door close gently, a tiny air-puff really. I heard water drip from Dufresne. Pictured him standing in the dark no more than five feet from me.

I heard a gun's slide rack. Dufresne *definitely* wasn't stupid—had a semi-auto, with a round in the chamber now.

Shit.

I pictured him listening hard, breathed slowly through my mouth. The gun changed things. I decided I had to take a chance.

I clicked the flashlight on, took loud steps, tried for the same voice I'd used on the phone. "Mr. Dufresne? That you up there?"

Nothing.

"You wanna hit the lights out here?" I said. "I banged the bejesus out of my shins once already." Walked toward the door as I said it.

It worked. Dufresne couldn't take the risk, couldn't walk in pointing a gun at a cop. He had stowed the gun in his raincoat by the time he stepped through the door, reached for the light switch, and said, "I thought—"

As the lights came on I flicked my heavy flashlight at his forearm, meaning to break it. But I missed, got the meat of his upper arm instead.

Dufresne was *most* definitely not stupid. He took one look at me and processed the whole scene before I could hit him again. He reached in the raincoat for his gun.

I closed fast, head-butted his nose, heard it break. He'd gotten his right hand on the gun, but his hand was hung up in the wet raincoat. I bear-hugged him to keep it there.

He was strong for a short guy. His left arm hung useless from the shot with the flashlight, and his right hand was tangled up in the gun and the coat, but he fought like hell anyway. He pushed up at my chin with the top of his head, nose-jetted blood into my shirt, stomped at my feet and ankles.

But his sneakers didn't bother my work boots. I poured on the bear hug, forced air from him, kept his right arm pressed against his chest.

Funny thing: As we fought, Dufresne's foot-stomps going weak, me squeezing and waiting for my chance to knock him out, I felt like I was up in the garage's rafters and to my left, watching it all.

That was new.

I used to forget everything in a fight. I used to lose myself in a red-mist fury that always meant bad things for the other guy—and good things for Barnburners. This was different. No red mist, no hate. I just wanted to weaken Ollie enough so I could take away the gun.

I was getting old.

I thought all this while I floated above and to my left, watching Dufresne's blood jet against my chest, watching myself crush him more or less to death.

He finally fainted. I could tell because his dead weight nearly pulled me over. I let him drop, making sure he didn't slam his head on polished concrete. I fished the gun from his raincoat. It was a Browning P35 Mark I, but different. I squinted, studied the piece, finally figured it out: The gun had been modified to fire beefy .40 S&W loads rather than stock 9 millimeter stuff. I'd heard you could mod the P35 that way, but hadn't seen it done.

I stuck the gun in the back of my pants, then realized I needed to black this place out right now, before a cruising cop spotted lights in Motorenwerk and swung by to check things out.

I killed the lights and checked Dufresne. He was out cold. I pocket-patted, found his keys, stepped out front.

The rain was slowing. Dufresne's 5-series BMW, mid-nineties, black or dark blue, was angle-parked. I hopped in and pulled it around the side of the building, between the Dumpster and the stack of old tires. Locked it, stepped inside, locked the office door behind me, stepped in the garage, flashlighted Dufresne.

His eyes were open. He stared at me, wheezed, squeezed his left fist like he was testing it. Twice he tried to speak, but wheezed and coughed instead.

I hadn't planned for this. The way I'd planned it, I would humiliate him, terrify him. I would zip-tie his wrists to the lift, slap him with an open hand, maybe pull down his pants. Pull a man's pants around his ankles sometime and slap—rather than punch—his face awhile; you'd be surprised how fast it can break a guy.

But it wouldn't break Dufresne. His hot-rod Browning, his street smarts, the way he fought with no arms and a broken nose: This was a soldier.

He took a huge, wheezing oxygen-suck and said, "What the fuck?"

"I was going to do the half-assed torture bit on you," I said. "I was going to scare you till you peed your pants. But you fight like a man, so let's skip the bullshit."

I took one step toward Dufresne, still prone on polished concrete, and set my left foot on his left shoulder. Applied steady pressure, watching pain flow to his eyes. He tried to kick me in the nuts, but it was halfhearted. I pulled the P35 and set it against his left temple. "You chambered a round yourself," I said, "am I right?"

"Fuck you." He looked me in the eye as he said it. I liked him.

"Tell me everything you can tell me about Tander Phigg and his Mercedes," I said, "or I'll put one of your own souped-up bullets in your head and walk out the door and drive home and sleep like a baby."

CHAPTER FIVE

Y ou have to mean it.

I thought I meant it. I tried to get a good mad on. I thought about getting whacked in the head and lied to and dragged to a Dumpster, thought about Tander Phigg hanging from a pipe stub.

But as Ollie stared at me, studying my face, I got that feeling again—sitting above myself and to my left, looking down at the whole scene. Knew I wasn't going to blow a man's head off, wondered if *he* knew it, too. I killed my flashlight and left us in sudden dark so he couldn't read my eyes.

We were silent a full thirty seconds.

"Can't do it, can you?" he said.

"Done it before," I said.

"But can you do it *now,* friend? Do you have it in you?"

He was a man, a fighter. "I'm not going to do it now," I said. "Not to you." I took the P35 from his temple.

"In that case," Ollie Dufresne said, "let's have a cup of tea and talk."

Ten minutes later, a bandage from the shop's first-aid kit covered Ollie's gashed nose—blood stained through, but only a little. He was hard to figure out. Short, round, looked soft, sat sipping tea he'd made on a hot plate. But he fought like hell, even with his arms pinned.

I leaned on a counter with his gun loose in my hand. "Tander Phigg died this morning," I said.

"Jesus. How?" His surprise seemed genuine. I wondered why Josh knew about the hanging but Ollie didn't.

"They say he hanged himself."

He shook his head. "That's rough. An old friend of yours, I presume?"

"He was a horse's ass."

"On that we can agree, though I hate to speak ill of the dead." He hesitated. "Given that assessment, what's your role? Your mission?"

"I promised to get his car back," I said, nodding toward the covered Mercedes. "And the thirty-five hundred he paid you up front."

"And now that he's gone," Ollie said, "you might as well help yourself. Spoils of war, eh?"

"No."

"No what?"

"No, I won't help myself. Still helping Phigg."

"Phigg's dead."

"I said I'd help him. I'll help him."

Ollie looked at me awhile. "We have here a rara avis," he said. "What's your intent? Send Phigg a money-gram care of the great beyond?"

"I'll sell the car, give the dough to his next of kin if he has any."

"And if he doesn't?"

"I'll donate it to AA. I think Phigg would be okay with that."

"Fair enough," Ollie said. "Let's move on to the next problem: I don't owe the late Tander Phigg a fucking nickel. He lied to you about what was going on with his car. Through his *teeth* he lied."

"So straighten me out."

Ollie folded his arms, pulled at his lower lip with thumb and forefinger, said nothing—a man considering his options. I took that as confirmation there was something dirty going on. Ollie had painted himself into a corner where he had to either tell me about it or let me keep believing he'd scammed Phigg. Maybe killed him.

"Or I could just point the cops your way, let *them* straighten it out."

His silence dragged. I needed to get him going. "I used to own my own shop," I said. "European cars, mostly German."

"I know," he said. "You invented tools for working on transmissions. You held patents and ran training seminars for Mercedes USA."

I popped eyebrows.

Ollie said, "I attended one of the seminars."

"Small world."

"Remarkably."

I spread my arms. "I'm guessing you used to do some good work here."

"I still fucking do!" he said. But then he looked around, dropped his shoulders. "Well . . . maybe not so much lately."

"What changed?"

He stared at nothing for a long time. I let him. I noticed the quiet and realized the rain had stopped.

Finally Ollie said, "What changed is that I got into something else."

"Chop shop?"

He shook his head, met my eyes. "Runs up to Canada."

"Cocaine?"

He said nothing.

"Heroin?"

"I'm not going to say it out loud," he said. "Not here, not to you. We made runs."

"Tell me."

"It's a long story."

"Shorten it."

Ollie half laughed. "That's not a bad idea, actually." He looked at the floor and rolled his chair in little circles while he organized the story. Then he told it.

Two years ago, Ollie had been running Motorenwerk, getting by on local projects but not building the big rep you need to get high-dollar restoration work. His shop was on a slow downhill slope, and he knew it. He could picture an eventual SPACE FOR RENT sign across the plate glass.

That's when Ollie got a visit from an old friend of his father. The visit was out of the blue: Ollie's father, a Quebecois, had died of cirrhosis fifteen years prior. The friend drove up in a Cadillac Escalade. He had a killer suit on, a layered haircut, a massive bodyguard.

At first, the dude tried a friendly-uncle bit—said he'd always kept track of little Ollie, had loved him since he was a pup, had made his dad a deathbed promise to keep an eye on him.

Ollie said that was a load of horseshit and they both knew it. He asked what the friend really wanted.

The friend's eyes went dark a few seconds. Then he laughed, slapped Ollie's shoulder, said he liked a blunt man, and got to it. He sold things in Montreal, he said. He'd done well. But after nine-eleven, it was hard as hell to get merchandise into Canada. He had an idea, a way to get back on top, that was right up Ollie's alley. Everybody'd win.

Ollie looked into my eyes. "We both knew what he was selling," he said. "Obviously, nobody wanted to say the word."

"Like now."

"Exactly."

"Jesus, it's just a word," I said. "Heroin or cocaine?"

Long pause. "The former."

The dealer had done homework. Everybody thought drug-sniffing dogs were impossible to fool, and cops liked to keep people thinking that way. In truth, the dealer had learned, mutts were mutts. If you wrapped heroin carefully and didn't leave sloppy residue everywhere, you could fool them pretty well. If you wrapped it *very* carefully and buried it deep enough inside the car that carried it across the border, you could fool them every time.

I said, "That's where you came in."

Ollie sat straighter. "You wouldn't believe the work I did. I could hide ten kilos in a brand-new Dodge Caravan. Turn the minivan over to the very engineer who designed it, I swear it would take *him* a week to find anything."

"Just a guess," I said. "Cut the gas tank in half, put the wrapped drugs inside, weld it back up?"

He wagged a finger. "Amateur hour, friend. That's the first place they look. Besides, a lot of gas tanks are plastic these days."

"Like everything else in cars."

He smiled. I'd won him over. Proud now, Ollie talked about his tricks. He stuffed thin ropes of plastic-wrapped heroin in a car's stiffening rails, covered by a panel that was sprayed and undercoated to match the body. He hollowed out truck batteries, stuck tiny motorcycle batteries in the shell, and packed the rest of the cavity with drugs. In some cars, he found he could stash a kilo in each windshield pillar. "It's all in the details, in how you cover your work to make it look factory," Ollie said. "In that sense, it's not so different from a true restoration."

I signaled "speed it up" with my finger. "Tie it all in to Phigg."

As the drug-packing business pushed aside the legit restorations, Ollie grew nervous. So did the Montreal dealer. After all, Motorenwerk was supposed to be a snooty, Germans-only shop. How long before somebody noticed most of the cars in the garage were now two-year-old Camrys, Accords, Caravans? Ollie needed a beard or two—genuine resto projects that could sit around the shop a long time.

On cue, along came Tander Phigg with his rare Mercedes.

Ollie touched the bandage on his nose, winced. "It was perfect," he said. "I saw immediately he was a rich sucker, the kind of guy who wants to be your pal so badly he'll swallow any line of bullshit just to keep the peace. You ran a shop yourself. You must know the type."

I knew. Nodded.

"That's when I hired Josh," Ollie said. "I told him he was going to lead the work on Mr. Phigg's Mercedes, and I encouraged him to take his sweet time. He was an eager beaver. So eager, in fact, that I began taking in dull little maintenance jobs."

"You keep Josh busy with the maintenance," I said, "so he never really gets anything done on Phigg's car."

"Indeed."

"He knows something stinks here."

"He does," Ollie said, "he does at that. Smart young man, and curious to boot. I'll deal with him when I absolutely must, and not before."

"Back up," I said. "You were making good money with this Montreal guy?"

"Of course. That's why the restorations ground to a halt."

"So why'd you ding Phigg for thirty-five hundred bucks?"

"I *didn't!*" he said. "With all due respect to the deceased, your friend was full of shit on that point." As he said it, Ollie's eyes cut down and left. He wasn't telling me the whole truth.

"Strange detail to lie about," I said.

"Care to see my copy of the original work order? It's three feet behind you."

"Sure." If it was a bluff, I was calling it.

Ollie stepped around me to a two-drawer filing cabinet that he must have stuffed in here when the office filled up. He rifled through the top drawer, pulled a manila folder, flopped it on the bench in front of me, and folded his arms.

I opened it and saw right away that Motorenwerk used the same software I used to. At the bottom of the eighteen-month-old work

order was Tander Phigg's authorization signature. There was no record of any deposit, no credit-card receipt, no staple where such a
receipt had once been.

If Ollie was faking me out, he was doing a hell of a job.

I shut the folder. Ollie gave me a "Well?" look.

"I'll buy your version," I said. "But like I said, it's a strange thing
to lie about."

"Your friend fell hard," Ollie said. I started to talk, but he waved
a hand. "Okay, so he wasn't your friend. He was a horse's ass. Whatever he was to you, he fell fast and he fell hard."

"Tell me."

"Early on he dropped by every two weeks or so, the way most
customers do. You know the routine. You show them the car, you
talk about how hard it is to find parts, you drop names, you make
them feel like their heap is the most important bloody thing in your
life."

I might have smiled.

"But then"—he squinted—"a year ago? Maybe a little less? He
started coming by every week, sometimes twice a week. He got angry when he didn't see enough progress to suit him. I got the feeling
he was under pressure, was perhaps getting squeezed."

"For what? By who?"

"I've told you all there is to tell, Sax," he said. He tried to look me
in the eye, but again his gaze dropped down and left. "I'm afraid you
need to either accept that or fight me again."

We stared at each other awhile.

Finally I used the gun to point at the window I'd climbed through.
"You'll want to fix that," I said. "It's how I got in."

He put a hand out. "Gun, please."

I shook my head. "Keeping it." I stuck it down the back of my pants.
"Not because I think you'll back-shoot me, but because I might need
it."

"As you wish," he said, making a fancy little bow. "Spoils of war."

I turned to leave.

"Sax," he said.

I stopped.

"Come here again that way, I'll kill you."

"I won't."

"I will."

"I know. So I won't."

I walked out the front door wondering what Ollie was holding back.

In the F-150, I checked messages. Had a text from Randall: *Call asap.* Checked my watch. Almost midnight. I dialed.

Randall picked up on one. "Little piece of intel for you," he said. Smug as hell, pleased with himself.

I took a guess. "You were right about that e-mail address? It belongs to Phigg's kid?"

"I was indeed right. But it's better than that."

"You contact him?"

"I'm looking at him," Randall said. "He's in your kitchen, eating tomato soup and a grilled-cheese sandwich."

Seventy minutes later, just after one in the morning, the soup was gone but Phigg's kid was still there. He was talking with Randall at my kitchen table when I came in. He rose, stuck out a thin arm. "I'm Trey Phigg." He almost whispered it.

While we shook I tried to superimpose his face on Phigg's. It wasn't easy. The son was whip-skinny, where Phigg was puffy; the kid was outdoors-brown, where Phigg was doughy. It took me a few seconds to see the biggest difference: During conversation, Phigg had always looked at your forehead or the bridge of your nose; the son looked you square in the eye.

The eye color was right, the height was right, the thick head of hair. The son's was the color of wet sand.

I started to introduce myself. Randall made a *keep-it-down* gesture and jerked a thumb toward the bedrooms. "Trey's wife and son are asleep."

I nodded and sat.

Trey Phigg said, "Randall tells me you were helping my father with something. And that you found his body."

"So you know," I said. "I'm sorry. New Hampshire state cops call you?"

"I called *them*. It would have taken them a while to find me."

"Why?"

"We've been overseas," Trey said. "We got back to the States late last night."

"Where from?"

"Vietnam. My wife's family lives there."

"How long were you there?"

"Four years."

"You must really like your in-laws," Randall said.

"No," Trey said. "I really hated my father." He stretched, yawned, looked at the wall clock. "It's nice of you to put us up, Mister Sax. We'll be out of your hair soon. I've got an appointment with a New Hampshire detective." He rose, yawned again. "My body clock is in a tizzy. Good night."

CHAPTER SIX

Randall and I looked at each other as Trey's footsteps faded. "Helluva strange homecoming," Randall said.

"You're telling me."

"Walk me to my car."

Outside it was cool, all mugginess washed away by the storm.

"So he hates his father's guts," I said. "He's gone four years. Comes back, boom: All of a sudden his father's dead."

"I figured you'd be thinking that way."

"Aren't you?"

"If Trey came back to the States, made a beeline for New Hampshire and hanged his dad, he sure picked weird accomplices," Randall said. "The wife knows maybe ten words of English, and the kid's three years old. Cute as a button."

"Still," I said. "What I'm thinking, you find out what flight he came in on and work up a timeline. That's an easy way to rule him in or out."

"And if we rule him in?"

I shrugged. "We keep looking at him. I'll hitch a ride with him tomorrow, pump him on the drive."

"What are you, Sherlock Holmes?"

"No," I said. "I'm just a guy with a dead Barnburner on my hands."

Randall looked at me awhile. "And why exactly is he on your hands?"

"You know why," I said as we eye-locked. "He was a Barnburner."

I woke up early the next morning to a fishy smell. Showered, dressed, headed downstairs.

Trey was in the same kitchen chair as last night. Next to him sat a cute little boy. The boy took one look at me, slipped from his chair, and hid behind his mother's legs. She turned, smiled, half bowed—and just about stepped on one of my cats. They were both eyeball-stalking her, the lady with the fish.

"This is my wife, Kieu," Trey said, rising. "My son, Tuan." Then he spoke rapid-fire Vietnamese, I guessed, and wound up saying my name. His wife half bowed again, plucked the skillet from the burner, extended it with a question in her eyes.

I looked at the skillet, which was full of a noodles-and-shrimp thing. I said sure. I was just being polite, but when she plated me up and I took a bite, I liked it. A lot.

While I ate I watched Trey watch his family. He was proud of them, and he didn't try to make the boy act like a grown-up. In a few minutes he glanced at my plate, saw it was empty, spoke to Kieu. She smiled and plated me up some more.

While I dug in Trey said, "I showed her the miraculous place where you can get all the exotic food you want, twenty-four hours a day."

"Where's that?"

"Stop and Shop."

We laughed. I asked where the New Hampshire Staties wanted him to go. He said the office was in Concord, the state capital. We decided I'd drive him.

While Trey got ready I texted Randall, who was on his way over to put new sash weights in a bunch of windows. He said he'd be happy to keep an eye on Kieu and the kid.

By seven thirty Trey and I were northbound in his rented Dodge Stratus. He'd insisted we take that car, probably didn't want me paying for gas. He asked me to drive. "You know how you see Asian drivers poke along in the fast lane, and everybody gets furious at them?" he said.

"Yeah."

"I hate to admit it, but that's how I drive now." He swept an arm at the Massachusetts Turnpike on a perfect day. "These roads terrify me. I need to get my sea legs back."

"Four years," I said. "Long time."

He said nothing.

"All to get away from your dad?"

"*All?* No. It's complicated."

I waited.

"We fought constantly," Trey said after a while. "Typical father-son stuff, but . . . I blew it out of proportion. I was a drama queen, if you want to know the truth."

"Teenagers and perspective."

"Yes. Any comment he made about my hair, clothes, grades was World War Three."

"Were you scared you'd make like your dad?" I said. "Take the easy road to the corner office?"

He looked at me. "Of course."

"To be different, you made a rebel stand. Took off for parts unknown."

"Just as my father had," Trey said. "Thus repeating the pattern in spite of my best efforts. The irony is not lost, I can assure you."

We were quiet for a few miles. When I hit I-495 North I said, "Well, you sure did one thing right."

He looked at me.

"You didn't name your son Tander Phigg the Fourth."

Trey laughed a long time. "You're fucking-A right I didn't," he said. "Pardon my French."

I said, "Yesterday somebody asked me what I thought of your father. First thing came to mind was horse's ass."

"Okay."

"But he did some good things," I said. "He got sober. He stayed sober a long time. Helped plenty others sober up, too."

"Huh."

"How much did Randall tell you about things?"

"My father hanged himself in Rourke, Hew Hampshire."

Randall had played it smart—had sketched things out for Trey, leaving me room to spin the details when the time was right and do some digging while I was at it.

I said, "You surprised your father killed himself?"

He took his time. Finally he said, "Yes."

"Why?"

"Ego," Trey said. "No. Almost ego, but not quite. Self-importance. He thought the sun would forget to rise if he wasn't around to remind it."

"That's about the way I see it."

"What are you saying?"

I shrugged, drove. Moved right to take I-93 North.

Keeping a peripheral-vision eye on Trey to gauge his reaction, I said, "Your father died flat broke. He was collecting cans and eating crackers in an abandoned shack."

"*What?* There is absolutely no way that can be true."

"It's true," I said. "I guess the cops and lawyers'll tell you more."

"How? Is there any chance he had a drug or booze habit? Prescription meds, maybe?"

"No."

"Gambling?"

"Not that I know of. It would've been hard for him to hide that, the circles he ran in."

"What, then?"

I shrugged and made a snap decision not to talk about Motoren-werk. Yet. "All of us Barnburners thought he was loaded," I said. I saw the question on his face. "It's an AA group. The Barnburners. Tight bunch. Your father must've mentioned it when you were a kid."

"I suppose so," he said. "I didn't listen to him much."

I nodded. "From what your father said, your grandfather ran a big paper mill and left your father a bundle. We thought he was set for life."

"Me too." Half laugh. "Truth be told, I thought *I* was set for life."

"You're taking it pretty well."

Shrug.

I needed to get him going. "Phigg Paper, was it?"

Trey straightened in his seat and put on a radio-announcer voice. "In 1928 Tander Phigg, Senior, a twenty-one-year-old immigrant from Liverpool, stood on the banks of the Nashua River. Phigg had the clothes on his back, four dollars, and a note from his father asking any fellow Liverpudlian to take on the youth as an apprentice. But he also had a dream: to dominate the market for paper receipts used in the fast-growing cash-register market."

"I guess you heard that story a few times around the dinner table, huh?"

"Worse," Trey said. "That was the intro to an industrial film my dad made about the company. He used to bring in a projectionist after Sunday dinner. We'd watch it in his study."

Trey was quiet as we crossed into New Hampshire. He was a smart kid. I could feel him organizing his thoughts, making sure he told it clean and clear, maybe crossing out details he didn't want me to know.

Trey's grandfather, Tander Phigg, Sr., launched Phigg Paper Products, Inc., in 1928, just in time for the Depression. Married a Catholic girl in 1932 despite her mother's promise to kill herself out of shame.

"Yikes," I said. "Different world back then, huh?"

Trey waved a hand. "Basic histrionics. She didn't kill herself, in case you're looking for a family suicide history."

Like I said—smart kid.

In 1934, the Catholic girl died while delivering her first child, Tander Phigg, Jr. Unlike virtually all men of the day, Phigg Senior never remarried. This led to rumors about the old man and the German housekeeper/nanny who raised Phigg Junior. The rumors were true, Trey had decided long ago.

Phigg Paper Products hung on through the Depression, then struck government-contract gold during World War II, then took off in the postwar boom. Tander Phigg, Sr., became an old-fashioned industrial baron. He was the biggest employer in Fitchburg, Massachusetts, for more than a generation. He kept his name out of the papers and gave wads of money to the University of Massachusetts at Amherst, even though he'd never set foot on campus and never would.

Trey went quiet again, staring up I-93 as it narrowed to two lanes. We had maybe twenty minutes to Concord, and I wanted more info. I thought of another guy I knew a while back, the son of a physicist. The son made 80 million bucks as a venture capitalist—and felt like a failure. "Your father was the son of a great man," I said. "That's not always an easy thing."

Trey nodded slowly and looked at me, maybe reevaluating me, before he went on.

Tander Phigg, Jr., was an only child, raised by the nanny he loved like a mother (and whom, most likely, his father loved like a wife). He went to a bunch of brand-name boarding schools but left them all suddenly and quietly. Nobody ever explained why, so he must've been thrown out, Gentleman Jim style. He finally scraped together a high school diploma and started at UMass Amherst in 1952.

Trey's tone made me glance over. I said, "What's wrong with that?"

"The sons of the rich did *not* go to UMass back then," he said. "Harvard, Dartmouth, maybe Bates or Williams in a pinch."

"Big deal."

"It was then, and my father, and *his* father, knew it. Trust me."

Phigg Junior graduated on schedule in 1956. As far as Trey knew, his father didn't do a single memorable thing in the four years. Diploma in hand, he tried the MBA program at UMass's Isenberg School. Dropped out after two semesters.

Long pause now. We were hitting the southern edge of Concord, didn't have a lot of time left. I said, "And?"

"At that point," Trey said, "I do believe my father rose up on his hind legs for the first and only time in his life."

"Finally."

"Yeah." Half a smile again, Trey cutting his eyes my way. "Yeah, finally."

Trey had pieced together the story while he grew up—his father refused to talk about that part of his life and got pissed whenever Trey tried to.

Tander Junior, miserable in the MBA program, had hauled off and told Tander Senior, a man who'd been working fourteen-hour days six days a week for thirty years, that he'd snapped pictures at UMass football games and turned out to have a knack for it. Tander Junior was dropping out of B-school and heading for New York to study photography.

"Can you imagine," Trey said, "the scene when my father laid all this on *his* father, a first-generation immigrant workaholic industrial baron who'd never so much as seen a talkie?"

I exited 93. State Police HQ was just a few traffic lights east. I said, "Friction?"

"*Beyond* friction!" he said. " 'You are not my son.' 'Never darken my door.' 'Where did I go wrong?' 'Was it because I never remarried?' The works."

But Tander Phigg, Jr., stuck to his guns, moved to New York City, and enrolled in photography classes. After a few months on broke street he called his nanny-mama, who figured out a backdoor way to get him trust-fund income.

I pulled into the lot. Trey and I swapped cell numbers. I had errands, said I'd pick him up when he finished with the detectives.

He popped the door of his rental, got a foot out. "There's got to be more," I said. "Give me a teaser."

"My dad had five happy years in New York," Trey Phigg said. "His *only* five, as far as I've ever been able to figure."

He slammed the door and trotted up the steps. I watched him. In Vietnam, he probably had the same build as most men. Here, he was a hell of a skinny dude.

I wondered how much truth he was telling.

As I drove strip-mall roads looking for a Home Depot, my cell rang. It was a New Hampshire number I didn't recognize. I picked up but said nothing.

"H-hello?"

The voice was familiar, but I wasn't sure where from. Said nothing.

"Mister Sax?"

I realized it was Josh from Motorenwerk. "Go ahead," I said.

"You said to call you if—"

"Go ahead."

"Something's going on at the shop. I made a coffee run. When I came back, a bunch of guys were climbing out of two Escalades."

"What guys?"

"I recognized Ollie's Montreal guy. He usually shows up with a huge driver who's probably a bodyguard, too. But today there were three *more* guys in another Escalade."

"Where are you?"

"I parked a few blocks over. When I saw all those guys, I decided to stay away from the garage and call you."

"Good."

"Should I call the cops?"

I thought about Ollie fighting his guts out even with his arms pinned and his nose smashed. He was a warrior.

Presented with something like this, the Rourke PD wouldn't know whether to shit or go blind. They'd slough the mess off to the staties as fast as they could. The staties would figure out the gist. They might not prove anything, but they could sure put Ollie out of the drug-running business.

I didn't want that.

Yet.

"Don't call the cops," I said. "Cruise past the garage every ten minutes, and call me again when the Escalades are gone."

"Are you sure?"

I clicked off. "No," I said to an empty Dodge. "I'm not sure at all."

CHAPTER SEVEN

An hour later, done at Home Depot, I sat parked in the state police lot and waited for Josh to call back. Trey bounced down the steps and hopped in. "The tail of my poor rental car is riding low," he said.

"Eighty pounds of drywall screws and a hundred pounds of joint compound'll do that."

We hit 93 South. I said we might detour through Rourke. Trey said that was okay by him. I asked what the detectives had talked about.

He said, "Not much—forms, releases, where should the body go. Like that."

I said, "Huh."

He turned to face me. "Okay, that's the second time."

I said, "Second time what?"

"The second time you've acted like you don't believe my father killed himself."

"You got all that from a 'Huh'?"

"Don't play dumb."

He was right. I hate when people play dumb. Might as well treat Trey Phigg the way I'd want to be treated myself. "The statie who showed up when I found your dad was a sharp guy," I said. "He didn't like the way your dad's necktie was knotted. Said it looked awkward as hell, hanging yourself that way."

"And?"

"Like I said, he was a sharp cop. And your dad didn't strike me as a suicide, and you said he didn't strike you that way either."

"So you think *I* killed him? Flew halfway around the world with my wife and my boy, hopped off the airplane, drove to New Hampshire, and fucking hanged a man I hadn't seen in four years?"

"It wouldn't be the dumbest way I ever saw a man kill."

"What about the other police, the detectives I just spoke with? Nothing but sympathy and filling out forms and arrangements to transport the body. Are they all idiots?"

Their sympathy might have been a play to get Trey talking, but I didn't tell him that. At the very least, they had to be doing the same as Randall—working up a timetable to see if he could have cleared JFK customs and driven to Rourke before I found Phigg's body. "Cop work is about clearing cases," I said. "Ninety-nine percent of the time, the obvious answer's the right answer. Look at your dad through a detective's eyes. He's an alcoholic. Sober a long time, sure, but no cop believes there's such a thing as a *former* drunk. Your father used to be rich, but lately he lived in a shack. To most cops, it's pretty simple. Tander Phigg fell a long way, burned through his money, decided to check out." I made a fist and thumped the steering wheel. "Case closed, what's for dinner."

We slowed, funneled into road construction. Trey looked out his window awhile. Finally he said, "You think somebody killed him?"

"Maybe."

"Who? Why?"

"I'll tell you," I said. "But first, you tell *me*."

"Tell you what?"

"Your dad's five happy years."

My cell rang. It was Josh. "Come quick," he said. In the background was a noise like a bear trying to bite through a trash-can lid.

"Ollie hurt?"

"He needs an emergency room, but he doesn't want to go."

"I'm in traffic. Be there soon." Click.

Trey said, "What was all that?"

I finger-drummed the wheel. "That possible detour to Rourke I mentioned? It's on. Tell me about those five happy years."

In 1958, Tander Phigg, Jr., moved to New York City and enrolled in a third-rate photography school run by a Brillo-haired man who walked funny because all his toes froze off in the Ardennes in 1945. He walked even funnier when he was drunk, which was most days. The student population changed every week because the drunk demanded tuition in cold cash, first thing Monday morning, and anybody who couldn't fork it over got the bum's rush down four flights.

To Phigg it was heaven. Once nanny-mama pulled her end run on Tander Senior and freed up trust-fund income, Phigg commuted from a doorman building on the Upper West Side to SoHo and Greenwich Village. He played Artsy Boho all day, then commuted back.

"What's boho?" I said.

"Bohemian. Hippies before there were hippies."

I nodded.

According to nanny-mama—who was Trey's source for the story—Phigg felt comfortable for the first time in his life. He caught Lower Manhattan Fever—poetry readings, basement jazz, very early pop art. (Trey said, "Warhol?" I said, "I know that one.") And photography out the wazoo, of course. He spent most days tramping around the city, shooting whatever struck him. Then he'd head back to the darkroom to experiment.

He was having a ball.

Trey smiled as he told it. We cleared the traffic and eventually sailed down Route 31. "There's even reason to believe Tander Phigg,

Jr., son of the paper baron of Fitchburg, Massachusetts, had himself a cohabitational-level fling," Trey said. "His nanny was sketchy on details, but I read between the lines."

He trailed off, looked at the Souhegan on his side of the car.

I said, "Then what?"

"Then his coach turned into a pumpkin."

I waited.

"Something happened," Trey said. "I'll never know exactly what. In 'sixty-two, my father came home with his tail well and truly between his legs. For the rest of his life he hated to talk about New York, and when he did, all he said was he'd gotten it out of his system."

"What happened at home? He sign on with the family business?"

"Eventually. First he finished up his MBA. Then it was straight to Fitchburg, with a corner office overlooking the river that by then looked and smelled like the Jolly Green Giant's urinal, thanks to my granddad."

"He stepped into his old man's shadow again."

"Never to emerge."

"Why'd he come back?" I said. "You must have wondered. The nanny say anything?"

"Not a syllable."

"You think we could talk with her?" I said, slowing for Rourke's three-block downtown stretch.

"She died four months after my grandfather did, back in 'ninety-six."

"Just like an old married couple. One goes, the other can barely wait to follow."

"You're not the first to make that observation."

We passed Dot's Place, a nail salon, a barbershop with a dead pole. As I turned onto Mechanic Street and eased toward Motorenwerk I made a note: When I checked in with Randall about Trey's timetable, I should ask if Phigg's address book included any pointers back to New York.

When Trey and I stepped into the office at Motorenwerk, we heard Ollie breathing but couldn't see him. I stepped forward, leaned on the counter, looked down.

Ollie sat with his back to a filing cabinet. His face was the color of a three-day-old bruise. He stared straight ahead and rocked a little at the waist, breathing like a train leaving an uphill station. His right pant leg, the one near us, was slit all the way up to plaid boxer shorts. His kneecap was three times as big as it ought to be. Josh knelt on the floor with his back to us. He heard me and turned. "I told him he's got to get to an ER," he said. "But he won't let me call an ambulance."

Ollie, focused on breathing, didn't turn his head. But he pointed a finger at me and said, "Get me the fuck out of here, Sax. I know a guy who can take care of me. No hospitals."

"No dice," I said, looking at the knee. "Listen to Josh. Go to the ER."

"No . . . fucking . . . hospitals." He said it slowly, concentrating on every word. Then he went back to breathing. He turned to look me in the eye, moving carefully, knowing he might pass out. "This guy I know, he'll do a better job than the hack hospitals around here. *Please.*"

He was right about the local hospitals. I said to Josh, "What'd they use? A hammer or something sharp like an awl?"

"Five-pound hammer," Ollie said.

"That's good," I said, nodding, thinking it over. "A hammer's the same as falling square on the floor. If they'd used a chisel or something, you'd have no choice but to go to the hospital."

Ollie fainted.

I said to Josh, "Take him wherever he wanted to go." I told him to fetch his car. Trey and I each got an arm beneath Ollie's meaty shoulders and dragged him outside. I noticed Trey's face was white, his lips pulled thin. He wasn't used to this kind of thing.

I wished I wasn't.

Working Ollie into the smallish backseat of Josh's Audi made me glad he was passed out: We were careful, but Ollie was heavy and he bumped around plenty.

We got the back doors closed. As Josh climbed into the driver's seat I said, "It was definitely Montreal's guys did this?"

He nodded and started the car.

"Why?" I said.

"Ollie wanted out," Josh said.

"How much do you know about what they've been doing?"

"I'm not sure what you mean," Josh said, putting the car in first gear. He damn near ran over my foot as he U-turned out.

Trey said nothing, all color still gone from his face. I pulled his Dodge onto the main drag, thinking about Dot's Place. "Hungry?" I said.

"Dear God no."

I looked over. Trey's body shook as he stared at me. "What the hell is going *on*?" he said. "What the hell *are* you? You talk about smashed knees like they were goddamn *paper cuts,* or *oil changes,* or . . . or . . ."

I needed to settle him down. Angled into a parking spot, killed the engine. I put myself in Trey's shoes. After a while I said, "Helluva twenty-four hours, huh?"

"I wouldn't argue with that."

"You've had more than your share of rough news. You've handled it well."

Trey said nothing.

I watched two old ladies step into the nail salon. "I was you, I'd want two things," I said. "One, I'd want to know what the hell *I'm* all about." Bumped my thumb to my chest. "Two, I'd want to get back to your wife and kid, make sure they're okay."

"You got two out of three," he said. "But there's something else first."

I waited.

"I want to see where my father died," he said, looking me in the eye, color returning to his face.

I put the Dodge in drive.

Except for fresh tire tracks in the clay, the Jut Road shack was just the way I'd left it . . . *yesterday*? That didn't seem possible, but yeah, yesterday.

We climbed from the Dodge and listened to the fast river, the angry bugs.

"From that," Trey said, gesturing at the skeleton of his father's dream house, "to . . . this?"

I started to tell him the shack was once a hydropowered generator for a big house. Then I realized there was no reason for him to give a shit. I shut my mouth instead.

There was no CRIME SCENE tape. The sagging door had been knocked clear off its hinges, probably by EMTs rolling a stretcher. I followed Trey inside, let him see and feel for himself.

Phigg's sad suitcase and sleeping bag were gone. On the floor sat a couple of Dunkin' Donuts cups that hadn't been here yesterday. Trey paced the room slowly, taking everything in. Then he turned to me and spread his arms. "This?" he said. "Only this?"

I nodded.

He paced again, found the milk crates. His eyes traveled up the north wall. When he spotted the pipe stub he pointed, turned to me, raised his eyebrows. I nodded. He cocked his head. He hesitated, then stacked the crates and stepped up. He wobbled, steadied, spun a slow 180. Now he was facing me. "Like this?"

"Yeah," I said. "Come down before you fall, huh?"

He ignored me. He touched his right index finger to the spot just below his throat, where a necktie knot would fall. Then he reached back with the same finger, feeling for the pipe stub. It took him a few tries to locate it.

Trey slow-panned the room. "This is the last thing he saw? This is what Tander Phigg Junior's life boiled down to?"

Tander Phigg the Third began to cry. Silent tears tracked both cheeks.

After a while he went back to the movie-announcer voice he'd used in the car. "Tander Phigg Junior. Mediocre son of a paper baron, fish out of water, expelled from the finest schools in New England. He did as he was told, occupied a corner office that should have been labeled 'Daddy's Boy,' spent his days signing papers presented by groveling employees who snickered behind his back."

Long pause. Trey dropped the fake voice, spread his arms wide, panned the shack one more time. "He died here," he said. "Master of a condemned pump house, pilot of a two-hundred-dollar Nissan, aficionado of three-for-a-buck potpies."

Then he shifted his ankles quickly to knock over the milk-crate stack. The move caught me off guard. I started to reach for Trey, then realized he'd done it on purpose. He rode the top crate to the floor like a surfboard, hopping off at the last instant.

"Let's get the hell out of here," he said.

If Trey Phigg had killed his father, he was one hell of a good liar. But then I'd known plenty of good liars. Hell, I'd *been* one.

Maybe I still was.

"I'll be damned," I said when we got outside.

A silver Jetta was parked beside Trey's rental. Between the cars stood the black woman I'd seen talking with Phigg the day before he died.

She was pretty. The short hair I'd noticed was nearly buzz cut, and she pulled it off because her head had a nice shape. I can never tell how old blacks are—she might be thirty, fifty, or anywhere in between. She stood an inch taller than Trey and held a red leather pocketbook in one hand and a little notebook in the other.

Trey and I stared at her maybe five seconds before she smiled and said, "Patty Marx, from *The Boston Globe*." She fished business cards from the pocketbook as she stepped to us, handed them over.

"I'm Trey Phigg." He shook her hand. Her face went from friendly professional to friendly sympathetic.

"I'm so very sorry about your loss," Patty Marx said. "I profiled your father a while back. I came today to pick up some atmosphere for a follow-up story. I didn't realize anybody would be here." She hesitated. "I'm sorry to intrude. It's my job."

"You wrote about my father?" Trey said.

She nodded. "A year and a half ago. Truth be told, it wasn't a straight profile. More of a look at the fates of old manufacturing towns."

Trey said, "Did he mention me?" Then he tucked his chin to his chest and turned red.

"Very much so," Patty Marx said, squinting. "You moved to . . . Vietnam, was it?"

While Trey nodded, I clicked through possibilities, wondering if I should mention the meet I'd spied on. I decided no—better to give *her* a chance to mention it.

"Why the follow-up?" I said.

"Tander's suicide," she said, looking me in the eye.

Twenty minutes later, after Trey showed the reporter the inside of the shack and set up a sit-down interview, I pointed the Dodge at Framingham and drove. We were quiet. Trey sat with his right elbow on the door's armrest, chin propped on fist, looking at nothing. I wondered what Patty Marx was up to, wondered why she hadn't mentioned her car-to-car meeting with Phigg. Talk to a man the day before he dies, that's a pretty big deal.

After half an hour Trey said, "You promised to tell me what you're all about. How you came by your intimate knowledge of shattered knees and hangings and police procedures."

I owed him that much, but didn't know where to start. "I'm a mechanic by trade," I finally said.

"Where do you work?"

"Well . . . nowhere, for now. I get some money from Charlene. I don't like it and neither does she, but there was a time she needed *my* help, and—"

"Who is Charlene?"

"My girlfriend. Sorry. Anyway, I'm fixing up the Framingham house. Going to sell it and use the cash to open another shop like the one I used to have."

"Which went out of business?"

"Torched by a douche bag."

Long pause. "Are you involved with organized crime?" Trey finally said.

"No. Look, I spent time in prison. Manslaughter two."

"Who did you kill?"

"Someone who fired an automatic pistol at me from six feet away and missed."

"You didn't miss."

"I had a shotgun."

"Wasn't it self-defense, then? Why'd you go to jail at all?"

"The DA thought I did a bunch of other stuff around the same time. He couldn't prove it. So he hosed me on the thing he *could* prove."

"Did you?"

"Did I what?"

"Do a bunch of other stuff?"

I said nothing.

Trey puffed hair from his eyes, frustrated. "We've gone off track," he said. "What I was trying to ask is how did you get started? How did you learn the things you know?"

I thought about that.

Then I talked about it, in a way I never had.

Funny how these things work. A skill—fixing BMWs and Mercedeses, say—leads you into a situation—running a chop shop that pulls air bags and interiors out of high-end cars, say. The new situation forces you to learn new skills—outsmarting cops, moving firearms around, protecting yourself against the wolves who want a piece of whatever you've got. It comes full circle when all anybody knows about you, all they *care* about, are the new skills.

After I drank away my NASCAR ride and my family, I spent a long time cycling through new skills, forgetting the old ones. When I sobered up, the inner-circle Barnburners—the meeting-after-the-meeting crowd, including Tander Phigg—made use of my more recent skills, but they also showed me the old ones were still there. Dust covered but there.

My story killed most of the ride. Trey Phigg listened well. When I finished, he looked at me a long time. I stared at the road but felt his gaze.

"Are you okay?" he said.

I said nothing.

When we got to Framingham, Kieu fed Trey warmed-over lunch. The kid, Tuan, played with Dale and Davey. Randall caught me eyeballing Tuan. Kids can be rough on cats. Randall made a thumb-and-forefinger circle, mouthed "He's okay." I appreciated that.

I nodded Randall away from the Vietnamese jabber. As we left the kitchen Kieu gasped at something Trey had said, rose, rushed around the table, hugged him. I figured he must have told her about the death shack.

I filled Randall in while he unplugged his laptop's charger and sofa-flopped next to me, holding the computer so we could both see the screen.

"First things first," he said, opening a Word document. "Understand I'm working with sketchy numbers on both ends here. I'm guessing it took ninety minutes to two hours for Trey and family to clear customs and rent a car the night Phigg died, and the newspaper reports on Phigg's time of death, per the New Hampshire Staties, have a three-hour window."

His document had links to the articles, copied Google maps, flight schedules, even a weather report from the day in question and EPA gas-mileage estimates for Trey's rental. Thorough as hell.

"Running the numbers in the most optimistic way possible," he said, then paused. "Or do I want to say *pessimistic*? Whichever, Trey Phigg could have landed at JFK, cleared customs, fetched his luggage, rented his Dodge, driven straight to Rourke, and hanged his father."

"*Could* have," I said.

"Yeah, if the murder happened on the late side of the state cops' window. And if he drove up I-95 like a bat out of hell. And if he brought the whole family along to watch. And if he figured out how to hoist a man twice his weight."

"You don't think he did it."

Randall shrugged. "If I were a cop or a DA, I might say I'm unable to rule him out."

"Huh."

"I went through the address book," he said, alt-tabbing to a spreadsheet. "You say you're looking for a New York City connection?"

"An address, maybe a two-one-two area code."

"You want to go back fifty years? What the hell for?"

"Curious," I said. "What chased Tander Phigg Junior back to

Fitchburg, a place he hated, to work a job he hated, for a father he more or less hated?"

"Oooo-kay," Randall said, tapping keys. "There are a bunch of area codes for NYC."

"This would be an old number," I said. "Trust me—two-one-two."

"There's just this one." He pointed at a number next to the name *Chas Weinberg*.

I said, "Google the number."

He was already opening a browser.

It was a business listing. Charles A. Weinberg, nothing else. Randall did a Switchboard.com search and found the business listed under Art Galleries & Dealers. Wooster Street, New York.

Randall said, "SoHo." He saw the question in my eyes. "Artsy-fartsy? Loft living? Galleries and coffee shops, Beat Generation style?"

I didn't know what he was talking about, but it squared with things Trey had said. I asked Randall to print the name and address. Looked at my watch. It was nearly four. My stomach growled as I dialed my cell.

A man answered. His words said, "Charles A. Weinberg, Evan speaking." His tone said, "You are a piece of shit."

I said, "Chas Weinberg, please."

"And your business is?"

"My business is put Chas Weinberg on the phone," I said. "If he's not there, I'll leave a message."

"Oh dear, a message! Let me . . . a pen! A paper! A most important message from an exceedingly butch caller! O happy day!" His voice started to fade. I pictured him playing for laughs, other people watching him. "Right! A pen! A paper! A . . . whoops!"

Click.

I stared at my cell. Then looked up, saw Randall staring at me. "Uh-oh," he said. "I've seen that face. What happened?"

"I'm going to New York."

"What happened?"

"Can you print me a MapQuest?"

"What happened?"

We stared each other down.

Finally Randall sighed. "Half a plan and your dick in your hand," he said. "Remember last time we tried it that way?"

I did. We had waded into a restaurant and started a donnybrook that wound up with six guys whaling on each other in a handicapped toilet stall. And we'd left with nothing to show for it. Huge risk, no reward. "This is different," I said.

"How?"

"New York's a long drive," I said. "I'll leave in the morning, try to get there around eleven. I'll have plenty of time to cool out."

"You're driving?"

"I don't like flying."

Charlene got home at six thirty. I was playing Trivial Pursuit with Sophie. TV Edition, the only version I stood a chance in.

Still, Sophie had earned all six of her pie slices and was moving in for the kill when Charlene kicked the front door open. She shouldered in with her purse, her laptop, and a steaming bag from an upscale Italian place.

Sophie and I popped up, went to the front hall, lightened Charlene's load. Charlene kissed Sophie. "Hey there, last-day girl!" she said. "How does it feel to be a seventh-grader?"

Sophie talked about how it felt while Charlene emptied the bag of lasagna, garlic bread, and a salad. I set the table. We paid a lot of attention to Sophie, egged her on, smiled more than we needed to. After Tuesday, we were grateful to have something to focus on other than each other.

An hour later we had to face each other. Charlene waved goodbye down her front steps as Sophie piled into a giggle-filled Honda

Pilot and headed for a sleepover. Charlene walked slowly back to the kitchen where I was stuffing dishes into the dishwasher. She grabbed a Diet Sprite—her big thrill; she's a drunk like me and the most disciplined person I've ever known—popped it, sipped it, set it on the granite countertop. "Well," she said.

I killed the water, wiped my hands, and leaned on the counter myself. It's a big kitchen. We were fifteen feet apart. I said, "I came over tonight because I wanted to say good-bye. Going to New York tomorrow."

"For how long?"

"Probably just the day. Maybe two."

"Flying or Acela?"

"Driving."

Half a smile. "You're scared to fly, aren't you?"

"Somebody once said a good race driver makes a lousy passenger."

"You like to be in control."

"Yes." I slipped my boots off and stepped to her, put my hands on her hips. She left her hands on the counter and said, "What's happening, Conway?"

"With this Tander Phigg thing?"

"No. With you." She cupped my chin. "Where *are* you?"

"I'm here."

"Technically you're here," she said. "Physically." She made a soft little intake as she said it—I was pushing a little now, hips on hips.

"I'm here right now," I said.

Charlene stroked my cheek. "No, you're not." She walked toward the stairs.

I slept on the couch, Trivial Pursuit shoveled beneath, dishwasher thrumming.

CHAPTER EIGHT

The next day about noon I found a parking space at the corner of Wooster and Spring Streets, New York City. I parked, tossed the MapQuest printout on the F-150's bench, rubbed my eyes, shrugged tension from my shoulders. It had been a rotten drive in heavy rain.

I hate New York. Too big. Too much.

I took it in. The street was paved with cobblestones. The building was right on the corner. Yellow brick, five stories. The bottom floor was a storefront: black aluminum-framed plate glass that had been tinted near-black. Matte-silver words on the door said CHARLES A. WEINBERG. The overall message: Extreme coolness here, tourists will be mocked.

That reminded me of Evan, my buddy from the telephone. I fished in the glove box for a Sharpie, pocketed it, got out, locked the truck, and hunched across the street through the rain.

I pulled the door and winced at the noise that hammered me. Music, I guessed, way too fast, way too loud. I stepped in and forearm-wiped rain from my face.

It was dark enough so that my eyes needed time to adjust. Once they did I saw that around the perimeter of the gallery, every eight feet or so, a spot shone on whatever they were selling—paintings and sculptures, mostly. In a far corner I swore I spotted an Ace Hardware wheelbarrow, rusted, lit like the *Mona Lisa*.

In the center of the space, two kids stared at me. College age? It's hard for me to tell anymore. Everybody under forty looks . . . unfinished. The boy was short and couldn't weigh more than a buck and a quarter. He had bleached and buzzed hair, rabbity eyes behind chunky black glasses. Big surprise: He wore a black shirt, black pants, black shoes.

The girl was dressed the same way. She was taller than me and as skinny as the boy. Looked like a vulture that hadn't found any roadkill for a while. She had a shaved head with a Chinese character tattooed above each ear. Her eyes were smarter than the boy's.

I pointed at him. "Evan?"

He either didn't hear me over the music or pretended he didn't. I stepped closer and said it again. He ignored me again. The tall girl shifted her weight.

Another step. I said, "Can you turn it down?" Had to more or less shout it, even though I stood two feet away.

The boy said, "The music?"

I cupped my hands. "Is that what it is? Thought it was three Germans banging on washtubs and shouting their times tables."

The boy gave me deadpan rabbit eyes, but the tall girl half smiled and stepped behind a partition. The music died.

"Thank God," I said. "Evan?"

He said nothing. The girl returned. I said, "I'd like to speak with Chas Weinberg. He around?"

The girl said, "Do you have an appointment?"

"No," I said. "Got a piece of paper?"

She found a slip. I pulled my Sharpie and wrote: *Tander Phigg hanged himself 2 days ago*. Folded the sheet. "If Weinberg reads this," I said, handing it to her, "he'll want to see me."

She turned and started toward the back of the gallery. I said, "Wait. Is this Evan?"

She stopped. "That's Evan all right."

Evan stared at me, arms folded across his chest. But not for long. I got my left hand under his chin, grabbed his throat, and jacked him to his tiptoes. The girl said, "Hey," but she didn't put much into it.

I quick-stepped Evan backward until his bleached head thumped drywall. I watched the fear in his eyes, tried to convince myself I took no pleasure from it. I bit the cap off my Sharpie and said, "Hold still."

On his forehead, in the neatest block letters I could make, I wrote: MANNERS.

He squeaked when I released him, rabbited off to the back where they must have a bathroom. As he passed the tall girl she read his forehead, smiled, covered the smile with a hand. "I'll be right back," she said.

I wandered. It *was* an Ace Hardware wheelbarrow. The tire was half inflated, and surface rust fought with the sky-blue paint. A card on the nearby wall said it was a found object by so-and-so. There was no price tag.

I heard steps, turned. The tall girl said she would take me to Chas. I thumbed at the wheelbarrow. "Is this for sale?"

"Of course."

"How much?"

"That piece is forty-six hundred."

New York.

The cheap elevator had obviously been added just to meet handicapped-access regs. While we waited for it I introduced myself. The tall girl looked at my hand a few seconds, took it. "I'm A," she said.

"A?"

She blushed some and nodded. The elevator doors rattled open. We stepped in. "What's your real name?" I said.

"Alexandra."

"Not cool enough for New York?"

"Apparently not."

"But a nice name back in . . . Wisconsin?"

Quick swivel. "How'd you know?"

"Don't worry," I said. "Give it six more months, nobody'll be able to tell."

The doors opened. I stepped into Chas Weinberg's apartment.

I'd expected it to be more or less like the gallery downstairs—cold, black, modern. It wasn't. The first thing I noticed was light, plenty of it: huge windows on the north and east sides. Even on a rainy day it was bright, especially compared to the gallery. The second thing I noticed was quiet music. No Germans banging on washtubs; jazz guitar instead, coming from hidden speakers.

It was a big space, this room alone an easy forty by forty. I wondered if Weinberg owned the building. If he did, he was a rich man.

Some of the furniture was squared off, modern, the way I expected. But some was old as hell and hand-carved. I saw walnut, ebony, southern yellow pine. The styles, ages, and woods were jumbled, but they all looked right together.

Here and there on the walls were paintings, perfectly lit. I didn't recognize them, but from the way they were presented I figured they were the cream of the crop.

As I scanned I did a double take: I'd nearly missed Chas Weinberg himself, sitting in a peach-colored chair not six feet away from me. Next to him were an end table and a matching chair.

He sat still, legs crossed, taking me in. I faced him and did the same. He was deep into his eighties, thin. Even sitting he looked tall, had to've been my height in his prime. Still-thick white hair flowed from a widow's peak, and his eyebrows matched the hair. His face was craggy in the right way.

Chas Weinberg motioned with a long hand. "Sit, sir, I insist. Sit and tell me why an old mediocrity like Tander Phigg bothered to hang himself."

His voice was higher than I expected, but it wasn't squeaky—was almost a singsong. Weinberg was used to hearing himself talk, and he didn't mind the sound.

As I sat, a man whipped silently past, silver tray in hand. He was dressed like the ones downstairs, black on black on black, buzz cut up top. But he looked older than Evan and Alexandra. Pushing thirty, maybe. He unloaded the tray on the table: coasters, two tall glasses, pitcher of water, no ice. He poured, then turned to leave. Weinberg snapped his fingers. "Wait here please, Esio."

Esio stopped, spun, stood at attention.

Weinberg leaned, extended a long hand. "Charles Weinberg, sir. You are?"

I said my name.

"A pleasure, Mister Sax. Before we discuss Tander Phigg, crashing bore and suicide, will you humor me on a point?"

"Sure."

He pointed at my T-shirt. "What is this?" He saw the question in my eyes. "This 'Champion Spark Plugs'? Que es?"

I looked down. "For crying out loud, Champion Spark Plugs are Champion Spark Plugs. The shirt's a freebie from when I ran my own shop. You know, the sales reps come by with stuff."

"Yes, but what *is* it? What is Champion Spark Plugs? I ask because that's a truly iconic logotype. And what sort of shop did you run?"

I looked at him awhile. I wondered if he was kidding around, decided he wasn't. Esio had produced a BlackBerry and stood with thumbs poised to take notes.

I said, "Champion and spark plugs is like McDonald's and hamburgers."

Weinberg nodded over tented fingers. "Esio," he said, "see if anybody's done anything with this Champion Spark Plugs." Esio was already on it, thumb-typing away.

I said, "My shop worked on European cars. Mostly Germans, but some Saabs and Volvos, too."

"Really!" He looked me up and down with smiling eyes. I half wanted to punch him in the face, or at least pull my Sharpie again. Weird thing, though: The other half of me wanted to please Weinberg, wanted to keep him interested. I said, "Before that I raced cars. NASCAR."

"Goodness," he said. "Were you a television superstar, walking around in one of those cute little billboard jumpsuits? Did you hold hands with your Implants Barbie wife and pretend to sing 'The Star-Spangled Banner'?"

"Drank myself out of a ride before I made the big time," I said. "That's how I met Tander Phigg. AA."

Weinberg sighed, sipped water. Esio left us. As he disappeared behind a Japanese-looking screen, his BlackBerry rang.

I gave Weinberg a two-minute recap on Phigg. He listened well. When I was done he tapped his teeth and squinted. "'Twas many years ago, and Tander Phigg was a barely memorable player during a very memorable time. Indeed, but for that awful name I doubt I'd recall him at all."

Esio returned, silent as usual. Weinberg sensed him and flicked a go-away hand, but Esio approached anyway and spoke in his ear, then stood at attention.

"Evan downstairs wants to call the police and report a hate crime," Weinberg said. "Please explain."

I explained. When I was done Weinberg looked at me ten seconds. Then he threw his head back and laughed like hell. Esio took the cue, laughing just as hard and for exactly the same duration.

Finally Weinberg took a handkerchief from the breast pocket of his blue suit and dabbed the corners of his eyes. He said to Esio, "Tell Evan to put down the phone, take the rest of the day off, and return tomorrow with a clean forehead."

"Bug and tar remover," I said.

They looked at me. "Bug and tar remover, like you use to clean the front of your car?" I said. "It'll take that Sharpie right off. You can get it at Walmart, if there's one nearby."

Weinberg cracked up again, doubling over, saying "bug and tar remover" over and over. When he had it out of his system he told Esio to relay the message. "And *do* get a picture of Evan before he leaves, please."

I let him settle down. After a while I said, "Tander Phigg."

"Of course," he said. "As noted, he was a mediocrity, a not-quite. I believe the current word is *wannabe*."

I waited. Weinberg sipped water and squinted at nothing, pulling memories. I listened to a jazz duo, guitar and bass, on the invisible speakers.

Finally Weinberg nodded to himself and told it.

He thought Phigg had appeared on the scene in 1960 or so. I asked if it could be '58. He snapped his fingers and said yes, it was before JFK.

By then, Weinberg was an established kingpin in Manhattan's modern art and queer scenes. He'd graduated from Yale in '43, had done a Navy stint counting crates on New York Harbor docks at the tail end of World War II. Then he'd launched one of the first avant-garde studios. In 1949, he said, he'd bought the building we were sitting in.

In 1958, when Phigg wandered down from Fitchburg and declared himself a boho photographer, carpetbaggers like him were a dime a dozen to New York's artsy types. "So predictable," Weinberg said. "The ghastly portfolio, the Charlie Parker fetish, the two-month beard, the Karl Marx phase, the Jackson Pollock phase. Of course, the gay tryst was often part of the checklist, and we didn't complain about *that*."

Weinberg meandered for ten minutes, rehashing stories from the time that had nothing to do with Phigg. I let him, hoping he'd talk his way around to a Phigg memory sooner or later.

It paid off. Weinberg snapped his fingers. "He was a photographer, wasn't he?"

I nodded.

"I remember because they were at the absolute bottom of the totem pole, all those boys from Indiana who bought Hasselblads because they couldn't draw a straight line." Weinberg nodded, remembering like hell now. "A few of us were forced to admit, bitterly and with no goodwill whatsoever, mind you, that this Phigg might have a dram of actual *talent*."

The memory led to others. There'd been rumors that Phigg's father was loaded, even more so than most carpetbaggers' parents. The rumors were confirmed when he invited a few of Weinberg's comrades to his apartment—that doorman building on the Upper West Side.

Weinberg looked at me like he'd delivered a punch line, but from my nonreaction he saw I didn't get it. "It was the worst thing he could have *done,* don't you see? Any credibility he'd built up through merit was dashed forever when we learned he was merely slumming down here."

"Why?"

"Because it was a *revolution,* dear heart. We were proud to live the way we lived. This was very early, before SoHo was SoHo, really. I'd bought this building with money I didn't have. I daresay it's the smartest thing I've ever done, but we didn't know that then. I didn't rent out lofts to be trendy; I rented out lofts to pay the mortgage."

"But the kids you rented to, the carpetbaggers," I said. "They *all* had rich daddies, didn't they?"

"Of course, but they had the decency to hide the fact," he said. "And Tander Phigg's failure to grasp that was indicative. He never quite *got* it. He was a born outsider."

I thought about that. "He wasn't enough of a phony."

"If you insist." He waved that long hand, thumbed his chin, remembered some more. "As I say, it just about dashed his credibility forever. Everybody froze him out for a year or more. And you haven't seen a proper freeze-out until you've seen one conducted by a bunch of art queens. Tander Phigg might as well have been invisible."

A gust slapped rain against the windows like bird shot, hard enough to make us both look.

After a while I said, "So you all gave him the cold shoulder for a year. Did he make a comeback?"

"He did, bless his heart, and a grand one at that. Some said it was calculated. Bosh and piffle, said I, Tander Phigg wasn't capable of such cunning."

He wanted me to ask.

I waited.

But he waited better: He half turned in his chair, picked up a glass and the pitcher, poured.

"You win," I said. "What was Phigg's big move?"

He poured himself water, sipped, looked at the glass, savored his moment. "He took up with Myna Roper."

I waited, watching Weinberg hide a smirk.

Finally I said, "Who the hell is Myna Roper?"

"Beautiful girl, an Amazon, six feet tall and the prettiest skin I've ever seen. She handled phones and filing for a piano mover down the block, if memory serves. But what made her interesting was that she sat as a model, here and in the Village, to augment her income."

I poured myself a glass of water, watched Weinberg smile at nothing. "She was sketched and shot by thousands of horny little carpet-bagger artist-boys," he said. "She had the surprisingly rare capability of working in the nude and maintaining some dignity about it, which tended to make the horny little artist-boys hornier, you see?"

"No."

"She played both virgin and whore in their sticky little dreams, and thus cowed the absolute hell out of them."

"So Phigg worked up the guts to ask out a cute model," I said. "Was it really that big a deal?"

"Oh dear, I left out a pertinent detail." Weinberg sipped to mask his smirk, then set down his glass and looked me in the eye. "Mister Sax, Myna Roper was a great strapping negress. Black as the ace of spades, in fact."

CHAPTER NINE

We felt another gust, watched rain rattle windows. "White guy dating a black girl," I said. "What year are we up to?"

"'Sixty-one. It's easy to pinpoint because we were all giddy over JFK and Jackie. Camelot, you know, 'Ahsk not. . . .' All things were possible, which is why Tander Phigg's timing was exquisite, whether by luck or design."

"So nobody held it against them?"

Weinberg laughed. "*Against* them? They became celebrities, an absolute must-have couple at parties and openings! They were instant A-listers, though we lacked the term."

"Invite the mixed couple, prove how . . . naughty you are?"

"I'm sure we all preferred 'progressive' or 'forward thinking,' but basically, yes."

"Phigg went from the shithouse to the penthouse, just like that."

"Well put!" Weinberg said. "I don't think he realized exactly *why*, second-rater that he was. We used to have endless arguments about the couple. Some styled Tander Phigg a Machiavellian mastermind, especially when he parlayed Myna into a couple of one-man shows. I said nonsense, the schlemiel simply loves the girl. You could see it in his dull little eyes."

Esio appeared and spoke in Weinberg's ear. Weinberg looked at his watch. "Five minutes," he said to Esio. "My apologies," he said to me, making a *what-can-you-do* shrug. "A telephone meeting."

I said, "What happened to Phigg and Myna Roper?"

"I was just trying to recall," he said. "And let me say I've enjoyed this, Mister Sax. I've hit that dreadful age at which memories from half a century ago are far preferable to today's. Not to mention clearer."

He sighed, stared at nothing, tapped fingernail to teeth. "There was a vague disaster of some sort, as there had to be. Nobody was certain what iceberg the SS *Tander and Myna* hit. The uncertainty led to bitchy speculation, of course. An abortion? A parental discovery? Who knows? But sometime in late 'sixty-one or 'sixty-two, Tander and Myna absented themselves without warning. I heard she headed south, where she'd come from, and he went back to Massachusetts and daddy's money."

"Do you know where she came from?"

"South Carolina rings a bell, but please don't hold me to it."

"How about I leave you my number?" I said. "Maybe somebody else from back then remembers. You can ask around."

"You may give the number to Esio, but whom, exactly, would I ask?" He spread his hands. "They're all dead."

I thumped northeast on I-95, wipers set on intermittent in fading rain. I wished my truck had an automatic transmission, stared at the ass end of a semi. Somebody had finger-written WASH ME on the semi's roll-up door. Underneath, somebody else had written BLOW ME.

It was just after four. I was tired, tired, tired. Felt like a week since I got cold-cocked at Motorenwerk, but it was just three days ago. There'd been a lot of action since then, which was okay. But there'd been a lot of talk, too.

People talk too much.

Traffic gained speed once I cut north on I-91. But not much. There was no sense jumping lanes; I tucked in behind the BLOW ME truck and rode, thought about what to do next.

I needed to check in with Randall and Charlene but decided to take four hours without palaver while I could.

I half smiled. *Palaver* was a word from my dad, the only fancy word ever used by the welder from Mankato, Minnesota. He ditched me and my mom when I was eleven, hooked up with a stock-car team in Massachusetts. When I was thirteen, I came east to live with him. That's how I learned to be careful what I wished for: By the time I moved in, my dad was drinking hard. I hadn't seen him but once since I dropped out during my junior year of high school.

The exit for I-84 surprised me. I cut off a semi and settled in for the run to Massachusetts.

Fathers and sons. Tander Phigg Senior, Junior, the Third. I thought about Phigg Junior's five happy years in New York.

It was easy to picture Phigg Senior the industrialist, getting pissed when his son ran off to play Artsy Photo Boy. It was easy to picture Senior keeping tabs on Junior—informally, through the grapevine, or not so informally, through a detective. When Senior learned about the black girlfriend, he must've hit the roof. It was easy to picture him laying down the law, telling his son to cut the bullshit and come home—or get cut out of the trust fund, the will.

As I thought this through I kept tripping over something. Figured out what it was while I crept toward the tolls where I-84 emptied into the Massachusetts Turnpike. Chas Weinberg was fuzzy on some details, but he'd been dead-nuts certain that Phigg was a second-stringer, a dime-a-dozen wannabe.

That didn't square with the Tander Phigg, Jr., I knew, the Phigg whose stories got bolder as time passed, who came on strong. The Phigg I knew was brash, a man who'd bragged about his river mansion and flipped up his polo-shirt collar even when he was living in a shack.

Far as I was concerned, brash was for the young. Hang around long enough, life stomps the brash out of you. But it seemed the opposite was true for Tander Phigg. Maybe that was why I hadn't liked him.

I wondered if there was more bad blood between Phigg and Trey than Trey had let on. Sure, Randall's timetable made him look like a long shot. But it couldn't hurt to learn more.

Mass. Pike East, homebound on autopilot while the sun set behind me. I faced a choice—Framingham or Shrewsbury? If I ran to Framingham I could fill in Randall, maybe get Trey to say more about his father.

But Shrewsbury meant Charlene, not to mention Sophie.

I smiled and headed for Shrewsbury.

Next morning. Saturday. The sun rolled across my chest as I woke up, stretched in twisted sheets, opened my eyes.

Charlene sat on the bed in a towel, staring at me and idly scratching my chest. I looked at her blue eyes, her damp hair. She bleaches it. I pretend I don't know.

I said, "Time?"

"Ten past eight."

"Wow." I'm usually an early riser.

"You slept like a dead man. You snored like a chain saw. I kicked you."

I grabbed at her towel. She held it closed. "This bed," she said, and bounced a couple of times to remind me how it squeaked.

"Didn't stop us last night."

Charlene didn't laugh, didn't open the towel as I expected. "You came back here," she said. "Why?"

"I was on the Pike. I thought about here, I thought about my house. Here was where I wanted to be."

She nodded, looked at nothing, finger-twirled my chest hair without knowing it. After a while she leaned over and kissed my cheek. Then she rose and went to her walk-in closet.

I gave myself three minutes in the sunbeam, then hit the shower.

I stepped out the front door with three waffles in my belly. The rain had pushed the heat past, made perfect weather. I needed a Windbreaker now but knew I'd spend most of the day in a T-shirt.

The weekend plan was to drywall a room in the Framingham house. But I checked messages as I climbed into my truck and found the plan blown up: Randall had texted he'd be gone all weekend. Hadn't said where.

I frowned at the message and started to get sore at him, then felt like a jerk. He'd done more for me than I deserved. I shot him a text with the bare bones of what I'd learned from Weinberg: Phigg's years in NYC, his affair with Myna Roper, a black gal probably from South Carolina, Phigg whimpering back to Fitchburg.

Two seconds after I hit Send, the phone buzzed. It was Josh from Motorenwerk. I picked up and asked how Ollie was doing.

"He wants to see you," he said, so quiet I barely heard. Then he said an address and a few landmarks in Mason, New Hampshire, a border town near Rourke. He clicked off before I could ask anything.

Last thing I wanted to do on a Saturday was slog north again, but I needed to hear whatever Ollie had to say. Hell, I needed to take a harder look at him for the murder—he obviously had bad blood with Phigg. It wasn't crazy to wonder if Phigg had learned about the heroin-packing scam and tried to work an angle somehow.

So seventy minutes later I was on Route 123, paralleling a railroad bed. I slowed and looked to my right for one of the landmarks Josh had mentioned—a mailbox set in a stack of steel wheels. Spotted it, pulled in, bounced a quarter mile down a dirt road. The road opened into a clearing.

I sat in my truck, looked around the clearing, didn't like the vibe. Two half-rotted F-100s and a Bronco were jacked up stupid-tall, monster-truck style. Jesus, one of the F-100s had a goddamn machine gun mounted in its bed, looking like something from the old *Rat Patrol* TV show. Four cheapo travel trailers, 1970s vintage, huddled in a half-assed semicircle. Three scrawny wild turkeys gobbled and pecked the hardscrabble.

The main building sagged like hell. It was white forty years ago and had cinder-block front steps. A TV satellite lay in the yard where it'd fallen off the roof and never been fixed. Farther off I saw an outbuilding. Miserable dog-yelps carried from it.

I didn't like it one bit. If Josh and Ollie had landed here, that was their problem. I put my truck in reverse and was easing the clutch out when a screen door banged. "Mister Sax! Mister Sax!"

Shit. It was Josh, waving, fast-walking toward me, grinning. The grin didn't make sense until I looked hard—it was the nervous type that masked big-time fear.

I sighed and killed the motor. "What the hell is this place?"

Josh's mouth fluttered like he wanted to cry. "You said take him wherever he wanted to go," he finally said, anger flashing through the fear. "This was it."

"I say again, what is this place?"

"Welcome," he said, sweeping his arm like Vanna White, "to the Beet Brothers' compound." Josh looked over his shoulder at the falling-down house, then leaned closer. "These guys are lunatics. Flat out fucking lunatics."

I took a guess. "One of them a half-assed doctor, a medic in the army or some such?"

"How'd you know?"

I shrugged. It was an easy guess. I fished under the passenger seat and came up with the Browning P35 I'd taken from Ollie at Motorenwerk. Stuck it down the back of my pants, grabbed my Windbreaker as I stepped from the truck, tied the Windbreaker's arms around my waist.

As we crossed sixty feet of dirt and weeds to the cinder-block steps, I told Josh to give me twenty seconds' worth of info on this shithole.

"The brothers that own the place are gone right now," he said. "Hunting or stealing or whatever. They've got fifty-sixty acres on either side of the old railroad tracks, they fuck around down there all day. One of them was a medic in Vietnam, just like you said. Ollie's on a sofa in the front room, been there since I brought him."

We stepped through the screen door. I about puked at the smell. I read somewhere that smell and sound are the senses that touch off memories. The Beet Brothers' stench touched off a doozy:

In my worst time, maybe fifteen years ago, I spent a summer in Lowell, Massachusetts, in a half-assed camp a bunch of us bums set up behind an industrial park. One of the bums, a huffer whose face was always gold-flecked because that was his paint color of choice, passed the time prowling for house cats and skinning them. He kept the pelts in the shack he'd built from cardboard and pallets. The rest of us gave the shack a wide berth, knowing he was even crazier than we were.

But one night, the huffer stole two dollars from a pal of mine. A half dozen of us got brave on Mad Dog 20/20, waited until the huffer passed out, and flooded into his shack to kick the shit out of him. It was mid-August, a hundred degrees easy.

When we swarmed the shack, the cat-pelt stench hit us like a mallet. Every one of us puked or passed out or both. I remember seeing one guy's eyes roll up as he fell forward. It was more than a smell in there, it was . . . an *immersion*. In death, hate, focused insanity.

This house smelled like that shack.

Ollie said, "You get used to it."

Behind me Josh said, "I haven't." He said it real quiet.

I followed Ollie's voice to my right. The front room was ten by twelve and had windows on two sides. The windows were wide open, thank God. An ancient console TV sat in the front corner of the room, set up with the first set of rabbit ears I'd seen in five years. On the tube: a court show, slightly fuzzy, a black woman saying her boyfriend had promised to split the rent but never did.

Opposite the TV was a couch, brown, older than the TV. Ollie Dufresne was propped up on it. He wore the same clothes I'd seen him in at his shop, his right pant leg split, that leg straight out on the couch. The leg itself looked much better than I expected, as if it'd been worked on by experts. A snow-white bandage wrapped the knee, an ice pack sat on top, and aluminum rods had been taped to hold everything straight.

Ollie wore half a smile as he watched me try to figure it all out. "Admirable field dressing, eh? One of the brothers did it, bless him. He's a sort of medical savant. He can't tell you who's president, but during a tiff in one of your more despicable African countries, I once watched him stuff ten yards of intestine back inside a man and sew him up with a safety pin and dental floss. The man was on his feet two days later, couldn't have gotten better care at Walter Reed."

I sat at the end of the sofa and breathed through my mouth. "Chrissake, what *is* this place?"

Behind me on TV, the woman's boyfriend said it was true he hadn't paid any rent, but he *had* made four payments on his girl-friend's car. Josh stepped to the TV and clicked it off.

From out back, maybe a mile off, we heard noise—a shotgun, at least two automatic weapons, a big-block motor, rebel yells.

Ollie and I locked eyes. At the exact same time we said, "Let's get the fuck out of here."

CHAPTER TEN

Three wide on my truck's bench seat isn't bad. Three wide with Ollie's leg sticking straight out was. Josh and I leaned him against the door, then set his leg across our laps. When I shifted into second and fourth, Josh had to pull the leg toward our bellies so the lever wouldn't hit it.

Nobody said anything for a while. I wanted to put some miles and some turns between us and the brothers, whoever they were. I checked the rearview a lot.

After twenty minutes and a couple of east–north–east–south jogs, I relaxed. "Where to?" I said.

"Enosburg Falls, Vermont," Ollie said. "Near the Canadian border."

I looked at my watch. "Take all day."

"Four hours."

"How about I take you to his car?" I said, chinning at Josh.

"We can really use you," Ollie said. "My Montreal guy is a tough bastard."

"Why would he still be looking for you? Seems to me he sent his message already."

"That he did," Ollie said. "But with the message sent, he promised he was going to look very hard at our recent . . . transactions."

"And once he looks them over?"

Ollie gritted his teeth as we hit a pothole. "He'll be back."

"What were you skimming?" I said. "Dope or cash?"

Ollie said nothing.

"Dope or cash?" I said.

Nothing.

I checked my mirrors, pulled over to the Armco barrier, killed the engine. "Get out," I said.

Josh said, "Here?"

Ollie said, "Knock it off."

"You want me to make an eight-hour round-trip, you'll tell me every damn thing," I said.

Ollie and Josh looked at each other. "It's not an unreasonable request," Ollie said.

Josh shrugged. "Your call."

"Drive," Ollie said.

I lit up the truck and pulled out.

Ollie said, "What do you want first?"

"How you knew those yahoos back there, the Beet Brothers. And that bit about seeing a man's guts blown out in Africa." I looked at his pain-white face. "You're not just some guy runs a two-lift garage in Rourke, New Hampshire."

"Believe it or not," Ollie said, "I did a stint in the French Foreign Legion."

I nodded. "Makes sense."

Ollie said, "Most people don't even realize it still exists."

"I've known some mercs."

"From the Legion?"

"No," I said. "But they talk about it. With respect."

Josh said, "He took an airport in Iraq in Gulf War One."

I said, "All by himself?"

Ollie laughed. "We were with the French Sixth, a light-armor division." Long pause. "You said you know a few mercs, so you probably understand that the world I used to inhabit was a small one. Nevertheless, try to imagine my shock when I ran into the Beets at Walmart a few years ago."

"Beets," I said. "Explain that. Nickname, or what?"

"Brothers," Josh said. "Bret, Bobby, and Bert Beet."

"You're shitting me."

"My mouth to God's ear," Ollie said. "Bert's the medical savant I described. Anyway, they spotted me in Walmart and we reminisced about the two or three hellholes we'd cohabited, and so on. When they learned I lived fifteen miles away, they had a virtual circle jerk right there in the pain-relievers-and-cold-relief aisle. I've been dodging them ever since."

"He has a standing invitation to ride around in four-by-fours with the brothers and shoot deer with machine guns," Josh said.

"Big fun," I said.

"For them," Ollie said, and patted his knee. "Anyway, when this happened and I awoke with young Josh trying to get me locked up by calling the gendarmerie, Bert Beet was the first man I thought of."

We were quiet a while. If half of Ollie's stories were true, he was one interesting dude. When we hit the on-ramp to I-89, I got us up to seventy-five, settled in, and said, "Tell me about Montreal."

Ollie puffed his cheeks out. "Where to begin?"

"Start with your father," Josh said.

"It always comes down to the father," Ollie said. "Doesn't it?"

Oliver Dufresne was born in Enosburg Falls. His mother was an American schoolteacher, his father a snowmobile tuner—a racer until he busted up his hips in a wreck—from Bedford, Quebec, thirty miles north of the border.

The father was a damn good tech and a damn lousy drinker. When things got tough in the marriage, he ditched his wife and kid and moved back to Bedford. He developed a pattern you could set your watch by. He would hook on with a snowmobile race team or tuner shop and be a model employee for six or eight months. Then he'd hit the bottle hard, would drink his way out of a job and onto the dole.

While growing up Ollie hated school, took his mother for granted, and daydreamed about how cool it'd be to live with his dad. I shook my head, thinking he was telling *my* story. Typical son, worshipping the bum who'd deserted him.

He spent as much time as he could in Bedford, wheedling visits though neither his mother nor his father wanted them. By the time his dad died of cirrhosis at age forty-four, Ollie had his legacy—a knack for working on engines and the ability to speak French.

"What about this?" I said, making the *glug-glug* drinking gesture. "You inherit it, too?"

"Never had a problem with it."

"Lucky."

"I know."

Ollie had no interest in school, said the best day of his life was graduation. He skipped the ceremony, didn't so much as leave his mother a note, and thumbed west because there was a Grand Prix race in Detroit that year.

"Formula One?" I said.

"Indeed. You a fan?"

"I know something about racing."

"Then you may remember they ran an F1 race in Detroit for a few years. It was one of those Mickey Mouse affairs through streets lined with Jersey barriers and chain-link fences."

I said I didn't remember—wasn't much of an F1 fan. Ollie said I hadn't missed much, not in Detroit anyway.

Once there, he'd surprised himself by talking his way into Team Brabham's garage, where he did scut work all weekend. When the race was over, Ollie got an even bigger surprise. The Brabham guys kind of adopted him, this short, round little guy who did all the shittiest jobs, never complained, and spoke French. They asked if he wanted to travel with the team awhile.

"You said, 'Hell, yes.'"

"Precisely." And away they went, once Ollie scrambled for a passport. He wound up spending a freebie summer in England, France, Germany, Portugal. Then the series doubled back to North America for races in Montreal and Mexico City.

Which was where Team Brabham dumped him. The F1 traveling circus was moving to Australia and Japan, and while the Brabham guys liked their mascot, they couldn't afford to take him that far.

Before getting bounced, Ollie had spent dozens of long nights with the other low man on Brabham's totem pole, a bashed-up Scot. The Scot had maybe three teeth left in his head, but he had plenty of stories. He'd been a coastal smuggler, had been one of the last men gang-pressed into the Merchant Marines, had joined the Royal Navy during the war. After, with no family to go home to, he'd done a long stint in the French Foreign Legion.

The guy told stories to impressionable Ollie that made his Foreign Legion years sound like a cross between time spent with the Hardy Boys and the Arabian Knights.

And so Oliver Dufresne, dumped in Mexico City, broke, barely eighteen, thumbed east to Veracruz, talked his way onto a cargo ship, rode to Norway, thumbed to Aubagne, France, and signed up for the Foreign Legion.

"You have to admit it's a cool story," Josh said.

"It is," I said, popping into the fast lane and passing two semis as we crossed over I-91. I glanced at Ollie. "When was this?"

"'Eighty-seven," he said, and smiled at nothing. After a long pause, he told some more.

The Legion turned him hard. He didn't say much more than that. I thought I knew why. The guys I know who've seen combat, you need a crowbar to get stories out of them. Or a dozen beers. The guys itching to tell war stories are usually full of shit. They were desk jockeys, administrators, assistants' assistants. They swipe stories told by line-of-fire grunts and make them their own.

Finally Ollie said, "I came back in 'ninety-one."

"Why?"

"What else? A girl. The love of my life, et cetera et cetera." He smiled to himself. "Egyptian girl. Very modern family, very wealthy. They sent her to Dartmouth. I followed her to the States."

"And?"

"And I found myself in New Damn Hampshire with no dashing uniform and no devil-may-care twinkle in my eye. I took a job as a grease monkey in Rourke. Oh, the ignominy!" He laughed. "Meanwhile my girlfriend was attracting a fair bit of attention up in Hanover. She was an exotic beauty of a freshman, and it didn't hurt when boys found out her father was a billionaire."

"She dropped you," I said.

"Like a hot potato."

One thing about the story: It made the time pass. I-89 carved west. I hadn't been this far north in years, but I remembered the road would cut north again pretty soon for the run to the border. Enosburg Falls couldn't be far.

Ollie read my eyes, read my mind. "Forty minutes."

"You haven't even gotten to your Montreal guy," I said.

"But I've laid the groundwork, as you'll see. May I fast-forward two decades?"

He did, to 2006. Ollie explained why Motorenwerk was going nowhere. I let him tell it even though I already knew.

You can put a high-end restoration shop in the boonies. The loaded customers will actually think better of you if you're in the middle of nowhere. They find it charming.

But to make it pay, you need a couple of high-profile projects to kick-start things. You need to build cars for TV stars or baseball players. Once those restos get written up in magazines, your phone rings off the hook.

Ollie never quite got his celebrity customer. He got plenty of nibbles—referrals and near-misses—but no takers. So Motorenwerk went sideways, doing thirty-thousand-dollar jobs instead of three-million-dollar jobs. Do that long enough and sideways turns into down.

Which is where Motorenwerk was in '06 when the old friend of Ollie's dad drove up in an Escalade and pitched his idea.

"What was his name?" I said.

"Call him Montreal."

"Why?"

"For now."

I shrugged.

Nine-eleven had put Montreal in a jam. Where his competitors relied on shipments to Atlantic ports, he preferred U.S. mules, and tight border security meant one out of every five mule-mobiles was getting busted. Montreal's supply chain was unreliable, *plus* he was constantly recruiting mules to replace the ones in jail, *plus* he was playing Snitch Roulette—and the odds worsened with every bust.

Bottom line: Montreal was slipping fast.

"Just like you," I said.

Ollie half smiled. "Fair enough. We both needed to get healthy."

He said they experimented with plastics and sealing techniques until their system was foolproof. Then Montreal invested in a better class of mules: mostly whites, a few Asians, no criminal records. Sometimes they registered for business conferences. Sometimes they brought their kids, made a family vacation out of it.

"Nice touch," I said.

"It worked," Ollie said. "Next exit."

We took a state road east through pretty hill country. Soon we hit Enosburg Falls, which looked like little Vermont towns are supposed to look. Ollie told me where to turn. We soon cleared the downtown, such as it was, and pulled into a country-road driveway. I looked at a small white clapboard house. It had a stone foundation, a deep porch, window boxes everywhere. The lower four feet of the shin-gled roof was covered with stamped aluminum to prevent ice dams.

I killed the truck.

"Mom's house," Ollie said, flushing.

We all felt as stiff as Ollie's leg. Josh and I stretched, worked Ollie out of the truck and helped him up the steps. Mom wasn't home. Ollie had Josh reach under a flowerpot for the spare key.

Inside we took turns pissing, then helped Ollie to the front-room sofa. I looked through a picture window that faced front. "What mountain is that?"

Ollie laughed. "That's no mountain at all," he said. "That's a *hill.*"

I said I was leaving. Ollie seemed surprised. He asked if I wanted to hear why things went bad between him and Montreal. I said it wasn't my fault he couldn't spit out the story in four hours, then opened the door to leave.

I wanted to hear the story, but I didn't want to get stuck here over-night; there was too much going on at home. I told Ollie he could fill me in later. I hopped in my truck, found a gas station, filled up, grabbed a coffee, headed south.

Thought about Ollie, a guy I liked, a grease monkey like me.

A guy who helped smuggle heroin and didn't seem bothered by it. A guy who maybe killed Tander Phigg. Who had a perfect little helper in Josh, who seemed ready to do whatever the hell Ollie told him to.

CHAPTER ELEVEN

Charlene was gone when I woke up the next morning. I had barreled down from Enosburg Falls, had gotten a snuggle and an "Mmm" when I climbed in bed beside her. She'd left a note on my bedside table: *Office—GD paperwork! Special BB meeting tonite, Tander memorial.*

I thought about the memorial while I drove to Framingham. These days, it seems a half dozen Barnburners die every year. The old joke: Dying sober is the only prize you get out of AA, and then you're not around to enjoy it.

I stepped into my family room. Kieu and Tuan were watching a kids' show. I pidgin-asked where Trey was. Kieu smiled and pointed past the living room. On TV, something green rode a unicycle. Tuan giggled and clapped.

I stepped through the living room into the narrow area—call it sixteen feet by six—that used to be a front porch. Some long-ago owner had slammed clapboards across it and turned it into a room, but the conversion was a hack job; the insulation was useless or non-existent, the windows were cheap, and there was one measly electrical outlet. Freeze in the winter, bake in the summer, electrocute yourself year-round.

I'd decided to strip it to the studs, bring the electrical up to code, insulate the hell out of it, and install decent windows. Randall and I had done most of the work and were ready to hang Sheetrock. That's what I'd hoped to do today, but Randall still wasn't answering his phone.

When I walked in Trey was squatting, taping craft paper to the floor. He looked up and said, "Does this look right?"

"What are you doing?"

"Randall called and got me started. He said you and I would be putting up walls today."

"How come he's calling you but not me?"

"He said he met someone."

Huh. "You know how to hang Sheetrock?"

Trey rose. "I'm stronger than I look, I'm good at taking orders, and I won't speak unless spoken to."

"Perfect."

"That's what Randall said you'd say."

"When does the not speaking start?"

He smiled.

As I turned to fetch Sheetrock and screws, motioning "follow me" over my shoulder, I might have smiled, too.

An hour and a half later, Trey sank the last drywall screw. I looked at my watch and said, "Not bad."

"There wasn't much to hang, when you got down to it."

"But lots of trimming and finessing," I said. "That's the hard part. Thanks."

He ran his hand along a wall. "I would think making all these screws and seams disappear is actually the hard part. I'll help with that, too."

"I went to New York City," I said. "Learned something about your father's five happy years."

His mouth made a soft O. After maybe ten seconds he said, "You *did*?"

"Let's take a break before we mud these joints," I said. "Walk down to Dunkin' Donuts?"

"My curiosity is beyond piqued."

"Let's take a walk."

When Trey told Kieu where we were headed, she had quite a bit to say. He said something back. She set hands on hips, pointed at Tuan in front of the TV, and made an even longer speech.

Trey turned to me. "She wants to know if they can come."

"Sure."

"They've been . . . we agreed they should stay inside as much as possible," he said. "This neighborhood." He half bowed as he spoke.

"It's a shitty neighborhood and getting worse," I said. "Don't be embarrassed to tell me that. Not exactly breaking news. Tell them 'Let's go.' "

He did. Big smiles all around. As Kieu wriggled Tuan's feet into tiny sneakers, Trey said, "I didn't want to insult you or your home, which incidentally—"

"It's not my home."

"Pardon me?"

"It belonged to a friend of mine," I said. "He left it to me in his will."

"I assumed from the thoughtful way you're revamping it—"

"I'm not revamping it. I'm bringing it up to code so I can get the hell rid of it."

I ignored his puzzled look and led everybody outside.

Tuan was all over the place as we headed west toward Union Avenue, the main drag. He juked like a puppy in a new park, right down to the sniffing, as his mother tried to herd him in the right direction. I looked at the houses, hundred-year-old Victorians mostly, and daydreamed of rehabbing them all—junking vinyl siding, replacing rotted trim, painting them in their funky old colors.

Framingham's a funny city. Its northern end is a solid suburb. Decent schools, lots of commuters to Boston and office parks. Splitting the town is Route 9, one of the original strip-mall roads. Fast food, car dealerships, furniture stores, traffic lights. Like that.

Down here, south of Route 9, it's a ground-down city. Former mills, former factories, train tracks that screw up traffic all day long. Methadone clinics, halfway houses, a hospital with a busy ER. Lots of illegals, lots of old folks who can't afford to leave. Most of the businesses in the downtown blocks have Brazilian flags or *Falamos Português!* signs.

Trey said, "How in God's name did you learn anything about my father?"

I told it, starting with the address book. The two-one-two number, Chas Weinberg, SoHo. It was a lot to dump on Trey, who'd obviously had problems with his old man. I wondered if it was too much at once. But he listened like hell.

We scuttled across Union Avenue and into Dunkin' Donuts. Tuan was overwhelmed by the noise, the choices, the tall people. Kieu picked him up, settled him, and started pointing at the shelves.

Three minutes later we were outside, Tuan holding a chocolate-chip muffin about as big as his head. We sat on a bench in front of a dentist's building. It had enough grass for the kid to run around on, and it was the closest thing to a park we were going to find in this neighborhood.

Medium regular for me, large black for Trey. We sipped, watched traffic bunch and ease. After a while I said, "The name Myna Roper mean anything to you?"

He shook his head.

"Your father and Myna Roper were an item in New York," I said. "Made a big splash on the artsy-fartsy scene around 1960."

Trey smiled and toasted. "That's gratifying," he said. "It's hard to picture my dad making a big splash in any way, shape, or form." He put his Styrofoam cup to his lips.

I said, "Myna Roper was black."

He jerked and spit hot coffee, which hit the side of my face, missing my eye only through dumb luck. I sleeve-wiped my face and turned. Trey was staring at me, coffee dribbling down his unwiped chin.

"You are shitting me," he said after apologizing for the spit-take. "*My father?* Are you *sure*?" He barked Vietnamese. Kieu hustled over, plucked a Dunkin' Donuts napkin from her sleeve, and handed it to me. It took maybe ten seconds, but that was long enough for Tuan to get close to the street. Kieu intercepted him and herded him toward grass.

I told more. I watched Trey's body soften as he learned about his father's New York years. I watched his head tilt, then watched him smile and weep at the same time. When I was done I let him cry. He wasn't embarrassed about it; he just sat sipping coffee and crying, wiping his eyes once in a while.

Finally he said, "I'm so proud of him."

I said nothing.

"I wish I'd known that before," Trey said. "I wish . . . I wish he'd been that man while I was growing up."

"What man was he?"

Long pause. "My mother died in childbirth," he finally said, "but she was a ghost even before that."

"*Your* mother died in childbirth?" I said. "Same way your father's mother died?"

"She did." He looked like he wasn't sure what he wanted to say next.

Trey watched Tuan wobble past, Kieu hot on his trail. He smiled, sipped. "Every other generation gets stuck in between, you know?"

"No."

"The lucky ones got the Summer of Love, Chicago 'sixty-eight, Woodstock. The ones born five years down the road got stagflation and the Ford Pinto. Hell, they got *two versions* of 'Muskrat Love.'"

I kind of liked that song. Didn't say so.

"Sorry to get on my hobby horse," Trey said. "The point is, my father got stuck in one of those tweener generations. At least I thought he did until two minutes ago. If he'd been born five years earlier he would've been a World War Two guy. Instead, he was a Korean War guy. And his dad made damn sure he stayed in college so he could give Korea a wide berth."

"Sounds like you're calling the World War Two guys lucky," I said. "The ones got killed might not agree."

"Touché." He toasted me. "But the ones who *didn't* get killed became the 'greatest generation,' as the book says."

I wondered what the hell book he was talking about. He read my face. "Here's where I'm going with all this," he said. "I always felt bad for my father. He was a little too young to be a World War Two guy and a little too old to be a sixties guy. He always seemed bitter about it."

"Now you're thinking maybe he was bitter about something else," I said, nodding. "About Myna."

"It looks as if he carved out something very nice for himself, then had it ripped away."

We were quiet awhile.

Finally I said, "What year did your mother die?"

"I was born in 'seventy-two."

"Your dad never remarried?"

He shook his head. "Another parallel between him and my grandfather, I realize."

I nodded. "Your dad was in his thirties, had plenty of money and a brand-new kid. Most guys in that position in 1972 would give it six months or a year, then snap up another wife. If only to clean the house and keep you fed."

From the sounds behind me, it seemed Tuan was about done having a good time. He bickered at his mom, and she scolded back. I rose, stretched, killed my coffee, took a few steps to toss the cup in a sidewalk garbage barrel. When I turned back, Trey was staring at nothing, tapping his lip with his near-empty cup.

I said, "Head back and mud that room?"

He stood. "You're a strange cat. You know a thing or two about the human animal, don't you?"

I said nothing.

"You're saying this Myna Roper was the love of my father's life. It's why he never remarried."

"I'm saying let's head back and mud that room."

Three hours later, I idled down Mechanic Street in Rourke, taking a long look at Motorenwerk.

Trey had been a natural with the putty knife and joint compound— we'd finished up earlier than I expected. With time to kill before the Barnburners' memorial for Phigg, and with Ollie and Josh way the hell up in Vermont, I wanted a look-see through the garage.

Ollie's BMW was parked next to the building. The street was dead on a Sunday afternoon except for my upholstery-shop Mexican pal. The guy worked hard, I had to give him that. His roll-up door was open. As I eased past, scouting the street, his pit bull went crazy. I U-turned at the railroad tracks and rolled past again. The pit bull's barking had pulled the Mexican out front. He stood watching in gray coveralls, wiping his hands with a shop rag, and shook his head when our eyes met. I nodded, thinking he meant there was nothing new on Mechanic Street.

I should have thought harder.

I put my truck next to the BMW, looked around, ducked around back of the garage. I found the unlockable window, pulled hard, and stepped through into darkness.

"That will be fine." The voice said *"Zat,"* and I knew right away it was Montreal.

I was caught in an awkward long step, my right foot on the shop floor, my left ankle on the windowsill. And the voice came from behind me, so I couldn't gauge the threat. And I'd left Ollie's P35 under the seat of my truck. And I'd ignored the Mexican's warning.

And I felt like a jackass.

"Just stepping in, okay?" I said, spreading both hands. "If I don't, I'm going to fall over." I hopped like the world's worst ballerina, got both feet planted, blinked fast to help my eyes adjust to the dark, and spun a slow 180 to face the voice.

What popped into my head was *lounge lizard*. He looked twenty-five years younger than I knew he had to be. His dyed-black hair was a slightly modern take on a pompadour, and his goatee looked drawn on. His getup was straight out of *The Dick Van Dyke Show*: narrow-legged black slacks, a shimmery blue-gray jacket with skinny lapels, an equally skinny necktie. It was all tailored and expensive-looking, so I figured the early-sixties look must be hip again.

The only thing that kept me from laughing out loud, picking him up by his ankles, and swinging him in circles was the dude next to him. The dude wore the same goatee as Montreal but was six inches taller and a hundred pounds heavier, with deltoids erupting from his yellow muscle shirt.

Across his chest he held a machine pistol with a banana clip. I'd never seen a gun like it, but it was flat, black, and ugly and I bet it fired twenty rounds a second.

I tried to ignore the muscle man, focusing on Montreal. "Where'd you leave your Escalade?" I said, playing for time. I was clicking through facts, thinking about what Montreal knew, what he *wanted* to know, and how much truth I had to spill to stay alive.

He flicked a hand and made a *pfft* noise. "Throw your wallet on the floor."

I did, staring down the muzzle of the machine pistol. Without taking his eyes or gun off me, the muscle man picked it up and handed it to Montreal. He found my license and said my name, DOB, address, and driver's license number. Then he said, "Do you have it?"

"Got it," muscle man said.

Montreal read my eyes. "Do not be fooled by appearances," he said, flipping through my wallet some more. "He has the best memory I have yet encountered. Say . . ." He held up a card. "You are on parole, Mister Sax. For what crime or crimes?"

"Manslaughter two."

He arched his groomed eyebrows, put the parole card back in my wallet, and tossed it to my feet. "So," he said—almost but not quite pronouncing it *Zo*—"what brings a convicted killer to Ollie Dufresne's little garage?"

"It's right behind you," I said.

Neither man turned.

"Under the cover," I said. "Mercedes 450SEL 6.9. It belonged to my friend Tander Phigg. Dufresne's been stalling, ripping him off. I promised I'd get the car back."

It was the best kind of lie—mostly truth. And because Montreal knew how Ollie was really spending his time here, it would be easy for him to believe Ollie was stalling Phigg.

Montreal head-motioned to muscle man, who kept an eye on me while he raised the car cover enough to open the passenger door.

Montreal said, "We will find the car registered to, what was the unusual name, Tander Phigg?" His poker face wasn't as good as he thought. The name lit him up, flared his nostrils, dilated his pupils for a few tenths of a second.

"Tander Phigg *Junior*, if you want to be precise," I said, confirming the flared nostrils.

"You said the car *was* his. Please explain the use of the past tense."

"He's dead," I said. Montreal raised the eyebrows again while muscle man shuffled through the glove box. I gave a thirty-second version of all the stuff he would confirm in the newspapers, leaving

Trey Phigg out of it. If Montreal knew about Trey at all, he thought he was in Vietnam. No need to correct him.

As I finished up, muscle man read the registration, nodded to Montreal, and began to button up the car and cover.

"If Mister Phigg is dead," Montreal said, "for whom do you want the car?"

I licked my lips and looked down. "I was helping Tander get it back."

"This we have established. But who is your patron *now*?"

"I put in a lot of time," I said, refusing to look him in the eye. "A lot of hours."

"You came to steal this car."

I said nothing. We all stood and looked at each other. I tried to act nervous—licked my lips, flicked my gaze from the gun to Montreal—and finally said, "Now what are *you* fellas doing here? Not that it's my business."

"Time for all of us to go, I think," Montreal said.

Montreal left first. Muscle man gestured me out next, then came after and had me close the window tight. As we rounded the building, he put on a black Windbreaker that had been tied around his waist, zipped it up, and tucked the ugly machine pistol inside.

While Montreal watched me climb into my truck, muscle man stood fifteen feet away in my blind spot. I could try to lean over, reach the P35 beneath the seat, come back up, and fling a half-assed shot at Montreal, but muscle man would cut me in half.

Montreal made a cranking motion with one long-fingered hand. I rolled down my window.

"He's memorized your license plate now," he said, flicking his head toward muscle man. "In addition to your other data. Please don't come back. If you do, he will kill you."

I nodded, rolled up my window, drove away. "Shit," I said out loud, pounding the wheel. I was pissed I'd gone inside without a gun. The address on my driver's license was Shrewsbury. Montreal now knew where Charlene lived.

The church basement we used for Barnburner meetings, Saint Anne's, was booked that night. But Mary Giarusso figured the Phigg name might still carry weight in Fitchburg and made a few calls. It worked: She got us the Odd Fellows hall on the cheap.

Me, Charlene, and Sophie rolled in at quarter of eight. There were only a half dozen Barnburners so far, and most of them stood around grumbling that the memorial was too far from our home base.

To offset the ingrates, my first move was to find Mary Giarusso and thank her for getting us the hall. She's the one who makes the Barnburners go: She updates the telephone tree, buys cards for sobriety anniversaries, keeps us in good standing with AA National. Like that.

She's slowing down some in her late seventies, forgetting things here and there. I worry about her. I worry more about what'll happen to the Barnburners when she's gone. The world ships us new drunks all the time, but even the ones that stick around don't want responsibility. Mary says getting them sober is the easy part these days; it's getting them involved that's hard.

Mary, Charlene, and a few others shuttled Swedish meatballs and pigs in a blanket from the kitchen to the stainless-steel warming trays. A DJ whose name I always forget set up his speakers. Barnburners filtered in. Sophie was in a corner with two other girls her age, sipping generic soda from cans and pretending not to look at a couple of boys somebody'd brought along.

I looked around and thought about what a weird tradition this was. Part AA meeting, part wake, part roast, part sock hop. Strictly a Barnburner thing—I'd asked around, and nobody knew of another group that did it. I'd invited Trey and his family, but when I explained how the get-together would go, he passed. I didn't blame him.

At the stroke of eight the DJ hit a button on his laptop and slammed out an old doo-wop song, *way* too loud. Mary Giarusso walked straight over and made him turn it down. He looked sour about it but didn't dare say no to Mary.

I spent the next forty-five minutes talking with various Barn-burners about Phigg. Everybody had heard some true things and some bullshit. I confirmed the true, waved off the bullshit. I didn't sugarcoat or minimize anything. That would be an insult to all drunks.

Butch Feeley, one of the oldest old-timers and the unofficial boss of the meeting-after-the-meeting crew, shuffled up, grabbed my sleeve, and said over a doo-wop song, "Tander's sponsor ought to say a few words."

"Who *was* his sponsor?"

"We were hoping you knew."

I didn't. Yelled in Butch's ear that I'd figured it must be him or one of the other old-timers.

He shook his head. "I sponsored Tander until 'oh-one," he said. "We had words over some foolish thing. He told me to go fuck myself, and we haven't spoken three words to each other since. I asked around, and most of the other old farts have similar stories."

I said, "Fucking Phigg."

Butch shook his head and looked at me with wet old man's eyes. "No, shame on us," he said. "All of us. He pushed us away and we let him."

We locked eyes for maybe five seconds. I wanted to fight Butch on that. But I couldn't. He was right. "Shame on us," I said. "Shame on *me*. I'll say the words."

He clapped my shoulder and shuffled off.

I stood alone and watched the party. It was jumping. Sophie and the other girls were chewing the DJ's ear, wanting newer songs so they could dance with each other. Little knots of people ate pigs in a blanket, drank from plastic cups, laughed.

Across the room, Charlene had been cornered by Chester Bagley, another meeting-after-the-meeting old-timer. His wig had slipped eight or ten degrees west. Every time he made a point, he put his hand on Charlene's waist. Every time she replied, he leaned in like he couldn't hear and slid the hand down to her rear end. The Barnburner ladies called him "Chester the Molester."

I waited for eye contact with Charlene and made a show of slapping my own ass, giving her a big thumbs-up. She about spit ginger ale on the floor, then used her free hand on her head to show how far Chester's toupee had slipped.

I laughed, went to the DJ, and asked him to kill the music.

The sudden silence got everybody's attention. They looked my way.

I waited for stray conversations to end, then said what we always say at these things. I'd been to maybe two dozen of them but had never spoken the words before. My throat tightened even as I started with the easy part. "I'm Conway," I said. "I'm an alcoholic and a drug addict."

"*Hi, Conway.*"

"Barnburner Tander has achieved the goal we all strive for."

"*What is the goal?*"

"To die sober."

"*We raise a glass to Tander.*" Everybody did.

"This is an anonymous program, but a glorious death deserves fame."

"*And fame means a last name.*"

"We drink to Tander Phigg Junior. Sober as a judge, dead as a doornail."

"*Sober as a judge, dead as a doornail.*"

Everybody drank.

The little ditty was a Barnburner tradition before I got here. The first time I heard it, I grabbed an old-timer's sleeve and asked what the hell we'd just said—and why. The old-timer, Eudora Spoon, had laughed and patted my hand. "Everybody asks that," she'd said, and walked away.

Now I looked around. The new drunks looked as puzzled as I had that night. I watched them buttonhole old-timers the same way I had. I watched some of the old-timers cry, watched kids stare because they weren't sure why people were crying.

The DJ played a doo-wop song. Either he loved doo-wop or he thought we did. I made my way toward Charlene but felt a tug at my sleeve. It was Sophie. She said something. I couldn't make it out over the doo-wop, so I cupped an ear and leaned.

She said, "Is that all he gets?"

"Who?"

"The one who died. Tander Phigg."

"I guess it is, yeah."

"It's not much, is it?"

"You'd be surprised," I said.

She put out her hands and smiled goofy. It took me a few seconds to see she wanted to dance.

Hell.

I took and danced her. Sheesh, she was almost up to my chest. I looked over at Charlene. She smiled and put her hands together over her heart.

We danced, me and Sophie.

An hour later, as the get-together broke up, I climbed into the passenger seat of Charlene's Volvo SUV. I'd left my cell in the cup holder. I had four missed calls and two voice mails, all from my house. Both messages were Trey saying call him ASAP. I did.

"Is your father Fred Sax?" Trey said. "Frederic J. Sax, let me see . . ." He said a Social Security number.

"What about him?" I said. Charlene and Sophie picked up on my tone, stopped talking, and looked my way.

"The hospital called," Trey said.

"What hospital?"

"Cider Hill State Hospital." From the way he said it, I could tell he'd Googled the place.

My insides slipped. My heart hurt. My eyes closed. I said, "Should I go there now?"

"Not at this point," he said. "They told me if I couldn't get hold of you right away, you might as well wait until tomorrow morning."

I clicked off.

Charlene said, "What?"

"My father's in the nuthouse," I said.

Sophie started to speak, then swallowed it.

"What?" I said.

"It's Father's Day," she said.

CHAPTER TWELVE

Next morning, big sun at my back, I drove west on Route 9. Soon I banged a right into the New England that leaf-peepers dream about—elms, oaks, some pines mixed in. As the road passed a big pond on my left and grew twistier, houses petered out.

I came around a corner and there it was, spoiling a pretty field: a big red-brick insane asylum. Mesh-reinforced doors, barred windows, uniformed security patrols, the works.

As I pulled in, I saw parking places marked PICKUP/DROP-OFF ONLY. I said out loud, "Just like Applebee's." Laughed, knew the laugh sounded wrong.

I killed the F-150, sat a minute to let my heart slow. I'd been here before on taxi duty, hauling people from the nuthouse to the private rehab up the street.

I climbed out into a day that was good and hot already, then pulled a door and stepped inside. At first, Cider Hill State Hospital looked no different than any other health-care operation: It was full of women with big asses who obviously hated their jobs. Everything they did they did slowly, almost cartoon-slow. Like it was a joke they played on outsiders, and the second you turned your back they sped up.

But I knew they didn't.

I stood at a counter while three of them keyboard-clacked and had a contest to see who could avoid making eye contact with me.

The loser was a black woman with a twenty-ounce Diet Dr Pepper on her desk. She looked at me for maybe an eighth of a second, but that was enough. "Morning," I said.

She sighed, probably kicking herself for that eighth-of-a-second eye contact. "With you one minute." Jamaican.

Twenty minutes and nine signatures later, I waited in a private room just back of reception. The Jamaican had said Doctor Lin would be with me soon.

I looked around the room—half office, half lounge—at a desk, a couple of chairs, an old sofa the color of a Band-Aid. The big window that looked out on the parking lot was barred.

Then I took the most comfortable looking chair, spun it to face daylight, and waited for my father.

He'd always claimed they called him "Fast Freddy" Sax, but in Mankato I never met anybody who remembered the nickname. He ran tracks in Rochester, Tomahawk, Sioux City, Sioux Falls, sometimes Waukesha. Quarter-mile, third-of-a-mile, some paved, mostly dirt.

When I was eight he stopped kidding himself about racing full-time and took a job as a welder.

When I was eleven he left me and my mom and moved to Milford, Massachusetts. Claimed he'd found work as an engine builder with a Late Model racing team that was going places.

When I was thirteen I bullied my mom into letting me move east to be with him. Whatever part of her wasn't broken when my father left finished breaking when my Trailways bus pulled out of Minneapolis. She's been fuzzy ever since. Pills, I think. She has her church group and Wednesday afternoons shelving books at Mankato Public Library and not much else.

Three days after the bus dropped me in Milford, I knew my father was a drunk and a liar. He hadn't been an engine builder for any race team—he was a gopher, sweeping the shop floor and fetching coffee. And he was drunk all the time, so he couldn't even do that right. They canned him.

A welder can always find work, but a drunk welder never lasts long.

I more or less flew solo from there on out. I ate a lot of grilled cheese. While my friends were looking forward to their learners' permits, I was shuffling checks and working collection agencies to keep the phone and electric and gas on—most of the time. I couldn't stop the eviction notices, but in Massachusetts an eviction notice doesn't mean shit. You can last eighteen months easy if you play it right.

When I was fourteen, I figured out the only sure way to keep Fast Freddy Sax around: I taught myself to drink. We had some good times.

Then some bad ones.

He's spent the past twenty years panhandling in Vermont during the summer, then in Jacksonville, Florida, all winter.

When I won my first televised race in Martinsville, Virginia, he saw it on ESPN and hitchhiked from Brattleboro to my race team's shop to ask for money. I guess he figured I was rich, or would be soon.

But he'd taught me more than he knew; by then I was a flat-out drunk myself. I lost my ride not long after, started my long slide.

I stared through the barred window, put my feet on the sofa, thought about the last time I saw him. Five years ago, six? He was begging at a stoplight near a Massachusetts Turnpike toll booth. Cars stack up at the light, so there are usually three or four bums working it.

The bums there are always black, so when I spotted a white one, he caught my eye. He wore a lunatic's beard, a real stranded-on-a-desert-island job. Underneath it, though, he looked familiar. I thought, *It couldn't be.* But my stomach, dropping away, was telling me something else. I needed a closer look, so I caught his attention and waggled a buck.

He saw it and hustled to the minivan I was driving back then. As he neared, he stuck out the HOMELESS MISSION can the bums use. We locked eyes.

It was my father. He'd dropped thirty pounds, and filth covered the part of his face that the beard didn't. But I recognized him, all right—he was my *father.*

He recognized me, too. And smiled.

It was a shy smile. Like when a kid moves out of the neighborhood, then visits with his family the next summer. The smile says *Everything's the same, but everything's different.*

The light changed. Boston drivers aren't patient: I got two seconds of courtesy before people started honking.

I ignored them. "Fast Freddy Sax," I said.

My father said nothing. Instead, he slapped the pockets of the raincoat he wore. Soon he pulled out a little notebook and a golf pencil.

More honking, some hollering, too, as the light went red. I ignored it all.

While my father worked his pencil I fished my wallet out again, pulled all the money I had, stuffed it in his can.

My father tore off a notebook sheet and put it in my hand, saying nothing but making that shy smile again. *Everything's the same, but everything's different.*

The light turned green. I gassed it. In the rearview, I watched my father step to the curb and wait for traffic to bunch again. Far as I could tell, he didn't look my way.

At the next red light I looked down at the paper he'd folded into my hand. It said *IOU.*

I thought there must be more, blinked away tears.

But that was all it said.

I heard a doorknob and took my feet off the sofa. Noticed I had my wallet in my left hand and the scrap of paper in my right. I carry it. I don't know why. I looked at it. *IOU.*

I stuffed the paper away, rose, turned.

Doctor Lin was a woman. She was Chinese and five-two, and she couldn't weigh more than a buck-ten. She was reading from an aluminum clipboard, stethoscope over her shoulders the way they carry them. She kicked the door closed as she signed the bottom of her clipboard sheet, then looked up.

Most doctors' eyes are hard. Smart, but hard. They don't let you in; they bounce you back. Doctor Lin's eyes were not like that. Instead they were warm, amused, like she was still thinking about a joke she heard out in the hall.

She said she was Vicky Lin and stuck out a tiny hand. We shook. I said my name.

"Only son of Fast Freddy Sax," she said. "The scourge of the midwestern NASCAR scene back when men were men and helmets were for sissies." Her eyes smiled. "To hear him tell it. Is there any truth to his story?" She looked pure Chinese but talked pure California. Not Valley Girl–Surfer Dude California. Educated California.

"A little truth and a lot of bullshit," I said. "Does he sell it well?"

"Well and often," she said. "He had a couple of patients asking for his autograph. Also an orderly."

I said, "So he's . . . how is . . . can he . . ." Then my knees went weak and I sat down hard.

She asked if I was okay, if I wanted water. I said yes to both. She ducked behind the desk, came up with a bottle of Poland Springs, and handed it to me. Then she sat behind the desk, watched me open and sip.

"I apologize," she said after a while. "I started off all wrong. This is a big deal, and I failed to treat it as such. When did you last see him?"

I told her about my father begging for a buck at the intersection. I almost told her about the IOU—she was the kind of person I wanted to tell that story to—but held back.

She asked more questions, medical-history stuff. I couldn't tell her much, but I could tell her he'd been a drunk at least thirty years. I didn't have to tell her I'd inherited that, but I did. She wrote while I talked.

When I was done, Doctor Lin tapped her teeth with her pen, the teeth white like in a toothpaste commercial. Everybody has white teeth these days.

"Given what you've told me," she said, "you may be pleasantly surprised when the orderly brings him in."

I waited.

She said, "Your father is stone-cold sober."

"No fucking way. Pardon my French."

"No fucking problem," she said, warm eyes smiling. "I've heard worse. Indeed, I've heard worse in the last fifteen minutes. But it's true." She glanced at her clipboard. "Your father was picked up at a rest stop on I-Ninety-one. He was digging through trash cans for food, scaring off customers apparently. The manager of the McDonald's called the state police."

"When was this?"

"Four days ago. Your father told the state police he'd hitchhiked from Vermont—"

"That sounds right."

"—and he was confused and agitated. They checked his record, found a long history of incarceration and institutionalization, assumed he was drunk or on drugs, and brought him here."

A long history of incarceration and institutionalization. My chest felt tight. I stared at nothing.

"We took him in Thursday, late," she said. "And here's where the glimmer of good news begins, Mister Sax. I observed your father, studied his records, and set in motion the usual tests. Your father remained confused and agitated. He maintained he was sober and had been for some time, but I didn't believe him. He was, after all, telling these fanciful stories, and he exhibited symptoms of delirium tremens. The DTs?"

"I know what they are."

Her eyes lingered on me before she went back to the clipboard. "The point is, we Doubting Thomases ran your father through the usual tests and procedures, and I'll be damned if he isn't sober."

"Hard to believe," I said, and thought for a few seconds. "So why was he Dumpster diving? Why was he confused, all that?"

"Malnutrition. Dehydration. Thirty or more years of intensive alcohol and drug abuse." She finger-ticked as she spoke. "Your father's not an active alcoholic at the moment, and I'm afraid he's not eligible for inpatient treatment here. But he's not doing well. Sometimes he's cogent, sometimes he's incoherent or childlike."

"You're saying he's a wet-brain."

"Thirty or more years of intense alcohol and drug abuse," she said, making a tiny shrug.

There was a quiet knock, a turn of the knob. A huge dreadlocked orderly stepped in. Behind him came my father.

He was smaller than I remembered.

"You're bigger than I remember," he said.

Doctor Lin nodded at the orderly. He stepped out and closed the door.

"No beard," I said.

"They shaved it when they deloused me." My father rubbed his chin. "Feels funny."

Neither of us said anything for a while.

It was like looking at myself. He was three, four inches shorter and thirty years older, and his teeth were a lot worse than mine. Otherwise, he looked like me.

"I'm off the sauce," he said.

"I heard. How long?"

His mouth started working, then stopped. He rubbed his hands together. He looked to Doctor Lin, then back at me. Then did it again.

She said, "Days and dates giving you trouble, Fred?"

My father nodded.

I said, "It doesn't matter, Pop." Looked at Doctor Lin. "Can we go?"

"After you sign thirty or forty more forms."

I thought she was kidding. She wasn't.

During the ride we were mostly quiet.

At a stoplight my father said, "Your truck?"

I nodded.

He looked around the interior. "Nice."

Then we were quiet again.

I took him to Charlene's and watched him eat two egg-and-cheese sandwiches from Dunkin' Donuts. He sat at the kitchen table wearing green scrubs they'd given him at Cider Hill, chewing like hell with his lousy teeth.

I said, "What's your shoe size?"

"I don't know."

"How can you not know your shoe size?"

"Go twenty years without buying a pair of shoes, that's how."

"What was your shoe size twenty-one years ago?"

"Ten and a half. Why?"

"I'll buy you some clothes."

He nodded and polished off the last sandwich. Then he looked around. "Nice house," he said. "Not yours, though. This is a woman's house. Your girlfriend?"

"Yes."

"You live here?"

"Kind of."

"It's not a kind-of question. Yes or no?"

"Fuck you."

He looked at me awhile, then nodded. "I won't begrudge you that," my father said. "Fuck me."

Twenty minutes later he was showered, naked, asleep in Jesse's room. I'd pulled the curtains while he climbed into bed. "Room dark enough?" I said, and heard snoring. He was out cold. "Guess so," I said, and headed for the door.

But stopped. I looked down at my father. He could use a haircut. His was mostly gray, but it was all there. And it was clean now.

I reached and touched my father's hair. His snoring hitched. I pulled my hand back, then soft-footed out the door and down the hall to Charlene's room. I pulled the curtains in that room, too.

I like to pray in the dark when I can.

I hit my knees, closed my eyes, set my forehead on the yellow comforter.

I prayed.

The praying turned into thinking. That happens a lot. I used to worry, thought I was praying wrong. Then Eudora Spoon told me there was no way to pray wrong. She said praying is praying.

So I thought and I prayed. Somewhere in there I started to cry.

When I finished praying, the comforter and my T-shirt were soaked. I rinsed my face, changed my shirt, stripped the bed, went downstairs, ran a load of laundry.

I watched a rerun of a World of Outlaws race while the washing machine ran. Called Charlene, got voice mail, left a message. Called Randall. Voice mail. Message.

I transferred the laundry to the dryer and was coming back to the family room when everything hit me. I felt my knees go, the way they had at the hospital. Got a hand on the wall, steadied myself. "What am I going to do?" I said out loud.

My cell rang. I squinted at the number. It was a 603 area code, which meant New Hampshire, but I didn't recognize the number.

I clicked on but said nothing. Somebody said my name, waited, then said it again.

It came to me: the New Hampshire Statie who rolled up on me at Phigg's place, the supersized Abe Lincoln. "McCord," I said.

"Hell of a way to answer your phone."

I said nothing.

"Where are you presently, Mister Sax?"

"My girlfriend's house. Shrewsbury, Mass."

"Been there awhile?"

"Why?"

"Been there awhile?"

"Sure."

"Folks there with you? Anybody to back up your story?"

"Sure," I said. "What do you want, McCord?"

Long pause. "Somebody tore the hell out of Tander Phigg's sorry little shack," he said. "Thrashed it and trashed it."

"Kids?"

"Doesn't look like it. Somebody looking for something, you ask me."

"Looking for what?"

"You tell me," McCord said. "I'll be here another hour or so, keeping my blue lights on while the detectives knock around."

CHAPTER THIRTEEN

I made it to Jut Road just as McCord was leaving.

It hadn't been an easy getaway. I'd had to figure out which friend Sophie was with, then call to make sure she could stay until Charlene came home from work. The mom said sure, the girls were reading pop-star magazines in the tree house and it'd take an act of Congress to get them down anyway.

Then I left a note for my dad. Then I called Charlene. I was grateful she didn't pick up—the message was that I'd carted a derelict she'd never met from the loony bin to her home, and he was sleeping naked in her daughter's room. Yikes.

After doing all this as fast as I could, I paused at the front door and thought about my father waking up alone at Charlene's place.

Most drunks won't keep booze in the house, but Charlene calls that scaredy-cat bullshit. She has business friends who enjoy a drink now and then. She keeps vodka in the basement freezer and a couple bottles of this and that high in a kitchen cabinet.

What should I do?

Decided to play it safe. I quick-stepped to the kitchen, grabbed the half-empty fifths of Scotch and bourbon, bounced to the basement, grabbed the vodka from the freezer. I stashed the works on a shelf behind a box of painting supplies.

After all that, a steady ninety miles an hour up Route 495 put me nose to nose with McCord's green-and-copper Charger as he got set to swing out of Jut Road. He backed away to let me in.

The hottest part of the day overpowered the thin shade in this overgrown spot. Souhegan noise battled insect noise.

I said, "Sorry I took so long." McCord waved it off and walked us toward the shack, pointing as we neared it.

"Building's got no business still being here," he said. "Used to be a house right over there, a big one. My old man remembers it. But the river floods every five years, and there's a natural bowl in this spot. Real bad flood when my old man was in high school. The owners said fuck it, never came back."

I told him I'd guessed most of that. "And Phigg was building on the same spot, more or less. Bad move?"

"Maybe not," McCord said, but his shrug told me he thought it was. "You can see where they tried to fix the grading."

"But a bowl next to a river is a bowl next to a river."

He twitched his eighth-inch smile.

"Brick support piers," I said, pointing. "That's why this one's still here."

"Miracle they're holding, uh? Place could fall any day."

As we stepped inside I asked about the break-in. McCord folded his arms. "Local lady drove by, spotted a vehicle. She wouldn't have thought twice about it, but Phigg's the talk of the town. She called nine-one-one. I was the nearest unit. Got here twenty-one minutes after she made the call, but they were gone."

"She see their car?"

"Black SUV, a big one she thought."

Montreal and his black Escalade. So I'd been right—Montreal *had* pricked up his ears at Phigg's name. I was glad my back was to

McCord. I didn't have to worry about a poker face as I clicked through possibilities, coming up with two questions: Why did Montreal care about Phigg, and should I tell McCord about the connection?

I answered the second one first: no dice. Felt guilty at the thought of jerking McCord around, but as far as I knew the cops had zero Ollie-Montreal-heroin info, and that seemed like a good thing.

The first question—What did Montreal know about Phigg?— would have to wait.

The shack didn't smell any better. The floor still sagged beneath me. All the same crap from the other day was here. It had been thrown in different spots, maybe, but the shack was such a mess to start with it didn't look any worse today.

"You sure it wasn't kids?" I said. "Looks like somebody came in on a dare, tossed things around, and took off."

"Detectives saw it that way, too," McCord said. "They didn't even want to come here, didn't want to fuck up their nice clean suicide."

"They find anything?"

He shook his head. "Showed up, bitched about the drive, smoked cigarettes, looked around a little, said I was a douche bag for hauling them out here. Then they drove back to Concord."

"You don't like detectives much."

"I don't like stupid ones." He stepped to the shack's northern side, where a sort of box, maybe four feet tall by two feet deep, jutted from the main wall. To me it looked like it must house a couple of axles and gears from when this was a pump house.

McCord pointed at the boxed section.

I said, "What?"

He motioned me closer and tapped brick. I saw it—an eighteen-inch horizontal line in the mortar, much whiter than the brick and mortar around it.

I looked at the floor near the boxed section. The floor was such a mess it took me a few seconds, but I spotted shards of mortar. A few of them rested atop a Dunkin' Donuts bag the detectives had tossed here the day Phigg died.

"Fresh," McCord said.

"You've got a helluva good eye."

"Wait here."

He trotted from the shack. I heard his trunk open and close, heard him trot back. He came in with a lineman's hammer. It was double faced, weighed maybe three pounds. It was new, the SKU sticker still on the shaft.

"Found it in the drive when I rolled up," McCord said. "I'd say they left in a hurry, uh?"

"You think they were chiseling at this wall."

He nodded.

"That's the wrong tool for the job," I said. "Why not bring an eight-pound sledge and bash right through this shitty old brick?"

"You know that. I know that." He shrugged. "Maybe they didn't know that. City boys, clean-hands boys."

He was right, though I still didn't want to tell him about Montreal the lounge lizard, who was looking more and more like a guy who could and would kill Phigg. I felt bad about holding back the info, but even a good cop is a cop. Trusting them doesn't come easy.

"What do you think they were looking for?"

"Stand back," he said. "We'll find out." McCord took a wide-legged stance and touched the hammer to the wall once, where the mortar had been chipped. Then he reared back and took a big-ass swing.

The bricks didn't give, but the shack shook.

Another swing. When the hammer connected this time, the sound was duller—mortar giving, shifting.

Another swing did it: Mortar flew, bricks shifted and caved, a hole appeared. McCord reared back again to widen the hole.

"Wait," I said.

He wiped his forehead.

"Listen," I said.

Then McCord noticed it, too: The river noise was louder. It made sense. If the brick box held axles and shafts, it must be open all the way down.

I told McCord to go ahead. He began pounding out individual bricks, told me to fetch the flashlight from his Charger.

By the time I brought it he'd made a hole you could stick your head through.

McCord knelt and motioned me to stick the flashlight through the hole. He put his head inside the box. I moved the flashlight around so he could look at whatever was in there.

A full minute later he pulled his head out and brushed at his hair with both hands. "Jack diddly pooh," he said.

"Nothing?"

"See for yourself." We swapped. I looked while he held the light.

Imagine what it'd look like if you whanged a hole in your chimney and stuck your head inside. It was like that, but instead of a fireplace at the bottom, the Souhegan swept past. And instead of soot, I got dirt and cobwebs in my hair.

I craned my neck and decided I'd been right about the box's original function: Gears had been housed in here. But the shafts they rode must have rusted through, and everything had long since fallen into the river.

I pulled my head out, finger-brushed my hair the way McCord had, shrugged.

We left the shack, McCord holding the lineman's hammer near its head. It felt good to be outside. We started toward the vehicles. I glanced at the Souhegan, took a step, stopped. There was something about those piers supporting the outer side of the shack—I wanted to look again. But I didn't want McCord to see me looking, so I caught up.

He said, "I was supposed to have my unit back"—looked at his watch—"forty minutes ago. Sorry to pull you up here for nothing."

"You think that's nothing? The hammer, the SUV, the chipped-out mortar?"

He popped the Charger's trunk, tossed the hammer in, shut the trunk, stepped to the driver's door. "You were probably right the first time. Punks. Maybe somebody looking for copper pipe. We get a lot of that around here."

If McCord wanted to think that, fine.

I didn't think that at all.

I also didn't believe *he* really thought it. He was a smart guy, more complicated than he let on. I wondered what he was holding back.

He started the Charger. I stepped to his door and squatted. He looked a question at me.

I said, "Jack diddly pooh?"

I got the eighth-inch smile as he drove away.

I drove out, too, but only to put on a show in case McCord was watching in his rearview.

I needed a look at those piers.

I killed time on back roads, making sure McCord was really gone. Thought about that chipped-out mortar as I drove. Punks or looters, my ass. Montreal had learned Phigg's address and had gone there looking for something. And not copper pipe.

But why had he and his muscle man attacked a useless brick box? And why had they taken off before they busted through? I hadn't been able to say it to McCord, but muscle man was plenty strong. The only thing that made sense was that they'd heard the nosy lady drive past and had bailed.

I thought this through while I hooked a left and drove northwest on an elm-lined road that felt like it would eventually drop me back near Jut Road.

They must have attacked the bricks because they didn't know where the hell else to look. There just wasn't much to the shack.

There was no cellar, and the rafters were open—no ceiling cavity to stash something in. The same went for the walls—plain-Jane brick, no studs or Sheetrock to create hidey-holes.

My guess: Montreal was pretty damn sure Tander had stashed something in that shack. City-boy lounge lizard that he was, though, he'd done a lousy job going after it. Bought a silly little hammer at the nearest Home Depot and started trying to bash walls in. And he couldn't even do *that* right.

I took a left onto the road that would take me to the shack, checked my watch. It had been twenty-five minutes since McCord left.

What the hell did Tander Phigg, living on crackers and Sam's Club soda, have that was worth hiding right up to the day he hanged himself? It looked like a dotted line ran from Montreal through Ollie to Phigg. I needed to press Ollie on that.

That made me remember some of the crap I'd found in the trunk of Phigg's car the day he died. Wading boots, mask, and snorkel. At the time it seemed random, a scavenger's pile of junk. Maybe not.

I pulled onto Jut Road thinking of the piers that held the shack up. They were off just a little, wrong somehow. They were what I'd come back to look at. Had McCord spotted them, too? Were they the reason he'd gone all cagey with the kids-and-looters bullshit?

No Charger in sight. Good: McCord hadn't doubled back.

But you never knew with him, so my priority was speed. I pulled my F-150 right to the shack, killed it, dumped my wallet and cell on the seat in case I got wet, and stepped out.

The riverbank dropped away fast, easily a forty-five-degree angle. It was a six-foot drop from where I stood to the river's surface, and there was no path. I spotted a place where the wild grass and scrub elm looked beat up, figured that was the best way down.

There was no sense being pretty about it: If I tried to walk down I'd probably fall on my ass anyway. So I sat and slid, using my hands as brakes.

I gasped when my boots hit the water. Even on a hot day, the White Mountains runoff was ice freaking cold. Now the wading boots in Phigg's trunk really made sense.

I got my footing and stood ankle-deep in the river. I couldn't believe how soon and how much my feet hurt. This was bad cold. The flow was quick as hell, too, a stout current trying to pull me to my right.

I realized I hadn't put any thought into getting back up the riverbank. Turned and looked. "Shit," I said out loud. "Make it quick."

I faced the river again and looked at the nearest pier, the one that supported the shack's northwest corner. It was only eight feet away, but that eight feet felt like a big deal all of a sudden. I stepped toward it.

And thought *Fuck me* as my boot came down on nothing and I went under.

Under.

My heart stopped.

My mouth opened.

I sucked in a lungful of Souhegan, kicked, sank, felt the current pull me, opened my eyes, saw only black. I thrashed, boots and arms flailing. I was drowning three feet from a riverbank. A corner of my brain felt embarrassed. I hoped they'd find me downriver in deep water. Maybe they'd think I died doing something worthwhile.

I flailed, kicked, my heart banging away now, lungs confused, sucking, getting only more water.

My left hand hit something. Very thin rope, some sort of cord maybe. Thank God. I grabbed it with both hands. I pulled. And again. And more, pulling upriver, fighting current.

My head hit something hard. I felt with one hand. A pier. I hugged it with arms and legs, shinnied, pictured a koala going up a tree.

And felt air on my head, then my face. My lungs went insane, coughing out water, trying to gulp air at the same time, racking me so bad I nearly lost my grip. I locked my right hand around my left wrist, hooked my right ankle across my left, hung the hell on.

Soon I heaved up one last mouthful of water and breathed. Breathed, breathed, breathed. I looked around. I was clinging to the northeast pier, the upriver one. I said out loud, "Did that the hard way." It came out a croak.

Now I had a fresh problem: I had to make that eight feet back to the riverbank, and from the waist down I was still underwater, numb as hell.

I remembered the cord I'd managed to grab, the cord that had saved my life, and looked down. It was underwater, had somehow gotten wrapped around my right thigh. I had to see what it was before I tried for that eight feet. I reached.

It was too thin for clothesline. I snaked it away from my thigh, pulled. Jesus, whatever was at the end of that line was heavy.

I finally lifted it from the river and stared at it—a mesh bag. The top of the bag formed a drawstring that had been looped around the pier and knotted.

Inside the bag were a pry bar, a carpenter's hammer, and a pointed trowel. They had plenty of surface rust but were basically sound tools, newish even.

I might have smiled.

I couldn't feel my legs at all, had to get out of the water quick. But I leaned back and looked at the pier. I'd been right: This wasn't a hundred-year-old hack job that could drop any minute. This was sound work. The pier was made of old brick that probably wrapped a cinder-block-and-concrete core. Somebody had put some time and effort into building these piers, then had beaten them up to make them look as old as the rest of the shack.

Somebody'd made damn sure this pump house wouldn't fall into the Souhegan. Why?

It was time to go.

I took three big breaths while I angled myself toward the river-bank. Then I jumped backward like a swimmer starting a back-stroke race.

But my numb, waterlogged legs pushed me barely three feet, and my boots were heavy as hell. My legs dropped, pulling me down. When my lips got to water level, deep panic grabbed me and I thrashed, willed my legs to kick, felt like each foot was a bowling ball.

I angled in and flailed and whipped and thrashed. Felt like a month, but it was probably fifteen seconds later that I finally grabbed an inch-thick tree root. I didn't wait, couldn't, all energy fading fast. Hands and knees up the bank, shivering, chattering, filthy by the time I clawed to the top of the rise.

I shivered to the F-150, aimed it south, and cranked the heat.

When the worst of the shivering was over, I called Trey at my house. "You speak with that *Globe* reporter yet?" I said.

"We've been playing phone tag. Why?"

I said I'd explain later, clicked off, dug Patty Marx's business card from my wallet. She'd crossed out the cell number on the card and written in a new one.

She picked up on one ring and said her name.

"This is Conway Sax," I said. "Remember me?"

"Of course."

"Want to talk about Tander Phigg?"

"Of course."

I was coming up on an exit I knew. "Take 495 North to 62 West," I said. "In about a mile there's a farm stand on your right."

Patty Marx walked toward my shaded picnic table in flat shoes, designer jeans, and a turquoise tank top with thin little straps that didn't cover her bra straps. The bra was black. She wore hoop earrings the diameter of a soda can. She was very pretty. As she sat, she glanced at the apple pie I was eating. "A whole pie?"

"They don't sell slices," I said, and handed her a plastic fork.

She hesitated, then took it and stabbed a piece of crust. "Why are you dripping wet?"

I ignored that. "How long you been at *The Globe*?"

"About a year and a half." She laughed. "Just in time for the industry collapse."

I didn't know what she meant. But I did know it was about then Phigg ran into hard times. I said, "How'd you meet Tander Phigg?"

"When I got to Boston I worked general assignment for three months, waiting for a beat to open up. I pitched my editor a feature on hard times in old mill towns. The long-gone manufacturing jobs, the vanishing tax base, the friction between townies and immigrants, et cetera." She waved a hand. "An evergreen, of course, you've read it a thousand times. But my editor bought it." She forked a bigger piece of pie and shrugged while she ate it. "Once I began researching Fitchburg, it didn't take long to catch on to Phigg Paper Products, hence Tander Phigg Junior."

"What was your take on him?"

Patty Marx hesitated a beat too long, looking at her white plastic fork, and I wondered what she was holding back. "He was his own worst enemy," she finally said. "His own harshest critic, too. That's a bad combination."

"What do you mean?"

"There's nothing wrong with having a rich daddy, okay?"

"You're asking the wrong guy."

She smiled. "Push a pencil, smile nice at the board meetings, and say a little prayer every time you cash a trust-fund check. What's wrong with that?"

"It's not enough," I said.

"For a lot of people it is."

"Not for . . . a real man," I said, and felt myself go red. I stared at a knot in the picnic table, waiting for her to laugh at me.

But when I looked up, Patty was nodding. "Precisely. Now imagine you're man enough to *know* you're not acting like a real man, but not quite man enough to *do* anything about it."

I thought about Tander Phigg, Jr. and nodded. A man like that would puff himself up, make himself out to be a big deal.

We ate pie and said nothing for a while.

Finally Patty shook her head and said, "He was dying to show me the big river house he was building himself. That's why I say he was his own worst enemy."

"What do you mean?"

"In a piece like the one I was doing, Tander Phigg Junior had *fall guy* tattooed on his forehead. And he should have known it."

"Why?"

She stuck her fork in the piecrust and ticked off reasons on her fingers. "The paper company's shut down, right? Tander Senior, the daddy who built the empire, is revered by all, the benefactor who employed the whole town for thirty years. Now that town is collecting welfare, food stamps. The men are crooks or drunks or both, the girls are knocked up by the time they're fourteen. The only player who's doing okay is Tander Phigg Junior, and what did *he* ever accomplish? He was daddy's boy, the company collapsed on his watch, and he's sitting on a fortune."

She built momentum as she said it and gave the table a good fist-thump when she finished. I wondered again what she wasn't telling me.

"Point being?" I said.

"The point is if he had a whiff of common sense, he would've seen he was destined to be the bad guy in my piece. He either wouldn't have talked with me at all, or he would have spun his story like crazy. He could have earned himself at least a little sympathy by telling me how awful he felt for the laid-off workers, for Fitchburg, for the region. Get it?"

"I guess."

"Instead, he showed me around the million-dollar timber-frame home he was building on the Souhegan! So into the piece it went."

"So you made him look like a jerk in your article."

"He made himself look like a jerk," she said. "I took pity and tried to soft-pedal him for his own good, but my editor knew I'd struck gold. Tander Phigg Junior, showing a reporter around his mansion-to-be while Fitchburg went in the toilet, was the lead anecdote when the story ran."

"How'd he react?"

"The way pissed-off sources always react."

I ate pie. Patty watched me. After a while she said, "What was *your* deal with Tander?"

"Friend."

"In pretty deep for a friend."

I told her a little about the Barnburners, about what I do. She listened with hard eyes, maybe buying it, maybe not. My story sounded weak even to me. I didn't like being on the defensive. Decided to go blunt, try to surprise her. "There's something heavy you're not telling me," I said. "What is it?"

"Thank you for the pie."

CHAPTER FOURTEEN

A hundred minutes later I pulled off my still-wet boots and socks on Charlene's front landing. I stepped inside, headed for the kitchen, and plopped two Walmart bags on the table.

Staring at me from great room sofas were Charlene, Sophie, and my father. He held a bottle of cream soda, his favorite from way back. Charlene didn't keep any in the house. Who does? She'd bought it special.

Charlene said, "What on earth happened to you?"

"Greeter at Walmart asked the same thing," I said. I patted one of the bags and looked at Fred. "Boots, socks, underpants, T-shirts, a button-down, jeans. Wranglers. Junior's brand. Thought you'd appreciate that."

He said, "Junior who?"

"Dale Earnhardt Junior."

"Earnhardt has a kid?"

Oh boy.

Sophie giggled. She knows her NASCAR. Charlene shushed her. Fred looked lost.

But as I headed upstairs to shower he perked up and started telling the gals about the time he raced against Dale Earnhardt's father,

Ralph. I was pretty sure the story was bullshit. He'd been telling it since I was a kid, and the details changed every time. Let him tell it often enough, he'd have himself winning the Daytona 500 with a last-lap pass.

I smiled as I thought it, squelching upstairs to the shower.

As I stepped from the bathroom, towel-wrapped, my cell rang. I grabbed it from Charlene's dresser, saw it was Randall. I picked up and said, "The hell you been?"

"I spent the weekend reposing on Cape Cod. At the lovely and exclusive Chatham Bars Inn, specifically." Big fake sigh. "Tennis, window-shopping, oysters on the beach. You know how it goes."

" 'Bout time you got laid."

"Philistine. Cad. Masher." Long pause. "Yeah, it was about time."

I shoulder-jammed the phone to my ear while I pulled on underpants and jeans. "Who's the lucky gal?" I said. "Anybody I know?"

"No, but you might be interested in what she does."

I ran a belt through the jeans, looked in the mirror that tops the dresser. I needed a haircut. Whenever it looks like it could use combing, I get it cut instead. Never have understood why anybody, man or woman, would want long hair. Pain in the ass.

Randall said, "Thanks for asking, dipshit. She owns an insurance agency in Bellingham."

"Okay." I wondered what the hell was interesting about insurance. I also wondered if Randall really liked the gal, felt bad about my getting-laid crack.

"The interesting thing about insurance," he said, "is that you need myriad databases for underwriting purposes."

"Myriad?"

"A shitload. And if you're whiling away a cozy Cape Cod weekend with a debonair man of the world, you may find yourself persuaded to surf some of those databases on your laptop while lolling about your handsome room that overlooks Chatham Harbor."

"Jesus, Randall."

"You're not much fun to tell a cool story to."

"When I tell you about my day so far you'll understand," I said. "Databases. Tell it."

"Myna Roper? Tander Phigg's former paramour? The one you texted me about?"

I'd been tugging on tube socks. I stopped. "What about her?"

"I found her."

"*What?*"

"She lives in Hebron Crossroads, South Carolina," he said. "Been in the same house since 1962."

"You sure it's the same Myna Roper?"

"I called to confirm. We had a short chat."

"Well I'll be damned," I said. "Can you come to Charlene's?"

"What for?"

"We'll fill each other in. We'll have some dinner. You can meet my father."

"*What?*"

I clicked off and looked in the mirror again. Caught myself smiling. Not as much as McCord, but smiling.

I wanted to talk with Charlene in private. I texted her: *Meet me lvngrm.* Then put on a T-shirt and my watch, headed downstairs.

She was just zipping through the front hall into the fancy room, which caps the western end of the house. It's stiff, formal. Crimson drapes, no TV, a pair of chairs that cost more than my truck. I think Charlene entertains serious prospects there, little parties I'm not invited to—the parties where she serves booze. Sometimes I wonder why she doesn't include me. Is it because of the booze, or because I'd embarrass her in front of the high rollers? Either way, it's probably a good idea all around.

She spun, folded her arms the way she does, waited.

"I'm sorry about my dad," I said. "If there'd been anywhere else to—"

"I adore Fred. Sophie does, too, I can tell. He's welcome here forever."

Jesus, she's hard to figure. A year or so ago, she bought Sophie two hamsters—and returned them three days later, saying they were disruptive.

I wondered why Charlene was looking at me that way if she wasn't pissed about having Fred under her roof. He had to be more disruptive than a pair of hamsters.

She said, "Why didn't you look for him, Conway?"

I said nothing.

"He says a few years ago, you spotted him at that intersection near the Allston/Brighton tolls." She softened her voice and stance. "Why didn't you *look* for him? He's your *father*."

There was so much to say.

I said nothing.

Charlene spread wide her arms. I stepped in.

I shook.

An hour and a half later, Chinese takeout wreckage covered the kitchen table. Me, Randall, and Charlene ate fortune cookies and orange slices. Sophie and Fred were sofa-splayed in the great room. The TV was tuned to a highlight show about last weekend's NASCAR race. Fred would point at the TV, then hold an imaginary steering wheel the way racers do. Then he would use body language to show Sophie how today's pansy-boy drivers would drive if they had a pair. Sophie sat rapt, loving every word, giggling when Fred dipped into dirty language.

"He's handing her a giant load of horseshit," I said. "You do realize that, don't you?"

Charlene slapped my arm. "Look at her. Look at *them*."

Randall said, "It's exactly like looking at Conway in thirty years."

"But a Conway that *talks*," Charlene said. They cracked up.

I said, "Assholes." But I might have smiled while I said it. I faced Randall. "Now you need to hear what I found at Phigg's shack, and I need to hear about Myna Roper. Who's first?"

Randall shifted his chair. "You."

I told it, starting with Montreal at Motorenwerk. Charlene listened in while she cleared the table.

When I got to the part about falling in the Souhegan, I lightened it, tried to make it a *Three Stooges* moment. But Charlene read my tone, read my eyes. She kissed the top of my head as she took the egg foo yong carton. "Thank God you're okay."

"You almost drowned three feet from the riverbank," Randall said. "How embarrassing."

I slapped the table. "That's *exactly* what ran through my head, even while it was happening."

"Very common." He knuckle-rapped his prosthetic. "I can't remember this myself, but the guys swear that while I lay there in the street, bleeding out with my foot blown over a wall somewhere, I asked if somebody could help me into the back of the Humvee. I said I'd just wait in the car while they mopped up, that I didn't want to be any trouble."

We were quiet awhile.

"This Montreal drug dealer," Charlene finally said, sponging the counter. "Did he kill Tander?"

"Maybe," I said.

"I keep coming back to the physical act of hanging a good-size man who was presumably struggling," Randall said. "Montreal's muscle-bound pal would certainly come in handy."

"What about Ollie and Josh?" I said.

Randall wiggled a hand in a *not-so-much* gesture.

"And the son, Trey?" Charlene said. "Randall tells me he's unlikely, but you can't be sure."

"That's true," I said.

"And yet he's your *guest*," she said, scrubbing a bit of invisible goop. "He's living under your *roof*."

I hadn't known until now how much that bothered her. "Well," I said, then didn't know what else to say.

"A classic Conway Sax conundrum," Randall said. "The Barnburner must be served, hence the Barnburner's kin must be served. Even if the kin murdered the Barnburner."

Charlene laughed at that. I was grateful to Randall for taking the pressure off me.

"Hey, Hardy Boys," Charlene said in a lighter voice, "don't leave me hanging. Do you think Tander stashed something?"

"Good question," Randall said, then gestured at me. "I defer to you, Brother Frank."

"What the hell are you talking about?" I said.

They looked at each other and laughed.

I said, "Bet your ass he stashed something."

"But what?" Randall said. "He didn't have a pot to piss in."

"We'll find out tomorrow. You, me, and Trey."

Charlene said, *"The Shabby Shanty Mystery."*

Randall said, *"The Secret of the Souhegan Shack."*

I stared while they laughed. Idiots.

A noise like the world's biggest crow strangling came from the great room. Fred rolled off the sofa and balled himself up, hands pressed to his stomach, twitching.

Sophie said, "What should I do what should I do oh my God what should I do?"

We all rushed in. Smelled it: Fred had shit himself.

"Sophie, come with me," Charlene said. Sophie didn't move fast enough. *"Come with me right now!"* Charlene got a hand on the small of Sophie's back, walked her through the dining area and up the stairs.

Fred's eyes were clenched shut. He was still spasming a little.

Behind me Randall said, "Too soon for Chinese food."

I nodded.

Fred's eyes opened and locked on mine. He tried to speak. Couldn't. Tears rolled.

I said over my shoulder, "Randall, maybe you can put leftovers in the fridge." I leaned and told Fred it was all right. He kept shaking, put a hand on my forearm and squeezed. "Right in front of everybody," he said. "Right in front of the *girl*." He cried.

I put my mouth to his ear, said again it was all right, asked if he could stand. He shook his head.

I got my arms beneath him, wrapped one of his around my neck, braced myself, rose, cradled him like a baby. Part of me wanted to make it look easy. Another part asked why.

I ignored the smell, ignored the shit transferring from the seat of his jeans to the front of mine. I told my father we would go upstairs and get him in the bathtub.

As we moved he kept saying, "Right in front of everybody." He was whispering, talking to himself.

Half an hour later I stepped into the great room again in sweatpants and a fresh T-shirt. Everything was neat as a pin. I palmed the sofa. It was damp and smelled of cleaning stuff. God bless Randall. He'd left a note on the kitchen table: *Long day. Rest. Call me AM w/plan.*

He was right—hell of a long day. I went upstairs, silently opened the door to Jesse's room, stuck my head in. I heard Fred breathing, fast asleep.

In Charlene's room, I listened to her breathe, too. I stripped, knelt, prayed, climbed in bed, slept like a dead man.

"Charlene Bollinger stayed home from work?" Randall said. "Now I *know* you're lying to me."

I said, "My mouth to God's ear."

"She must love your old man."

"I figure it's like having me around, but he doesn't paw after her."

"As far as you know."

It was the next morning, Tuesday, and we were northbound in Trey Phigg's rented Dodge. Trey had volunteered to drive, saying he needed the practice. He kept up with traffic, but you could see he was white-knuckling it.

I rode shotgun, and Randall took the backseat. The trunk was loaded with stuff we'd picked up at Lowe's and a sporting-goods place.

Fred had woken up at seven, had come downstairs acting like nothing had happened. Charlene, Sophie, and I had gone along with that. Before I left, Charlene had pulled me aside and said she'd stay with Fred today. It was the first time in six years she wasn't itching to get to the office.

Before climbing in, Randall had made a bogus excuse to speak with me alone. "Why the hell are we bringing Trey?" he'd said. "As far as we know, he killed his dad for whatever we're looking for."

"If he did, I'd rather have him up north with us than screwing around in Framingham," I said. "And if we do find anything, let's see how he reacts. It could tell us a lot."

Randall grumbled but went along.

Now, the Dodge had a good vibe as we headed for Rourke. Why not? We had another sunny day and an adventure to boot. We were digging for buried treasure. As a bonus, Trey was enjoying his escape from the Framingham house.

Randall read my mind. "Sure beats taping and mudding that office."

I nodded. "Myna Roper. We got interrupted last night. How'd you find her?"

"Once my friend showed me how to manipulate these insurance databases, it was easy," he said. "I doubt it took fifteen minutes.

Roper's a common name down there, but with the first name, the race, and the approximate DOB, she rose to the top pretty soon."

"Race?"

"For the actuarial tables, yeah." He leaned forward.

"You called her up?" I said. "Just like that?"

"And she picked up and talked. Nice lady. Born and raised in Hebron Crossroads, went to New York in 'fifty-nine, sowed her wild oats—her very words—came home in 'sixty-two, married, raised a family. Husband died thirty years ago, she's been on her own since."

"What line did you use to get her talking?"

"Semitruth. Laid on some dialect, made it clear I was a brother." He said it *"brotha,"* sneering. His father, Luther, sneers the same way at the street/ghetto bit. They both talk like they went to Yale. "And I may have let slip that I'm a wounded veteran."

"Laid it on thick, huh?"

"With a trowel," he said. "I told her Phigg had died, and said we found references to her in his papers."

I pointed. Trey turned right onto the road that paralleled the Souhegan. We'd be at the shack in five minutes. I said, "How'd she react?"

"She went quiet," Randall said. "Then she got more polite and more formal, and I knew I was a goner. I would've liked to probe deeper, but all I had to go on was the text message you sent me."

"You did fine." I turned to Trey. "Slow, but don't pull in." He eased past Jut Road. We saw no sign of a vehicle. Trey drove a quarter mile while I looked at the river to my left. Finally I said stop, pointed. "See that clump? Three dead birches? Keep watch for us here, just in case things turn to shit."

"Good call," Randall said. "It wouldn't take but two minutes to float down here, and there are plenty of branches to grab for."

Trey nodded, turned the Dodge around, idled back to Jut Road, stopped.

While Randall cleared the trunk, I recapped Trey's job. I watched him close while I did it, making sure he wasn't jittery. We'd figured it wasn't safe to have a car here: The lady who called the cops yesterday when she saw an SUV had proved that. So Trey would cruise up and down the road, staying nearby and we'd call when we needed him. He would buzz my cell if he saw anything sketchy.

I climbed out, thumped the roof, watched the Dodge pull off. Randall asked if Trey was okay. I said yes, then led the way.

The Souhegan was running high and fast, runoff jacked up a notch by the warm spell.

In two minutes, we dumped gear at the riverbank and I pulled on the fisherman's waders we'd bought. Randall took off his shoe and his ankle—I never got used to that—and began working his way into a royal-blue wet suit. The sporting-goods place hadn't had one big enough for me, so I was stuck with the waders.

I hate fishing in general. I especially hate waders.

After Randall zipped the wet suit, he tied a knot in its right ankle—to keep it out of the way, I guessed. I eyeballed it. "You sure that'll work?"

"It has to," he said, shrugging. "I'm not larking around in some freezing river wearing my hundred-thousand-dollar prosthetic." He sat, pulled an air pump and a pack of D batteries from a bag, and installed the batteries. Then, from the same bag, he pulled the smallest inflatable boat the sporting-goods shop had. It was more of a heavy-duty pool toy, really—circular, three feet across. The guy at the store said kids climb in them and get pulled around by boats—water-skiing for people who can't water-ski.

The pump made a racket, but in three minutes the boat was inflated. While Randall loaded it with tools, I took my cordless drill and fifty feet of climbing rope to the waterline.

I was clumsy in the boots. Just wearing them on land felt like walking through Jell-O. I worked my way west until I was beneath the shack, in a spot where the drop-off wasn't as sudden. Trying not to think about what happened here yesterday, I stepped into the river.

Once I stopped worrying about falling in, it was easy to move around in two and a half feet of water. Funny feeling, wading boots: You're not cold, exactly, but you never forget how near the cold is.

Yesterday I hadn't looked hard at the underside of the shack. Now I did. It had been built on two-by-ten ribs that ran perpendicular to the river. The five ribs were stout, the kind of lumber you can't get anymore. Along with the rebuilt piers, they explained why the shack still stood.

The important thing right now was that the strong ribs would hold the rigging I wanted to set up. I used a half-inch bit to drill a bunch of holes, ran rope through the holes, then tied off the rope.

Randall said, "Catch."

I looked up the slope and saw he was getting set to release our little rubber boat. I nodded. He let go. The boat slipped down the steep bank. Top-heavy with gear, it wanted to overturn when I stopped it, but I managed to keep everything dry. Randall ass-slid down behind the boat and looked over the rope rigging. " 'T'will serve," he said.

"Fucking A it t'will."

Randall looked at the piers eight feet away. "You sure those things have been fixed up? They look grungy to me."

"That just means whoever rebuilt them did his work well. Get closer." I realized it was kind of nice down here if you weren't drowning. It was cooled by shade and river water, and there was enough of a breeze to keep bugs away.

Randall grabbed a handful of rope as a safety line and hopped into the Souhegan, just like that. I saw the current hit him, saw him counterbalance. Two hops later he was swimming. He made it to the northwest pier, the same one I'd about died at, in maybe six seconds. He was a natural athlete. Must've been something when he had two feet.

He turned and looked at me, silently rubbing it in.

Then he turned again to check out the pier. He looked it over and nodded. "Okay, from here I see it," he said, raising his voice above the river rush. He pushed off the pier with one leg, swam a few strokes, and was sitting on the riverbank a few seconds later.

By then I was checking out the underside of the shack.

"What are you looking for?" Randall said.

"Not sure." But I kept looking.

The shack had been built long before plywood existed. The flooring, six-inch-wide planks set across the supporting ribs, ran the same direction as the river. The age-gray planks had tiny flakes of paint—orange or brick red, hard to tell—clinging here and there. When I stuck a thumbnail in them, they were a little mushy but basically sound.

I froze, thought, looked again. I stepped back, made a sloppy measurement with my hand-span, stepped back under, and measured again.

"If I had a dictionary with me and I looked up *shit-eating grin*," Randall said, "I do believe I would find a picture of you as you look right now."

"Wait here."

I pistoned up the slope, walking in slow-motion due to the waders. Stepped across the clay drive and into the woods, looking for the remains of the main house. When they started Phigg's dream house, the contractors had regraded heavily to fight flooding, so it took me a while to find what I was looking for. I bashed through the woods until I found remnants of a brick foundation, then hit my knees and cleared leaves, moss, dirt.

Finally I found it: a plank, six inches wide. I rubbed dirt from it, held it up, squinted.

And saw paint flakes. Burnt orange, maybe brick red.

I ran back and butt-slid down the slope so fast I was up to my knees in water before I got myself stopped.

Randall said, "What?"

I pointed. First at the plank in my hand, then at the shack floor-board.

Randall tried. He looked back and forth. Then again. Then he gave up, looked his question at me.

"You don't paint the underside of a pump house floor," I said, and pointed again—at paint flakes this time.

Randall said, "False floor."

"Want to hand me that pry bar?" I said.

CHAPTER FIFTEEN

Two and a half hours later we were hot, waders and wet suit long removed, shirts peeled off. Trey had backed the Dodge to the edge of the drop; he stood next to the car's open trunk. "You want me to come down there and help?"

I craned my neck to look at him. "Stay. We'll do a bucket brigade."

I pulled out my multi-tool, cut down the climbing rope, and gathered gear. Randall was wedging bogus floorboards back in place. He wrist-wiped sweat from his forehead and looked over his work to make sure he hadn't missed anything. "What an absolutely ingenious setup," he said.

It was. The southernmost section of floorboards, the downriver side, had been cut where they rested on a rib, so you couldn't see the cut from below. We'd poked around fifteen minutes before we figured out the rib had been rigged to pivot. To make that happen, we had to pound out a couple of dowels way over on the outboard side of the shack, where the fast water was over my head. Phigg must've figured nobody would ever get to those dowels without scaffolding. He was almost right: Randall had barely reached them by setting his good foot in our rope rigging and stretching. I'd worried he'd fall backward and whip downriver.

He hadn't. When he'd popped the second dowel out, the far end of the rib had pivoted eight inches, enough for us to see where the bogus planks had been added. A four-foot-square section had been glued and screwed together. It fit so well Randall and I both had to lean on a cat's paw to pop it out.

Once it was out, you could see why Phigg had rigged it this way: The false floor was low enough so that the real one sagged and squeaked the way a hundred-year-old floor should.

It was a hell of a hidey-hole.

And a well-packed one.

We hadn't told Trey yet. I wanted to eyeball his reaction. He stood next to his trunk, trying to be cool but knowing something was up. Finally, as Randall and I stacked gear, he said, "Anything?"

We pretended we didn't hear. I tossed one rope end up to Trey, tied the other to the boat, put most of the gear in it, and told him to pull. He did, then dumped the gear and sent the boat back down the slope. We filled it with the rest of the gear and sent it up again.

Randall began whistling while we loaded the rubber boat a third time. It took me a few seconds to recognize the tune: "Money," by Pink Floyd.

I said to Trey, "That'll do it. Haul away." While he pulled, Randall and I scrambled up the bank. We made it as the boat crested the rise. Trey looked inside. Came to a dead stop. Did a double take. Grabbed a packet to triple-check.

Randall and I eye-locked, both thinking the same thing: No matter what anybody's timeline said, Trey Phigg hadn't known about any pile of money, hadn't killed his father.

Finally he said, "What the *hell*?"

The rubber boat held four packs of money, each pack sixteen inches by sixteen by the width of a dollar bill. They were machine-wrapped in industrial plastic. Everything was vacuum sealed, professional quality—the way you'd protect money if you planned to store it four feet above a river.

Trey looked at me, then at Randall, then at me. "What is this?"

"Hard to tell until we count it," I said. "We were hoping it was all hundreds, but if you look close you can see everything from fives on up."

"Which is good news," Randall said. "It means your father already laundered it. The only thing better than money is money Uncle Sam doesn't know about."

Trey's mouth made an O as his head swiveled from me to Randall and back again. "But what *is* it?"

"It's *yours* is what it is," I said, glancing at the main road. "We're vulnerable here. Let's finish loading and split."

Two hours later in Framingham, I sat on a couch with Tuan and watched a TV show about sharing and the letter *P*. Trey and Randall had taken the money upstairs to count it. I was lookout.

On TV, something purple said sharing only works if everybody does it.

I pulled my cell and dialed Charlene's house. She picked up.

I said, "How is he?"

"Hang on a sec," Charlene said. I heard footsteps and pictured her moving from the great room into the living room, wanting a little privacy.

"Shaky," she said. "Grand and expansive one minute, then dead quiet. He . . . he goes away, inside his head, and when he comes back it takes him a few seconds to remember who we are. Then he goes in his room—Jesse's room—with the phone and calls that guy. That seems to calm him down."

"What guy?"

"I was going to ask you," Charlene said as the purple thing on TV shared an ice cream sandwich with an orange thing. "Fred says you know the guy. I assumed you'd hooked him up with a sponsor."

Huh. "No. What's the number he's dialing?"

"I'm embarrassed to say I checked, or tried to. He's masking that somehow."

Huh. Fred barely knew his shoe size; no way had he figured out how to erase call logs without instruction. Who the hell was he talking to? Mental note: Find out.

"He have any more accidents?" I said.

"No, but he's paranoid about that. Strictly saltines and ginger ale so far. I'm trying to get some lunch into him. How was your little adventure?"

"Phigg had a big pile of money stashed in his shack," I said. "We found it."

"I'll be damned. How much?"

"Randall and Trey are counting it right now."

"Trey's in on the count? You trust him with that?"

"He didn't kill anybody."

Long pause. "The thing about you," Charlene finally said, "is that you don't trust anybody until you trust them. And then you trust them too much."

I told her if she'd watched Trey the way I had, fired questions at him the way I had, she'd understand.

She didn't sound convinced.

I was relieved when Randall and Trey clomped down the stairs. Said I had to go.

The three of us hit the kitchen, where Kieu was cleaning the countertop like it was the president's shoes. Trey shot some Vietnamese at her and she went to watch TV with Tuan.

"Seventy-five K," Randall said as we sat. "Ratty old bills, everything from fives to hundreds. Fully laundered money."

I whistled and clapped Trey on the back. "Nice score."

"Like hell it is," he said, slapping the table.

The room went quiet.

Trey looked at my face, then at Randall's, then around the kitchen. His face turned red as he realized how his comment had come across.

164 | Steve Ulfelder

"I'm sorry, guys," he said. "It *is* a lot of money, I guess. It all depends on your expectations."

"What were yours?" Randall said.

"High six figures, maybe seven," Trey said. "I knew my father was drawing down the Phigg Paper Products legacy, but I didn't know he was actively *squandering* it."

We were quiet awhile, Randall and I thinking about how to respond to that.

"Once we get this house fixed up, I'll be lucky to get a hundred grand for it," I finally said, then nodded at Randall. "He's driving around in his dad's twenty-year-old station wagon with rust holes you can step through."

Trey got it. "I hear you, and I'm sorry about the dilettante bit," he said. "In my defense, I just spent four years with four generations of in-laws in an apartment no bigger than this kitchen. I'm not exactly a silver-spoon kid."

"Or maybe you were, but got past it?" I said.

"Maybe."

That was enough for me.

From the family room came a song about the letter *P*.

After a while Randall said, "So what the hell was he doing with seventy-five K stashed in his floorboards?"

"And living like a bum?" I said.

"Who the hell killed him?" Randall said.

"Where the hell do we start?" Trey said.

Randall and I locked eyes, said it at the exact same time. "Hebron Crossroads, South Carolina."

Eight hours later I sat in a rented Ford Focus at the bottom of Myna Roper's driveway, wondering whether to knock on her door or backtrack to a Motel 6 I'd passed twenty minutes ago.

My Seiko said 9:05. Purplish daylight hung tough to the west, this being one of the longest days of the year, but the eastern sky was black. I squinted up a rise at an unlit house—a small ranch or a big trailer—and wriggled my shoulder blades. The flight to Charlotte, then the three-hour drive south, had more or less locked up my back. Stiff, hungry, and tired, I wondered how the pizza was down here and lit the Focus. As I got set to U-turn north and head for the Motel 6, a light went on in the house. "Hell," I said out loud, wriggling my shoulders again as I pulled up the asphalt drive.

I'd spent most of the flight trying to think through my approach to Myna Roper. How would I establish trust? What info should I use? What should I hold back? But my brain doesn't like to work that way, so I'd mostly read *Racer* magazine and watched the college girl next to me play a game on her laptop.

As I climbed three wooden steps, I saw the house was a double-wide trailer, but a nice one: Mature bushes and flowers hid the bottom, and the vinyl siding was no more than a couple years old. I heard a TV, hesitated, knocked.

The TV went off or mute, and after a few seconds of scrabbling—dog?—the trailer turned quiet. I figured Myna Roper didn't get a lot of callers at this hour. I knocked again and said her name.

No movement, no sound. Just a frightened old lady keeping still and wishing she hadn't turned the damn light on.

"I'm here about Tander Phigg," I said, and waited.

It took her a full minute to crack the door. "Pardon me?" she said.

"He hanged himself last week in New Hampshire," I said, wishing I was better at planning these things. "Can I come in?"

She opened the door wide, took two steps backward, and hit a light switch. By the time I stepped in and closed the door behind me, Myna Roper was leaning on a Formica counter, one hand over her mouth.

A spiky gray dog no bigger than my cats sniffed my ankle. I was grateful it hadn't barked the way those dogs usually do. I dropped to one knee and petted it and waited for Myna Roper to say something.

But she didn't. I rose and took a good look at her.

Chas Weinberg had called her an Amazon. You could see why. She was five-ten, even with an old woman's stoop; must have been very tall for her time. Her hair had been straightened and was cut in a very short pageboy, like something from an old Motown girl group. She wore no makeup, but her eyelashes were long and her dark skin was pure. Her flannel nightgown touched the floor.

"I'm sorry," I said. "I don't know how to do things like this. He killed himself, and I'm working with his son to figure out why, and we both thought I should talk to you."

She looked at me another ten seconds, then uncovered her mouth and nodded. "He did have a son, didn't he?"

"Tander Phigg the Third," I said. "He goes by Trey."

She put the hand over her mouth again—tried to make it a casual gesture, but I'd already noticed she didn't have her teeth in. "Pardon me," she said behind the hand, "but who did you say you were to Tander?"

I said my name and told her I'd known him a decade or more from AA. She nodded, waved to a brown-and-tan sofa, and asked if I'd like to sit while she made herself decent. The wave pulled my eye to an end table. Atop it were a short lamp and a tall mixed drink with two cherries. Her eye followed mine to the drink.

Her dark skin couldn't hide the blushing.

I waited ten minutes. At first I sat near the lamp, but I could smell the drink and it bothered me. It was a Manhattan. Funny the things you remember, the things you can't clear from your head.

I moved to the opposite end of the sofa and looked around. The walls were paneled, the TV an off-brand plasma, a thirty-two-incher. The dog sat beneath the TV and stared at me, head cocked. On the walls were a clock made to look like a compass, a framed thank-you from a church youth group, and a twin frame with two pictures: a high-school graduation shot of a girl who had Myna's eyes and lashes, and an uncomfortable-looking man with a broad nose and a half-assed Afro.

There was also a black-and-white photo, framed, of young Myna Roper.

She'd been stunning. In the shot she wore a black dancer's leotard and posed on a stage or platform, right thigh tucked beneath her rear end, left leg extended straight before her. The twist of her arms and the way her neck swanned made her look like a hurdler, a ballerina, and a warrior all at once.

"Tander shot that one," she said, stepping from the bedroom at the end of the narrow trailer. "It's the only memorabilia I keep from that time."

She'd put on black stretch pants, a baggy T-shirt that said CLEM-SON, and her teeth. She must have gotten over her embarrassment about the drink while she changed, because she plopped into her spot on the sofa, hefted her Manhattan, and took a pull. "To the memory of Tander Phigg Junior," she said, toasting, and took another. "You said he hanged himself? Dear God. Please tell me the circumstances."

I did, while she drank.

When I finished, Myna Roper said nothing for a long time. I watched her play movies in her head. Her eyes would crinkle, then soften as she moved from scene to scene. "My, that was a long time ago," she finally said. "I imagine you've got quite a story to tell about how you managed to run me down. Are you a detective?"

"Just a friend of Tander's, Miz Roper."

"Myna, please. Just a friend, and come all this way?"

"We were in the same AA group," I said. "Tight bunch. We help each other out."

"How do you plan to help a dead man?"

"His son's not dead."

"What is the son like?" she said. "Did the apple stay good and close to the tree, the way they tend to do?" She sipped, watched me close. I made a quick decision to go for honesty.

"I've only known Trey a week," I said, "but I think he's a much better man than his father was."

Myna smiled big, showing me bright white dentures. "How so?"

I thought about it. "He knows who he is," I finally said. "I'll bet he knows what he's good at and what he's bad at, and I'll bet he's okay with both."

"Hmm," she said, maybe looking closer at me. Then she sipped and went quiet and reached a hand down for her dog to lick.

It hadn't taken her long to get to the bottom of a big drink. I needed to get her talking soon, especially if she was planning to build herself another Manhattan. I said, "How'd you end up in New York?"

"In 'fifty-six, when I was fifteen," she said, rising and taking the three steps to the kitchen, "two Jewish boys and a Jewish girl came to school and talked all afternoon about civil rights. They were from Columbia University, and, my God, they were the wisest, smartest, kindest things I'd ever laid eyes on." She splashed the dregs of her Manhattan into the sink and assembled ingredients for a fresh one. Her movements were efficient and swift, the way they get when you practice a lot and live by yourself: She knew within a quarter-inch where everything would be.

"You were what, a sophomore?" I said. "A junior?"

"I was the teacher!" she said, the word sounding just a little like *teashur.* "I learned everything I was going to in the colored school here by the time I was thirteen. After that I more or less ran things."

"You went to New York because of the Jewish kids," I said. "You bought what they were selling."

"Yes I did," she said, pouring vermouth. "I was reasonably bright, and I knew if I didn't get out of here soon I'd be stuck running that colored school the rest of my life. I spent two years up in Olanta getting the quickest degree I could, and off I went."

"So you got to New York when?"

"Nineteen fifty-nine," she said, pausing as she held an ice-filled shaker. From the way she smiled I guessed she was remembering the day she stepped off the bus.

"Full of piss and vinegar."

"You read my mind," she said, laughing and shaking her drink.

A minute later she was on the sofa, still remembering but not smiling anymore. "It took me two days to learn my first hard lesson," she said, licking her index finger. "All those white boys and girls, the college crowd, were more interested in theoretical Negroes than the genuine item."

"I wouldn't mind a soda or a glass of water," I said.

"I am so rude!" she said, more or less shrieking it, spilling some Manhattan as she slapped my shoulder. "Help yourself." *Heppy shef.*

I rose, stepped to the fridge, found a Diet Sprite, sat.

"I looked up the Columbia kids who'd visited Hebron Crossroads," Myna said as I opened my can. "How their faces fell when I told them who I was and why I'd come to the big city! They couldn't hustle me out of there fast enough. They were all in favor of educated, self-confident Negroes, but introduce them to one and they didn't know whether to shit or go blind." She giggled, covered her mouth. "Pardon my French."

I needed to push before the second Manhattan wiped her out. "You found work as a receptionist," I said, "and modeled for art classes on the side. You met Tander Phigg and started dating."

"How on earth did you learn all this?"

"I spoke with Chas Weinberg."

"Goodness, the King of the Queens. He's still alive?"

"Still runs the gallery on Wooster Street, still owns the building. Sells rusty wheelbarrows for forty-six hundred dollars."

Myna laughed and punched my shoulder. "It was a racket fifty years ago and it's just gotten worse, hasn't it?"

"Did you love Tander?"

That shushed her, straightened her up. She thought and sipped. "I loved the respect he had for me," she said. "I had plenty of offers from young white men, especially when I began working nude, but they were all wink-and-a-nudge offers. They were willing to be seen in a restaurant with me—they all assumed it was what I wanted—as long as I was willing to go to bed after." She slowly twirled an index finger. "Big damn whoopee."

"Tander was different?"

"Oh, yes. He was earnest and stumbling and stiff, just as he would have been with a white girl." She plucked a cherry, popped it in her mouth, and faced me. "Did I love him? No, I did not."

"I think you were the only girl he ever loved," I said. "For what it's worth."

"Really?" Myna touched her hair. "Now why do you say that?"

I told her Trey called his father's time in New York his "five happy years." Told her how Phigg had come home to Fitchburg like a whipped dog, had spent the rest of his life going through the motions.

When I said Phigg's wife had died in childbirth and he'd never remarried, she put her hand over her mouth and nodded fast. "Goodness," she said, "a brand-new baby and he didn't find himself another woman?"

"That's what hit me, too. You'd think a guy like Tander, in 1972, would remarry on the double, find somebody to take care of his only kid."

After a very long pause Myna Roper said, "His only *son*."

I looked at her, then at the girl in the high-school graduation photo on the opposite wall. "Well I'll be damned," I said.

CHAPTER SIXTEEN

We were quiet awhile. Myna finished her Manhattan but was sharp now, focused. I didn't know how long that could last.

"Chas Weinberg still wonders why you and Tander left New York in a hurry," I said. "He talked abortion."

"That was the plan, actually. That's how I broke from him. He kept saying he wanted to 'be there for me,' the fool. I told him he'd do no such thing. I told him I'd get it taken care of, and go back home, and I never wanted to see him again. I was doing my very best—" *ver besht,* the booze creeping back into her speech—"to be a modern Manhattan missy."

"What happened?"

"It was 1962," she said, jiggling ice, "and I was a Southern Baptist, and I *wasn't* a modern Manhattan missy. And I couldn't go through with it."

"You came home and had your baby."

Myna half laughed. "There was more to it than that. I came home, latched on to the lightest-skinned Negro bachelor in three counties, and made damn sure I had him hooked before I showed."

"Did he know he wasn't the father?"

"Bobby died in 'seventy-nine," she said, avoiding the question, eyes cutting to her empty glass. "Maybe he wasn't the smartest man, but he was a fine man, a railroad man. And do you know what, Mister Sax? Other than that one thing, I was a good wife to him."

I didn't see any Kleenex, so I stepped to the counter, tore a paper towel from a roll, and handed it to her as I sat. "Now Diana," she said, nodding at the photo and blotting tears, "*she* figured things out."

"How'd she manage that?"

"Smart and nosy," she said, pushing off. It took her two tries to stand, and she fought for balance before starting toward her Manhattan-building area.

The dog whined just a little—he'd seen this routine, probably saw it every night. "You want me to let your dog out?" I said.

"How sweet. Sometimes I forget."

I bet she did. I let the dog out, looked closely at the dual photos. "You said her name was Diana?"

"Diana Patience," Myna said, taking small, precise steps to the sofa, fresh drink in hand.

"Smart as a whip, huh? I can see it in her eyes."

"Yes, sir, she was," Myna said. Her new drink was two-thirds as tall as the others. Moderation. "She got a partial academic scholarship to Clemson. Studied journalism and communications."

"Those smarts made her wonder if your husband was really her father."

Myna set slippered feet on the small oak coffee table and closed her eyes and said nothing for a while. Just when I figured she'd passed out, she smiled, eyes still closed. "Both of them wondered. She was born in a little house down the road, not in a hospital, and the midwife fudged the birth date a few months." She opened her eyes. "I told Bobby it was so my family wouldn't know she was conceived early, and I suppose that was partly true. But he knew something wasn't right."

"And went along with it?"

She nodded. "Bobby Marx wasn't complicated and he wasn't demanding. He knew something wasn't right, but he behaved as if Diana was his to the day he died."

Holy shit. Now *I* froze up. Finally I said, "Bobby *Marx*?" I rose to take a close look at the twin photos.

"Robert No Middle Name Marx," Myna said, eyes closed.

Holy shit. Now I saw her in the high school graduation photo: Diana Patience Marx, aka Patty Marx.

"You say Diana was curious?" I said it loud to keep her awake. Myna's drink had listed, her breaths had lengthened.

"Curious, yes." *Curioush, yesh.* "Once she hit fourteen, that was her hobbyhorse. Oh, we had knock-down-drag-outs when Bobby was at work! She was persistent to a fault. 'Show me this.' 'How about *this*?' 'And then there's *this*.'" Myna laughed, slopping some Manhattan onto her lap. "I finally told her the summer before she went off to college that Bobby wasn't her father. She cut me dead, said I was eight years too late. And I still wouldn't say who *was* her father, and that just turned her persistent again. I think she studied journalism mostly so she could dig around and find her daddy."

"Did she ever figure it out?"

"Course she did." *Courshedid.* Myna raised an index finger. "Mister . . . sir, would you be a dear and bring over my trash can?"

As I stepped to the kitchen and grabbed a pale yellow plastic can with a white liner, I said, "What's Diana doing now?"

But Myna left the index finger in the air, gesturing *wait a sec*. She nodded thanks for the trash can, pulled her feet from the coffee table, set the can on the floor in front of her, leaned forward, and vomited once into the trash. I turned my head.

When she was finished Myna took one more dainty sip of her drink, set it down, rose. "And with that," she said, "it's off to bed." *Anwishatishoftabed.*

I said, "Are you all right?"

"Oh, yes. Toodle-oo, sir."

"Miz Roper," I said. "Where is your daughter now?"

She opened her bedroom door, swayed, waved a vague hand. "Up north somewhere," she said. "Doesn't come around much anymore, damn her."

Her door clicked shut.

When I stepped from the trailer, the little dog was sitting not three feet away. I held the door open. He hesitated, then made a wide arc around me and went inside. As he passed I said, "Take good care of her, pal." It seemed he wagged his tail, but I may have imagined that.

"How's Ollie's knee?"

"Coming along," Josh said.

"Let me talk to him."

"Nah, he's upstairs."

"So run the cell up to him."

"Nah, he's talking with his mom. You know how it goes."

I was in the rented Focus, heading to the Charlotte airport. I'd spent the night in the Motel 6 near Hebron Crossroads. Got up at four, was making the long drive to Charlotte for the morning flight. The night before, I'd texted Randall and Trey that I had big news. Hadn't wanted to say more in a text—the Patty Marx bombshell was too important.

I'd considered driving back to Myna Roper's house this morning, catching her sober, and talking again. I wanted to know more about Diana-slash-Patty.

But that, plus a later flight, would have eaten up most of the day, and Charlene would be stuck babysitting Fred.

So northbound it was. I'd waited until six to call Josh and Ollie.

Josh was holding back. I didn't like it. "I bumped into Ollie's Montreal guy," I said.

It grabbed him. "When? Where?"

"I'll tell Ollie."

"*Fuck* Ollie! Tell *me*!" Long pause. "I'm sorry. Cabin fever. Cooped up."

I said nothing.

"It's just that . . . Montreal is bad news," Josh said. "It'd sure be nice to know what kind of threat he poses. Ollie's mom is in the phone book, you know? I worry he'll find us here."

"I think I've got a plan for Montreal," I said.

"What is it?"

"Have Ollie call," I said. "Happy to share. With him."

"Is it my imagination," I said, "or did he gain ten pounds in a day?"

"Cereal, cold cuts, and cream soda," Charlene said. "I had to run to Stop and Shop *twice*."

Lunchtime, Shrewsbury. We stood on the deck watching Fred push Sophie on a creaky old swing set that should've been hauled away five years ago. Sophie was too big for the set, and Fred was pushing her past horizontal, saying things that made them both laugh.

"So everything's okay?" I said, looking at Fred and Sophie. "No . . . accidents?"

"Nothing like that," she said, setting paper plates on a table. "Open the umbrella, will you? This heat."

"What's he like? He talk much?"

"Ask him what he's like, for crying out loud," she said, popping open a bag of chips. "He's *your* father."

I said nothing.

Charlene looked at me, stepped to me, rubbed my arm. "I'm sorry," she said. "It's not that simple, is it?" Then she put thumb and pinkie in her mouth and whistled loud enough to make my ears hurt.

Fred said, "Soup's on!" He began to slow Sophie on the swing.

"He's so good, so *normal,* that you forget sometimes," Charlene said, leaning into me. "But then he just goes away. The thousand-yard stare comes into his eyes, and his mouth shakes, and he forgets where he is."

We ate—sandwiches for me, Sophie, and Charlene, just a stack of cold cuts for Fred. When she finished Charlene stood, said she had to get to the office before they forgot what she looked like, kissed the top of Fred's head, and left.

"You look good," I said.

"I *feel* good," he said.

"You want to hit a meeting?" I said, checking my watch. "Salvation Army has a one o'clock we can make."

"*Fuck* that," Fred said. "Got no time for AA sob sisters. You said you were gonna show me your place in Framingham. Pardon my French, missy."

Sophie giggled.

"I look like a sob sister to you?" I said.

"Why, yes," he said, winking at Sophie. "Yes you do, matter of fact. What color are your panties, sister?"

Sophie giggled some more, then looked at me and stopped. I felt bad for her. Her specialty was getting along with whoever was in the room. Right now she was whipsawed.

"It's okay," I said to her. "The man wants to pass on a meeting, that's fine by me." I turned to Fred. "So what do you want to do after we see the house?"

"Same thing every man wants to do, 'specially when it's been a while," he said. "I want to *drive*."

An hour later, after I showed off the Framingham house to Fred, we sat three wide in the F-150. I drove, Fred hung an elbow out the passenger window, Sophie took the middle. "Where are we going?" she said.

"You'll see," I said, swinging onto Route 146 South. No way in hell was I going to let Fred drive on a public road. But a Barnburner owned a dairy farm in Sutton, fifteen miles southwest of Shrewsbury. He was a race fan, and for kicks he'd dug and graded a quarter-mile dirt oval in a far corner of his property. He had a couple of beat-to-shit former cop cars, and once in a while some of us headed out there for half-assed races, laughing like idiots the whole time.

I explained this to Sophie and Fred as we drove. Thinking about Myna Roper, her daughter, and Trey, I let my head go where it wanted to go.

Until Sophie pointed at a sign and said, "Ooooh, sounds ominous."

The sign said: PURGATORY CHASM STATE RESERVATION 1 MILE.

Fred and I stared at each other. I hadn't thought about the place in thirty years. Hadn't *let* myself think about it. From Fred's face, I guessed he felt the same.

Sophie picked up on the vibe, swiveled. "What?" she said. "What about it?"

"Nothing!" I said.

"Shut up!" Fred said at the same time.

We each patted her knee. I felt bad about yelling at her. I guessed Fred did, too.

The rest of the ride was quiet.

My Barnburner friend wasn't around, but his foreman was. When I leaned in and told him I was going out back to drive around like a jackass for an hour, he gestured *be my guest.*

I killed the AC and switched to the recirc setting to keep dust out of the F-150's interior, then bumped over dirt roads that were rutted enough to force a walking pace. I'd always liked the property. It had been an apple orchard until forty years ago, and even though most of the untended trees were dead or dying fast, the straight rows and regular spacing made me peaceful every time I drove through.

We were just starting to wish for the AC when we cleared a long rise and saw the dirt oval below us.

"Well I'll be dipped in shit," Fred said.

Sophie laughed and clapped her hands twice.

At only a quarter mile around, the homebuilt track had no straights to speak of—just a couple of arcs where the 180-degree turns opened up. The start/finish line was marked only by a pitchfork rammed into the dirt, and four or five feet behind that were a half dozen scrounged lawn chairs and tree stumps for spectating.

A few feet back of the chairs sat an old orange road grader—my buddy won it in a poker game—and a pair of ugly Chevy Caprices, the ones from the mid-nineties that looked like beached whales. They were old cop cars picked up on eBay. I never was a Chevy man, but I had to give those cars credit: We'd been doing our level best to kill them for three or four years now, and they just kept going.

I rolled the F-150 down the hill, took a hard right onto the track in the middle of turn one, and racked up easy laps while I explained the place to Sophie and Fred. At first I drove gently, but soon instinct took over. With its empty pickup bed, the truck had almost no weight over the rear wheels. No weight meant no traction, which meant it was easy to kick the back end out and drift through the turns.

After a few laps like this, Fred said, "*Now* you're talkin'."

I upped the pace, notched a few more laps, and treated myself to a rebel yell. I looked down at Sophie to see if she was enjoying it, too.

She wasn't enjoying it at all. Her face was paste, her teeth were clenched, her left hand was clinging to my shirtsleeve for dear life.

I felt like a jerk. "Sorry, honey," I said, jumping off the throttle. "Sorry sorry sorry, that's enough of that, huh?" I coasted off the dirt oval and bumped over flattened grass to where the Caprices were parked.

"It's okay! I'm okay!" Sophie said, her voice too bright, her smile too big. I felt even worse.

"Jesus Christ," Fred said. "Things were just getting good out there."

"I had enough," I said, looking him in the eye, then cutting my eyes to Sophie.

He didn't get it. Folded his arms. "Pussy."

"For crying out loud," I said. "Pardon his filthy language, Sophie."

"Yeah, sorry," he said, rubbing his chin. "I meant to say 'fraidy cat.'"

Funny thing, family. I felt my face go red, felt the red-mist pulse start in my head, knew I was being sucked in, but couldn't help myself. "Choose your weapon, Fred," I said, pointing at the Chevys. "Let's see who's a fraidy cat."

"I'll take that one over there," he said.

"Good idea. That one's got a little more juice, and you'll need it."

"This is going to be awesome," Sophie said.

CHAPTER SEVENTEEN

My buddy leaves the keys in the Chevys and dumps five gallons of gas in their tanks when he remembers. Far as I know, the only maintenance they get is when somebody spits on their windshields to clean them off.

But they fired right up. Sounded pretty good, too: They had the 305 V8 that came with the police package, and we hacksawed their mufflers off two summers ago.

Fred and I agreed on three warm-up laps, then a ten-lap race. It would be easy to lose track of the lap count, so I aimed my truck at the oval, put Sophie in the driver's seat, and told her to flash the lights when there were two laps left.

Following Fred in counterclockwise circles during the warm-up, I felt like a jackass: I'd been too nervous to let him drive on the roads but had let him goad me into an idiotic race.

Only family could do that.

The dust was going to be brutal. Usually, we put a couple of kids on hose duty to keep the track damp between races. But I hadn't seen the hoses as we pulled up. Hell, just the slow laps in my truck had made it hard to see one end of the track from the other. It would get worse.

Jackass or no, I cared enough about the race to take a good look at Fred's line through the corners. He spent the warm-up figuring out just how hard he could toss his Chevy into the turns. He was planning an old-school approach: He wouldn't touch the brakes at all, would instead chuck the car into a big hairy skid to slow himself down. That was a classic old-timer's line around a dirt oval.

I had a better plan. I hoped.

As we passed the pitchfork to start the last warm-up lap, I pulled even with Fred. I stayed to his right, giving him the inside line.

We eased around the oval, jockeying for a good start, and Fred tried every trick he knew to get an edge. First he put his fender on mine, just to show who was boss. When I cranked my wheel left to tell him "knock it off," he pulled away sharply, hoping I would get crossed up. Then he played the start-stop-start-stop game.

I was ready for all of it. I dragged the brakes with my left foot, winding up the revs with my right. We were supposed to hit the gas as we cleared the pitchfork. I knew he would jump the start; the question was how early. The answer: way early, just as we entered turn three off what passed for the backstretch.

Fred beat me to the throttle by a tenth of a second and cranked his steering wheel hard right, trying to flat run me off the outside. It wasn't a traditional NASCAR track ringed by a concrete wall, but there was a two-foot buildup of loose dirt that the Chevys had been known to get hung up on.

"Prick," I said out loud, stabbing the brakes. I didn't have much choice. Got right back into the throttle and took off after Fred, but he'd built an instant three-car-length lead.

Not for long. I'd guessed right about his approach. As he neared each 180, Fred would yank the wheel left, kicking the back end out to scrub speed. Then he'd get right back to the gas, elbow-flailing the car sideways through the corner. It was a fun way to drive, and it looked cool; that's why stunt men do it in movies.

But it wasn't the fast way around. Not on this track, not in these cars. The Chevys didn't have limited-slip differentials, so Fred spent most of his lap spinning his inside rear tire, looking for traction that wasn't there.

Where he was pitching his car sideways, I was tapping the brake and turning the steering wheel gently, giving all four tires a chance to grip. Where he was hammering the throttle, I was easing it down like there was a baby duck between it and my foot. To Sophie, I wouldn't look nearly as dramatic as Fred.

But I was catching him.

In two laps I gained enough to watch the individual rocks his tires flung at my windshield. In two more laps I was on his bumper, and he knew it. When we came off the corner he goosed the gas too hard, put his car good and sideways, and could only watch me nip underneath him.

Now *I* was three car lengths in front. I knew I couldn't pull away much, not in five laps—the Chevys were junk to begin with, and they got worse once you put a few hard laps on them. I was smelling brake pads and transmission fluid already.

So I drove my line and wondered what Fred would try. Because he sure as hell was going to try *something*.

I recognized a new smell, glanced at the dashboard. The temp needle was pegged; even with its heavy-duty radiator and transmission cooler, the Chevy was running red hot. Engines hate heat: I could feel the power loss every time I came off a corner.

Fred was closing hard. Wasn't within ramming distance yet, but he was getting there.

I flashed past the pitchfork with maybe an eight-foot lead, saw my truck's headlights flash. Two laps to go. I eased into the corner, staying low low low. If Fred was going to pass me he was going to do it the hard way, on the outside.

He was close enough to bump me now, spin me out. But he didn't, which meant he was saving the move for the last lap. I ran my low line, then let the Chevy track wide on the tiny straights, blocking as hard as I could. A lot of drivers don't like blocking, think it's un-sportsmanlike. But in the last few laps, anything goes.

Fred waited until we entered the final corner. I knew it was com-ing, so when he nosed inside me and put his right fender on my left rear quarter, I was prepared. I felt my back end wash out to the right, cranked the wheel the same way, and mashed the gas. I heard, watched, *felt* Fred's car pull alongside and then ahead of me, our miserable small-block engines screaming for mercy. I manhandled the wheel, fighting for rear grip. Found some, built a little momen-tum.

Then I turned hard left and mirrored the move Fred had pulled on me, catching his right rear with my left front. It worked: I watched his back end sway left, knew he was keeping his foot deep in the throttle, shooting smoke and dirt and rocks everywhere.

He couldn't save it: I'd spun him out. I took my foot off the gas and coasted to the pitchfork. Sophie was flashing my truck's lights like crazy, honking the horn. I pumped a fist and eased my way into a victory lap.

Until Fred straightened out his car, hit the gas, and flew after me. Short-track instincts had risen to the top: He was going to ram me, let me know what he thought of that last move. I'd seen the old-school payback a hundred times. Hell, I'd *done* it.

While I coasted around the turn, he closed the gap fast, thirty-five hundred pounds of Chevy blasting my way. I waited until it was too late for him to change his line on the tractionless dirt, then goosed the throttle just a bit. It worked—he missed my rear bumper by maybe three inches. Frustrated, Fred cranked his wheel hard left, but it was too late. He was sliding broadside toward the buildup of dirt and stones that marked the track's outer edge.

I knew what was going to happen before it happened. I sighed, mashed the brakes, threw my Chevy in park. I didn't even need to watch to know that when the sides of Fred's right tires hit the outer berm, his car was going to roll. I just hoped it didn't go all the way onto its roof. I had half a second to wonder if he'd fastened his seat-belt. I was pretty sure he hadn't.

By the time I closed my door and walked toward Fred's Chevy, it was all over. Just your basic quarter-roll: The car had flopped onto its right side and was showing me its underside like a dog showing his privates. The rear tires spun, the motor screamed.

So did Sophie. I felt bad; it must have looked like a serious wreck to her. I hollered that Fred was okay, but she couldn't hear over the engine. So I motioned for her to come over and see for herself.

I put my hands on my hips and stood in the car's shade, staying far enough away so it wouldn't crush me if it righted itself. "Fred!" I said, shouting over the small-block.

Nothing.

I cupped my hands to my mouth. "Fred! Kill the motor before something blows up."

The motor died.

"You okay in there?" I said, hearing Sophie's footsteps.

"No!"

"Are you truly hurt, or just embarrassed at the way I spun you?"

"Fuck you."

"Got an arm pinned in there?" I said. "A leg?"

He said nothing.

Sophie took my hand. "Should I call nine-one-one?"

"Nah. I think he's just pouting."

"Something's pinned," Fred said. "Maybe crushed a little."

Sophie began to cry.

I sighed. "Hang on, I'm coming." I pointed at Sophie. "Stay away in case it tips back over."

I walked around the other side of the car, squatted, looked in the windshield. Sure enough, Fred was folded up on the front passenger-side door, which was now acting as the floor. It looked like all his weight was on the point of his right shoulder. "That's probably not good," I said.

"Come get me."

I straightened and pushed on the Chevy's roof. Didn't like the way the car rocked. Squatted again. "If I climb up to the driver's door," I said, "it might tip."

"So kick out the windshield, dumbass."

That was a good idea. The safety glass shouldn't bother Fred if we were careful. I told him to close his eyes, stepped back, and stomped with my left boot. Took me half a dozen kicks to knock a third of the windshield from its frame. While I did, Sophie came around, sniffling. "Are you okay?" she said.

"Fine, sweetie," Fred said. "Now watch out you don't get glass in your eye."

I took my T-shirt off and was surprised to see it sweat soaked, until I thought about what I'd spent the past twenty minutes doing. When I ran the Busch Series, back before they put suit coolers in the cars, we used to sweat off fifteen pounds a race.

I used the T-shirt to protect my hands, grabbed a handful of safety glass, and rolled it up toward the left side of the car like it was a sardine-tin lid. I flopped it over the left fender, made sure it wouldn't slip and hit me, dropped to hands and knees.

Now I had my head inside the Chevy. I smelled gas. "It would be a damn good idea to get you out of here," I said. "Where are you pinned?"

"It's this side. Feels like maybe my right hand is between the seat and the door. Can you see it?"

"Well . . ." I wriggled in, extending my neck.

That's when my father cold-cocked me. The right hand he'd been playing possum with came at me like a cast-iron skillet, caught me flush on the nose. I saw a white flash, then got a thump when my head dropped and hit the windshield pillar.

"Hey," Sophie said. "*Hey!*"

"Wreck *me* in the last corner, you dirty homo?" Fred said, trying to grab my hair. "I'll show you dirty . . ."

But my hair was too short to get a grip on. I waggled my head to clear the pain, then popped him in the nose with a couple of rights. I was on two knees and my left hand, so I couldn't get much on the jabs, but they slowed him down.

"Ha!" Fred said. "You still punch like a girl!" He pulled his left knee to his chest and let fly with a flat kick, going for my nose again. I shifted, but his boot caught my right ear and tore it some.

"Come on, Dad." I put both hands up to surrender.

"Fuck *you* I'll come on!" Fred pistoned the leg again, caught me in the chest, knocked the wind out of me.

That pissed me off. My nose, my ear, now my wind. I got the red-mist feeling around my eyes that meant deep trouble as often as not.

While I tried to catch my breath, Fred went for the kill shot, kicking with both legs this time, aiming at my face.

I caught an ankle with each hand, tightened my grip, felt the red mist taking over my head.

When Fred saw my face, he stopped cussing me out. "Hey now," he said.

"Conway?" Sophie said.

They were too late. I got a foot under me and rose, still grasping Fred's ankles. I pulled him straight through the empty windshield frame, not caring much if I cut him up on the way out.

I dragged him through dirt, screaming at him, calling him a stupid old rummy cocksucker who couldn't drive for shit. As I dragged, his shirt rode up all the way to his neck. His belly was loose, his chest scrawny, the whole mess fish-belly white except for lots of black hair.

Something about that hair lit off half a memory—shirtless Fred fixing a clapboard in Mankato, me looking on, maybe eight years old, wondering if I'd ever have chest hair like that, my father smiling as he explained how he got the butt joints just so—and ratcheted my red-mist fury. I dug my heels in and set my weight against Fred's.

Then I began to spin like a discus thrower. Fred slowly rose from the ground, flailing, grabbing at nothing, saying things I couldn't hear while I whirled him in circles, did a couple of full 360s . . .

. . . and let go, tossing my father in a dumb little arc that carried him ten or twelve feet. He landed on his back, then snapped the back of his head to hard-packed dirt. His arms and legs splayed. He didn't move.

I breathed myself calm, felt the red mist drain from my head, replaced instantly by a Jesus-I'm-an-asshole vibe that I know too well.

Sophie rushed past, and the way she looked at me was worse than anything she could have said. She knelt next to Fred, turned to face me. "His eyes are closed, Conway!"

I said nothing.

"I think you killed him!"

"Doubt it." I needed to move away while the worst of the shame washed through me. I walked over to Fred's Chevy, leaned on the roof, pushed. It rocked a little. I pushed harder. The car rocked three inches, but when it settled back toward me it rocked four. Damn thing might fall over on me.

I deserved it.

I glanced at Sophie and Fred. He was propped on his elbows. I'd just knocked the wind out of him, maybe put him on queer street a few seconds.

I kicked little ruts to set my heels in. Then I put my back against the Chevy's roof and spread my arms.

Then I pushed.

My boots locked into the ruts, and I felt the push start deep in my thighs. The push rose through my rear end, into the small of my back.

When the Chevy tipped a foot and a half, I got my fingers around its drip rail, and that helped. I rose, gripped, rose. That might have been when I began to scream.

My thighs screamed back, wanting to quit.

I pushed and I screamed.

The car came up another foot but didn't want to move any farther. I'd run out of leverage: My knees were nearly straight now. I let
the scream die, watched my right leg quiver. Sweat stung my eyes. If
I bailed out now, I could quickstep out of the way before the Chevy
tipped toward me.

I'd be damned if I was going to bail out.

I breathed three times, then pushed again. I pushed with everything I had. This time the scream started deeper and rose higher.

I pushed. I screamed.

And felt the car shift past the tip-back point as gravity became my
ally. The Chevy fell away fast, bounced once on all four tires, groaned,
squeaked.

And came to rest, the only sound a drip-drip-drip as neon-green
antifreeze hit dirt.

In the quiet I leaned forward, breathed, put both hands on knees,
watched my legs shake.

After a while I walked to Sophie and Fred. They were staring at
me. Sophie's eyes were huge. Fred looked old and small and scared. I
extended a hand. He looked at it for maybe ten seconds, then took
it. I pulled him up.

"I'd do it again," my father said.

I thought he was talking about trying to wreck me.

CHAPTER EIGHTEEN

Quiet drive to Shrewsbury. Sophie, sitting in the middle again, said nothing and tried not to touch me. Fred jammed himself against the passenger door, arms crossed, and mumbled to himself. Every few minutes I glanced over without turning my head, and it made me sad. What with his stubble and his dirty chin and the mumbling, he looked like what he'd been for twenty years or so: a bum. One time, his torso shook enough to make me nervous. But when I asked if I should pull over, he waved me off, rolled down his window, and sucked air.

Charlene's SUV was in the driveway when I pulled up, so I just dropped the two of them off. As Sophie slipped across the bench seat, I said her name.

"Don't worry," she said before slamming the door. "I won't tell her."

Smart kid.

Alone in the F-150, headed for Framingham, I called Randall.

"'Bout time," he said when he picked up. "You teased me with your text last night. Big news from Hebron Crossroads?"

"You going to see your insurance lady soon?"

"Seven tonight for dinner. Is that soon enough?"

"Think you can get your grubby paws on her laptop again?"

"Note that I'm bypassing the easy joke regarding my date and my grubby paws," he said, then paused. "The thing is, I like her a lot. I'm not sure I want to push my luck and monkey around with her databases every time we're together, do you see? It's a big deal, a firing offense."

"Myna Roper had Tander Phigg's kid. A daughter."

"Wow."

"That's nothing. The daughter is Patty Marx."

"*What?* Nonsense."

I told him about Myna's shotgun wedding to Bobby Marx, her daughter's lifelong nosiness, the picture I'd seen. Each time I clicked in a new fact, he whistled. "So write this down," I finally said. "Diana Patience Marx, born late 'sixty-two, graduated from Clemson in I guess the early eighties."

"That may be worth pushing my luck for." Click.

In Framingham, Trey Phigg's rented Dodge was gone and there was nobody home except Dale and Davey. They were happy to see me. I let the three of us into the upstairs apartment, figuring I should give Trey and his family the downstairs for now. I spent ten minutes catching up with the cats, stripped off clothes that were filthy from the dirt oval, and hit the shower. Left the clothes on the bedroom floor, knowing Dale and Davey would have a ball sniffing them.

As I rinsed dust from my hair I remembered there was more to Ollie's story about his Montreal connection. He'd tried to tell it in Enosburg Falls, but I'd cut him off because I wanted to hit the road. Dumb. Mental note: Call again, see how Ollie's knee was healing, ask him to finish the story. I wished I had a cell number for Ollie, didn't like the way Josh had blocked access last time I called.

I wouldn't tell Ollie about Tander Phigg's seventy-five grand. Keeping some info tucked in your back pocket is a hard habit to break. Montreal was looking more and more like the one who took out Phigg, but I couldn't rule out Ollie—maybe working with Josh, maybe not.

I dried, dressed, and brought a load of dirty laundry downstairs. Tossed it in the washing machine and was headed upstairs again when the kitchen door opened. Trey, Kieu, and Tuan came in, laughing and chattering.

"Hello?" I said, not wanting to surprise them, as I headed toward the sound. When I stepped into the kitchen, Tuan rushed me. He had a red balloon from T.G.I. Friday's, the string looped around his wrist, and I guessed it was what he was jabbering about.

"The miracle that is helium," Trey said, laughing some more as his son tugged on the string, then let the balloon float to the ceiling.

"Good dinner?" I said.

Kieu nodded, cut her eyes to Trey, then back to me. "Very good," she said, putting a hand over her belly. "Very . . . *big*, very *much*." It was the first English I'd heard her speak, so I nodded to show I understood. She blushed and put two Styrofoam leftover containers in the fridge.

When Tuan calmed down some, I motioned Trey into the living room. We sat.

"Five happy years," I said.

"How was your interview?"

"Myna Roper is a nice lady. Drinks too much, probably the only way she can fall asleep. But nice. Solid."

"And?"

"She lives in a trailer," I said, "but it's a *nice* trailer, you know? Down south, folks plant a double-wide somewhere and call it home, and nobody looks down on them."

"It's not your style to hem and haw, Conway. Please tell me whatever there is to tell."

"You have a half sister."

His mouth opened. "Pardon me?" he finally said.

"Your father loved Myna Roper. He got her pregnant. They didn't think that would fly in 1962, even in New York City. That's why your father caved to his father's threats and came back here."

"And Myna Roper had a baby girl."

"She was supposed to have an abortion. Your father always thought she did. But she couldn't go through with it."

"Well," he said, half smiling at something far away. "Well, then."

"You're cooler about it than I expected."

He traced a finger along the back of the sofa. "I've had a long time to think about my father's New York years. You run through possibilities, especially when the old man keeps everything a deep dark secret. Was he married? Was he gay? Was he talented? Was he miserable?" Trey shrugged. "I guess it would take a hell of a lot to surprise me."

"Do you want to know about her?"

"Of course I do," he said, dry-swallowing, his voice so quiet I barely heard.

"You've met her."

"Nonsense."

I told him. Diana Patience Marx aka Patty Marx. Curious, college, journalism. Figured out on her own that Tander Phigg was her old man. Climbed the journalism ladder, wound up at *The Globe*. Her mother claimed to have no idea where she was, and I believed her.

"They had a falling-out?" Trey said.

"Guess so," I said. "Myna puked in a trash can and passed out before she got that far."

"*Pardon* me?"

I told him about Myna's Manhattans, her routine, her polite vomiting, her dog.

"That's sad."

"Yes."

We were quiet.

"What next?" Trey finally said.

"Randall's digging up info on Patty Marx. Maybe we'll learn something."

He nodded. I watched him work through possibilities, staring again at something far away. Then he locked onto my eyes. "The big question—"

"—is what the hell does all this have to do with seventy-five grand stashed in your father's floor?"

"Well?" he said.

"No goddamn idea." I rose, stretched, checked my watch. Charlene never got dinner on the table until seven. I could make it.

"Are you going?" Trey said.

"To Shrewsbury, yeah."

"I thought you came here from there."

"I did," I said. "But I should go back. I *want* to go back."

The words surprised me.

Twenty minutes later I surprised Charlene. "I'll be damned," she said. "Your father said you dropped them and took off. I thought you were gone for the night."

"I'm here."

"And showered to boot," she said, hugging me and kissing my hair. "How lucky can a gal get?" When she turned away she had a little smile that meant she was happy but didn't want to advertise it.

Charlene grabbed a butcher's knife and attacked something on a cutting board. It looked like she was trying to kill a mouse. She goes through domestic bursts once in a while, and I wondered if Fred had triggered one. The problem is that when the bursts come along, she cooks and bakes—and we all suffer.

With her back to me, still whacking away, she said, "What did you Three Musketeers do this afternoon?"

So she didn't know about the idiotic rat-racing, and was trying to milk me. I silently thanked Sophie.

"Three Stooges is more like it," I said. "We took a ride out to Purgatory Chasm. Fred wanted to see the place again."

She stopped whacking, turned. "Did *you* want to see Purgatory Chasm again?"

"Of course not," I said, feeling bad about the lie. "Anyway, we weren't there long. Fred's rock-running days are over."

"Huh." She looked at me awhile, smelling a rat. Sophie saved me; she came in with wet hair and clean clothes.

"I was telling your mom about Purgatory Chasm," I said. "How Fred wanted to see it but wasn't up to hiking the trails."

"I *told* you it would be too much for him," Sophie said, smooth as that. Smart smart smart. She hollered out the sliding-glass door, and Fred came in. He was smiling, a clear drink in his beat-up hand, until he saw me. Then his eyes went dead.

Soon we were eating kielbasa. Charlene proudly set out the dish I'd watched her whack at. She said it was potato salad. It looked like dice covered with Elmer's glue. I took a double portion and smiled while I ate it.

The talk was stiff and sparse. Charlene knew something was up but couldn't break any of us down. Me, Sophie, and Fred mostly kept quiet for fear we'd blab about what had happened. If Charlene found out I'd taken my wet-brain father and a twelve-year-old to screw around on a half-assed racetrack, she'd kill me—and I wouldn't blame her.

Besides, eating the potato salad took all my concentration.

I always volunteer to do the dishes, and Charlene always says yes. Not tonight: She and Sophie would clean up, she said, and why didn't Fred and I relax on the deck?

So we faced west in Adirondack chairs and looked over the backyard. We were quiet awhile.

"You okay?" I said.

"Sore."

"I'm sorry I threw you."

"You should be sorry you *spun* me."

"You were trying to spin *me*."

Long pause. "I guess I was."

We looked at each other and started laughing. We let the laughter roll, forced it to go on longer than it wanted to. Once I caught Sophie peeking at us through the screen door, a dish towel in her hand.

"A racer's a racer, huh?" I said.

"Fucking A. Daytona or a cow pasture, it don't much matter."

We tried to laugh some more, but that was over. Shade deepened as the sun dropped.

I said, "You don't seem like a wet-brain. Except for that one accident, you seem pretty good."

"I can't always remember things. Maybe that's the wet-brain part."

"Or maybe there's stuff you don't want to remember."

"Lots and lots."

"Do you, ah, want to go to an AA meeting with me?"

"I tried that," Fred said. "It didn't take."

"What didn't take? You sit in a room on a folding chair. About the time your ass falls asleep, you get up and go home."

"The God part, the higher-power bullshit. It never worked for me."

"That's okay."

"It is?"

"You don't need a higher power to sit on a folding chair," I said, checking my Seiko. There was an eight-o'clock at the Episcopalian church up the road. We could make it. "Although near the end you might find yourself praying for a pillow."

A little over an hour later, as I started to take a left from the church parking lot, Fred took hold of my right forearm. "Want to drive around some?"

I said sure, hooked a right instead, and drove.

"What are you thinking?" I said after a while.

Face turned away, he said something I couldn't make out.

"What?" I said.

"Brave," he said. "To stand up and tell your story, your sins."

"Sometimes it feels good to get it off your chest."

"Do you do that? Tell your story to a church basement full of strangers?"

"Sure."

"Do you tell *everything*?" He shifted to stare at my profile.

"The meetings are only an hour."

"Don't joke about it!" He grabbed my forearm, and his intensity made me turn to look. We drove beneath a streetlight, and I saw his eyes were wet. "Think about the worst thing you ever done," Fred said, and paused a long beat. "Is it part of your story? Do you stand up and tell it?"

I felt his hand on my sleeve, watched the road ahead, made an honest inventory. "I guess not," I finally said. It came out half rasp, half whisper.

Fred's hand relaxed some. "Why not?"

"Some things . . ."

"Yes," my father said. "Some things."

I drove a long clockwise loop, each of us thinking our thoughts.

As we paralleled a reservoir, getting set to turn south and head back to Shrewsbury, Fred said, "If you ever fell off the wagon, what would you fall into?"

"What do you mean?"

"What would you drink?"

"Knock it off."

"You gonna tell me you never think about it?"

After maybe half a mile I said, "I used to."

He slapped his thigh. "Well okay, then. You tell me yours, I'll tell you mine."

"First few years I was sober," I said, "I had a two-days-to-live plan. You know, if the doc said you had two days to live, what would you drink? Jesus . . ."

"Keep going."

"It was a long time ago. It was a crutch, a game I played so I wouldn't have to think about the rest of my life coming at me."

"Tell me."

"I had two options," I said, shifting in my seat, surprised it was kind of fun to talk about. "A summer plan and a winter plan."

"Summer plan first."

"Simple," I said. "Rolling Rock longnecks. No cans, no shorty bottles. Got to be the longneck."

"How many?" Fred said. "Six? Twelve? A case?"

I laughed awhile. Looked over, saw Fred wasn't laughing: It was a serious question. "Never got that far," I said. "Once I took that first sip, the daydream kind of faded away."

He folded his arms and stared through the windshield. "What was the winter plan?"

"Take a highball glass," I said, "and fill it almost to the top with crushed ice. Not big ice cubes from the fridge, not those crappy little gas-station cubes with holes in them, but real crushed ice from a decent bar. You know what I mean?"

I glanced over. He was staring like I was a circus freak. "I know," he said.

"Then slow-pour Wild Turkey over the crushed ice. Bring it this close to the brim." I showed him a quarter-inch with my thumb and finger. "There you have it. Summer plan, winter plan."

He said nothing for a long time.

Finally I said, "Fred?"

"The sound the bourbon makes when it hits the crushed ice," he said, eyes dead ahead. "That's the thing."

I nodded. "Warm on cold."

Now *I* was looking straight ahead, but I felt Fred turn to face me. "You got both of those from me," he said.

"Did I?"

"You know goddamn well you did." He put a hand on my shoulder. "My legacy."

I said nothing.

"I'm sorry," he said.

I said nothing.

Later Charlene and I sat in her bed, pillow-propped against the cherry headboard. She wore sweatpants and a T-shirt and designer reading glasses that cost more than a good riding lawn mower. I watched her read a three-hundred-page magazine about keeping life simple. I liked the lines that radiated from her eyes and bracketed her mouth.

"You look cute," I said.

"Don't get any ideas. Sophie will be awake another two hours." She flipped to an article about suitcases. "Fred go to bed?"

I nodded. "Tired as hell."

"Did he enjoy the meeting?"

"Nah. He zoned out."

"Old dogs."

"Yes."

"You two were gone awhile. Did you go for coffee after?"

"We drove around." I didn't want to say more.

Charlene closed the magazine and set her glasses on it. Then she put her left hand beneath my chin and thumb-stroked my cheek.

"I need a shave, I know."

"Shush." She stroked some more, ran the thumb around my lips, kept her eyes on mine. "You came back, Conway."

I said nothing.

"You came here. I don't care why. Maybe you were worried about Fred, or maybe you were worried Sophie would blab about whatever you all did this afternoon that's such a big damn secret." She leaned and kissed me, a soft kiss on the lips. She smelled like moisturizing stuff. "Thank you for coming here." She set her magazine on the bedside table, clicked off her lamp, and lay down with her back to me.

I clicked off my lamp, stood, stripped, climbed into bed, spooned her in the dark.

"What's on tap tomorrow, Charlie Chan?" she said, yawning.

"Trey and Kieu want to talk to me about something or other," I said. "And I need to deal with Montreal and his muscle-head."

"Is that safe?"

"Got help."

"Care to divulge a bit more detail?"

"Mmph," I said into her hair.

After a while she swatted my hip. "I said no funny stuff."

"Ain't nothing funny about *this,* baby," I said, and wriggled.

When she giggled, I knew I had her.

Trying to keep quiet made it even better somehow.

CHAPTER NINETEEN

After, Charlene fell asleep, still on her right side. I lay on my back, my hand on her left hip, waiting to sleep.

But didn't, and knew why. Rolling Rock and Purgatory Chasm.

It's a state park—hiking trails, scenic views, like that. The big feature is a half-mile-long canyon with granite walls.

When I was thirteen and moved to Massachusetts to be with Fred, he wasn't completely gone yet. He was a guy who couldn't hold a job because he drank too much, but he wasn't a pants-pissing, grate-sleeping, panhandling bum. That would come later.

He'd bragged about crewing for a race team, so one evening at dinner, mostly to make conversation, I said I'd like to drive race cars. Jesus, I was thirteen. I wanted to play center field for the Twins, too.

"Stand up," he said, rising himself. He was buzzed already, and his knees banged the card table we used for dinner. His Rolling Rock longneck tipped one way, then the other, but he snatched and drained it before it went over. "I said stand!" He thumped down the bottle.

When I did, he said, "Hands like this," and extended his arms, palms up.

I copied him.

"Don't let me slap 'em," he said—and then slapped my palms, hard, before I knew what he was talking about.

"Don't let me *slap* 'em!" my father yelled, slapping my palms again. "Reactions! Quickness! Instinct!"

I got it. I was supposed to whip my hands away and avoid his slaps.

So I did.

Easily.

My father got madder and madder, his slaps wilder and harder, as I made him whiff. He stood there in blue Dickies and a matching work shirt with his name on the breast, beer breath rolling off him, just about falling down now each time he lunged at my hands.

"Quick little fucker," he finally said, and turned his own hands palms up. "Now you do me."

It was too easy. I nailed him four times in a row.

Finally he said, "Think that's quick? That ain't quick. Come on." My father plucked his keys from the card table and a Rolling Rock from the fridge, started out the door, backtracked, grabbed two more beers, and led me from the apartment.

It was early July, the end of a hot day. We rolled down the windows of the pickup—a beat-to-shit Dodge that looked like whoever'd painted it turquoise had used a roller—and hit the road. My father showed me how to hold his extra beers by the top of the neck, to make sure they didn't get any warmer than they had to.

After a while, I asked where we were headed.

"We're gonna do a little rock running at a place I know," he said. "See how good your reactions really are. You wanna be a racer? This'll give you a taste."

I never learned how he found out about Purgatory Chasm himself. Probably went there with work buddies to kill a six-pack or two.

Soon we pulled in, parked, climbed out. At seven thirty on a hot weekday, we had the place to ourselves.

A short walk brought us to the mouth of the canyon, which ran downhill from where we stood. Its floor was fallen rocks, some the size of my head, others as big as my father's truck.

My father worked on his second Rolling Rock. A cooling breeze swept up from the far end of the canyon.

"What are we doing here?" I said.

"Pay attention." *Paytenshun*. He drained his beer and flipped the bottle to shatter on a rock way to our left. "So you wanna be a racer."

I nodded, but wished I hadn't brought it up. Wished we were back at the apartment for a typical summer night: me building a model while my father watched the Red Sox and drank himself to sleep. Wished I hadn't badgered my mother into letting me move here. Wished I was at home in Mankato, throwing a tennis ball at the back of the house while she washed the dinner dishes.

My father squatted to set his face level with mine. He teetered some but held the squat. "When you're racing," he said, "things come at you every second. You got to think big and think small at the same time, see? *Can I beat that prick into the corner? If I do, will he get a better run off it than I will? Is his car heavier? Whose tires are better?* Like that. You wanna know what it's like, making decisions like that?"

I nodded.

"Run, then."

I said nothing.

"Run!" he said, pointing. "Down the hill. Best way I know to build the reflexes, what they call the muscle memory."

I cut my eyes down the slope, wondering if he was trying to kill me, or at least make me break a leg. You'd want to be careful *walking* down that slope, those rocks, most of them jagged, some of them loose—and no way to tell which until you put weight on them.

Run? Maybe a mountain goat could do it.

"Run, Mister Quick Hands!" my father said, his smile torqued, his breath Rolling Rock. "Test yourself! Run!"

I hopped downslope to a rock that looked like it wouldn't move. Then to another, then another.

My father laughed. "You call that *running*? Looks more like a bunny hop."

I spun. "Why don't *you* do it then?"

His smile went even tighter, and I thought he'd come down and hit me. He had a couple times before.

But instead he shook out his arms, limbering up, and tightened his belt one notch. "Watch this." He slipped the last Rolling Rock from his pants pocket, bit the cap off, spit it out, and drank.

And he took off.

And he was beautiful. Weightless, fearless, doing what he was born to do. The mean drunk in blue Dickies disappeared, replaced by something that was half dancer and half gazelle. I watched him dab from rock to rock, barely touching each. By the time the less steady chunks of granite shifted, my father was already gone two strides. He disappeared behind a stand of trees faster than I could have run the same distance on the middle-school track.

I waited, thinking if this was a test of race-driver reflexes, my father must have been a damn good racer.

Five minutes later he strode around the corner with a near-empty beer in one hand and sweat beneath his armpits. "You still here?" he said. "Didn't try it yet?"

"I can't believe how fast you went."

He tried to hard-ass his way past the compliment, but his mouth twitched. "The key," he said, pointing down the hill with his bottle, "you don't think about the moves. Your brain needs to trust your feet to find the right spots. Get it right, you'll be surprised how fast you can go."

I looked down the slope and tried not to feel dizzy.

"Three," my father said, and drained his beer.

"Two," he said, and belched.

"One," he said, and lobbed the green bottle over his shoulder. The moment it smashed on a rock he said, "Go!"

And I did. Three paces in, my head figured out what he'd meant about trusting your feet. Another three paces and I felt my shoulders loosen as I bounced from rock to rock. Three paces after that, my feet got the message.

I flew.

I didn't even look at the rocks my feet were touching. Instead I looked far down the hill, picking the path I'd be following in the next five seconds or so. My feet acted on their own, touching, adapting, springing, my ankles always rolling just right.

Before I reached the bottom I knew I looked just like my father, that this was what *I* was born to do—reacting, skimming, racing, moving. Moving fast. Faster than anybody. Maybe faster than my father.

When the stones petered to swampy grass, I slowed in three choppy steps, cool beneath oaks now. I trotted uphill smiling. I wanted to do it again.

I cleared the corner at the final rise, took one glance at my father, and tried to hide my smile. Probably didn't, though, because he cut loose with a big laugh I hadn't heard since I was six years old. "Not bad," he said. "Not bad once you got the hang of it. Feels pretty good, huh?"

I wanted to talk about the feeling. I wanted to ask how he discovered this place, these rocks, this running.

Instead I nodded and said nothing.

We stood side by side. Once I thought my father was going to put his hand on my shoulder. But when I half turned he scratched his side instead, put the hand on his hip.

Soon I said, "Again?"

"Energy," he said. "I remember when I had some. Three two one go!"

I took off, bounding faster than I had before. After thirty yards I felt, rather than heard, something behind me and knew my father was on my tail. So I moved even faster.

"You've . . . got . . . the reflexes," he panted, his drinking and smoking catching up with him. "But can . . . you . . . do it . . . with a hungry driver . . . right on your ass?"

We built momentum until we were skimming down Purgatory Chasm at a dead-nuts sprint. My father's longer legs paid off and he pulled alongside me, needing only two strides for every three I took. "Can . . . you . . . do it when . . . the money's . . . on the table?" he panted, and squeezed ahead half a pace, then a full one. With thirty yards to the finish he decided he'd won and eased into a fast jog, trying to win with style.

But I dug up the last bit of air in my lungs and exploded, running absolutely as fast as I would have on a sidewalk. Two strides, four, and I was catching him, his wind too far gone to let him accelerate again as I floated past, eight strides from the finish—

My father hit me in the ribs with an elbow.

He would spend that night, the next three years, maybe the rest of his life explaining how it had been a dumb accident—a wheezing geezer flailing, a showboating son squeezing a little too close in the excitement of the race.

It wasn't any fucking accident. Fast Freddy Sax watched me pull alongside, knew he had nothing left in the tank, and threw an elbow that was meant for my left arm but caught me high in the rib cage instead.

The pain-burst blew up my instinctive running. I took an ugly flat-footed step with my left sneaker, one with my right, and sailed through space. Airborne, I actually reached forward with my left hand like a football player trying to extend the ball past the goal line. I was still thinking about winning.

My right elbow was the first thing that touched down. It shattered on a chunk of granite the size and shape of a straight-six engine block.

An instant later, my head hit the same rock. But I think I was already knocked out.

At seven thirty the next morning, Sophie and I sat in my truck in the Shrewsbury High School parking lot. We were waiting for a bus; Sophie was headed for a Girl Scout camping weekend down on Cape Cod.

The parking lot was a nuthouse: thirty or more minivans and SUVs spilling girls, dads hood-leaning and chatting, moms smearing sunblock on their daughters, pressing money into pockets, triple-checking things they'd double-checked at home.

I'm no expert, but I could see almost all the girls were a year or two younger than Sophie. She was quiet for a change, nervous. I thought I knew why.

Her first two years, she was more or less raised by her sister, Jesse, who was seven when Sophie was born. Those two years were the tail end of Charlene's meth-and-crack career, when the state Department of Social Services took her daughters away and placed them with her sister. It was the kick in the ass Charlene needed; she's been bootstrapping ever since. Now she owns a transcription-and-translation company that's worth a couple million, easy.

For the most part Sophie acts grown up as hell, but since the girls went back to their mother nearly a decade ago, she's never been away for anything more than a one-night sleepover.

As two yellow buses rolled in nose to tail, I touched Sophie's head. "Thursday, Friday, Saturday nights, home by dinner Sunday. Piece of cake."

"This is training-wheels camp," she said. "This weekend is to get all the *little girls*"—she made a slicing gesture at the minivan in front of us—"ready for the real three-week camp in August."

"So?"

It was quiet thirty seconds. Finally Sophie said, "So what if I don't want to *go* for that long?"

"Then you won't."

"Mom will make me."

Hell. She was probably right about that. Charlene was happiest at work, didn't like it when kid schedules got in the way. She probably should've hired a nanny a long time ago but had refused for the same reason she stayed in her smallish house: She didn't want the girls feeling like they were something special.

I put my arm around Sophie, let her lean into me, kissed the top of her head. "I'll talk to your mom, okay? I'll remind her this is a try-out camp."

"Thanks." She slipped from my one-armed hug, popped her door open. "And be nice to Fred, okay?"

"Okay."

"Promise?"

"Promise."

"Now help me throw my camping shit on the bus."

I cracked up. Did as I'd been told, kissed Sophie again, watched her climb on the bus, waited with all the parents. Sophie had found a seat on my side and pretended not to see me. But along with all the moms and dads, I waved like an idiot when the buses pulled out—and at the last second Sophie turned, smiled shyly, waved her fingers once.

I headed north.

There was another jacked-up truck in the Beets' compound—a thirty-year-old International Harvester pickup on some sort of home-brewed chassis, so tall I could have walked under it. Other than that, the place was the same as when I'd fetched Ollie here five days ago: slow-rotting trailers, swaybacked house with cinder-block front steps, miserable dog wailing out back.

As I rolled to a stop I fist-bumped my horn, trying for a friendly *toot-toot*. It wasn't nine yet, and if I had to wake these guys I preferred to do it at a safe distance. I fished Ollie's Browning from beneath the seat, stuck it down the back of my pants and climbed out, slamming the door as loudly as I could.

"Hello?" I took three slow steps toward the house.

"That's close enough."

The voice came from the living-room window. I couldn't see inside: Against all odds the window still had a screen.

"Friend of Ollie Dufresne," I said, keeping my hands loose and at my sides, feeling a cold spot on my chest where I knew a long gun was pointed. "Here to see the Beets."

The voice said nothing, but in a few seconds I heard a tiny *zzzing* and knew what the sound was: the barrel of the gun dragging as it was pulled from the screen. The cold spot on my chest vanished.

Ten seconds later the front door opened. The man who stepped through was at least six-four, with a tangle of filthy hair adding another couple inches. A beard owls could nest in ran halfway down his torso. He wore plaid boxer shorts only, no shirt, so it was easy to see he was a once-strong guy gone to pot: sagging tits covered with gray hair, medicine-ball belly, small scars and bruises everywhere.

He was big enough so the sawed-off shotgun in his right paw looked like a kids' toy.

He tweaked his boxers with his left hand and popped his cock out. I saw he had half a morning-glory boner and looked away while he cut loose with a long piss off his porch, staring at me, smiling at his little gross-out.

When he got himself stowed away I said, "I'm the guy came and took Ollie away the other day."

"Bert wasn't happy 'bout that."

"Where is Bert?"

The man nodded toward the living room. "Asleep, with Bobby," he said, and smiled, showing me three black teeth and two brown ones. "I'm Bret, the smart one."

Thing is, he *was* pretty smart, once you got past the sight and smell of him. I got him to come off the cinder-block porch and tell me about the home-built four-by-fours, and that warmed him up some. Soon we were comparing notes on mercs we might both know, and that led us around to Ollie, and when that petered out, Bret Beet stood, one shoulder against a massive tire, sawed-off shotgun over his shoulder like a fishing rod. "That's why you're here," he said. "Ollie."

"He's in trouble."

He waited.

I decided it'd be stupid to hold back. There didn't appear to be much that would shock Bret Beet. "Drug-running trouble. Heroin."

"Heroin," he said, scratching his beard. "Bad shit."

"Ollie was running heroin north for a dealer in Montreal," I said. "He wanted out. Montreal wants him in."

"Montreal bust up his knee?"

I nodded. "And he'll do it some more, he can find him." Paused. It was soft-sell time. "Montreal's the one who killed my friend, too."

"You've got Ollie stashed away for now."

I said nothing.

"Maybe at his mom's house," Bret Beet said. "Up-country Vermont."

"Shit." He *was* smart.

"I'm not that smart," he said, reading my mind. "If I can figure it out, ain't no reason this Montreal cat can't."

"Want to run something by you," I said. "What if Montreal pulled right up your driveway? Just cruised up in his Escalade like a swinging dick?"

"On the Beet Brothers' property?"

"Like a swinging dick, demanding this and that, where's Ollie, where's my money."

"Killed your friend, huh?" Bret Beet pulled at his beard, then made a slow brown-teeth smile. "Live free or die," he said.

When I pulled into my driveway in Framingham and Trey, Kieu, and Tuan bubbled from the side door, I saw right away they had something up their sleeve. Trey wore khakis, a short-sleeve button-down with green stripes, and a necktie. Kieu had on a sundress the color of honeydew melon, and Tuan wore short pants, a white button-down, and a clip-on bow tie that had already popped from one side of his collar.

As I climbed from the truck I said, "Jeez, are we going to church?"

Trey blushed. "The attire was not my idea."

Inside, Trey escorted me into the living room, where snacks and drinks had been laid out, and barked over his shoulder at Kieu. She trundled Tuan from the room.

Trey stood before me like a brand-new Bible salesman who'd finally talked his way into some lady's home and wasn't sure what came next. He gestured at the coffee table. "Would you like a drink? A soft drink?"

"Trey," I said, "are you going to sell me some Amway?"

"What's Amway?"

"Never mind. Whatever it is, get to it."

"Your kindness to myself and my family has been overwhelming, and so I find it nerve-racking to ask another favor. But I understand it's your intention to sell this home in the near future, is that correct?"

"Sure."

"Kieu and I spent some time researching prices of comparable homes in the neighborhood," he said, pulling and unfolding a sheet of notebook paper. "As you may know, prices have been falling steadily here for the past—"

"Jesus Christ, are you looking to *buy* this place?"

"Well . . . yes, actually. We could use most of my father's cash for a significant down payment, and by renting the apartment upstairs, we're quite—"

"Sold," I said, standing. "Now go change into some real clothes. We're going to sand the joints in the office. It's dirty work."

It took Trey a while to change—once he told Kieu the house was theirs, they spent some time being giddy. When he did join me, Trey explained there were more Vietnamese in downtown Framingham than I'd known. Kieu had discovered this little community and made a few friends, and she wanted to stay put. Trey told her this wasn't much of a neighborhood, especially for Tuan, but she wouldn't budge.

We got the windows open and a fan running. I showed Trey how to use a sanding pole so he wouldn't have to climb up and down stepladders, and he pitched right in.

We were about done when my cell rang. It was Randall. I slapped dust off myself and picked up.

"The case of Patty Marx," he said, "grows curiouser and curiouser."

I waited.

"These reporters fret about their bylines like seventh-grade girls, did you know that?"

"You mean their names?"

"Their names as they appear in the paper," Randall said. "I guess those bylines are about all they've got, so they want them to pop. It's understandable. Who wants to be John Smith of the *Fresno Fishwrap*?"

"What the hell are you talking about?"

"It just made her a bit trickier to back-trace," he said. "She went by D.P.R. Marx for quite a while. I suppose she thought the three initials in a row added some heft to her byline." I could feel him savoring something. "Or maybe she wanted readers to think she was a man, thought she'd be taken more seriously."

"Where is she?"

"Her first job out of Clemson was at a weekly in Swainsboro, Georgia. Sewer-commission meetings and flower shows. But she worked her way north pretty quickly, and the papers got bigger. A black woman, you know, that's a prize employee these days."

I said nothing, figured that was the best way to move him along.

"From Swainsboro she moved to a decent-size paper near Nashville," he said. "Then *The Columbus Dispatch*, then the *Pittsburgh Post-Gazette*, then *The* by-God *Boston Globe*."

I said nothing.

"You're lucky I'm observant as hell," Randall said. "Because this all comes down to a single word. You know those bylines I mentioned?"

"Yeah?"

"Until about six months ago, hers read 'Patty Marx, *Globe* Staff.' Then she became 'Patty Marx, *Globe* Correspondent.'"

"What's that, a promotion?"

"Hell no," he said. "It means she went freelance."

"She's still passing out *Globe* business cards."

"Of course she is. They probably gave her a thousand of them. Right before they laid her off."

I was thinking it through. "The cell number on the card was crossed off, changed."

"Because they took away her company cell." Randall was enjoying this. He'd probably predicted my objections in his head—in order. He's smart that way.

"But the e-mail address was still there."

"A courtesy," he said, "for laid-off hacks while they scramble for their next job."

"You seem pretty sure about all this."

"I called Patty Marx's former editor," he said, and I could feel him breaking into a smile.

"She definitely got laid off six months ago?"

"Most definitely. And that's not the best part."

"Chrissake, can you get to it?"

But you can't hurry Randall, can't make him do anything any way but his, and he was slow-playing the story.

"I got the editor on the phone, a very nice woman," he said. "I teased all this info out of her. Said I ran an antiques newsletter in the Berkshires, and Patty Marx had written three pieces for me, and I was damned if I could find her address."

"That was pretty clever."

"Obviously this editor wasn't supposed to give out the address, but she felt rotten about all the layoffs, and who wants to hold up a starving freelancer's check?"

"The address, Randall. What was the address?"

"How about the Alta Vista Inn?" he said.

"Where's that?"

"Rourke, New Hampshire."

So many ideas, so many facts to click through. As I pulled into Charlene's driveway, I tried to push away ugly thoughts I was having about Patty Marx—living in Rourke on the sly, it looked like. And her car-to-car meet with Phigg just before he turned up dead. I needed to talk with Ollie, too. I needed to move.

Randall and I had decided to hit Rourke first because it was closer. Then maybe a run to Enosburg Falls. I just wanted to shower off wallboard dust before we split.

As I stepped in the front door, though, I heard footsteps, saw Charlene step away from a dining-room window. She narrowed her eyes. "Where's Fred?"

I stopped cold. "I left him here. Why?"

"Your note."

"What note?"

Charlene's eyes went wide. She turned and fast-walked to the kitchen, then returned with a blue Post-it stuck to her fingertip. "I came home to catch up on spreadsheets," she said, holding the note up, "and found this. I thought you wrote it."

WERE AT F'HAM HOUSE, HOME BY DINNER. Block printed, it just about could have been written by me.

But it hadn't been.

Our eyes met. We sprinted upstairs, flew into Jesse's room.

The bed was made.

The curtains were pulled back just so.

The windows were both open eight inches.

All the clothes I'd bought Fred, which he'd kept atop Jesse's dresser rather than mess up her drawers, were gone.

My father had taken off.

CHAPTER TWENTY

We spent the next ninety minutes in a full-court press, trying to find Fred before he got far. I had Charlene check the family luggage stash, which she kept in the attic. It was all there. "What does that matter, anyway?"

"A man with a rolling suitcase," I said, "is a whole 'nother thing than a man lugging his gear in a green trash bag."

She said I was right about that.

Charlene called the four cab companies that worked Shrewsbury while I dialed the local cops. Said my dad had slipped from the yard, might be confused, could be wandering down the main drag. Had anybody reported seeing him?

No dice.

Then I called the state police, Framingham barracks, got through to the detectives, and asked for Vic Lacross. "Ha!" said a nasally man's voice. "Year too late, friend. Long gone, good riddance." Click.

"What was that about?" Charlene said.

"Cop I used to know," I said. "I guess he's not a cop anymore. How about the taxis?"

She made a thumbs down.

We sat. Charlene drummed long fingernails on the telephone

receiver. "An old man, no longer unkempt but hardly genteel-looking, carrying a Hefty trash bag. Such a man is not invisible in this town. How is he getting around, Conway?"

"He's got a ride," I said. "He must."

"Unless . . ."

Then we were both up, flashing down basement stairs to the garage beneath the kitchen. Two years ago, when Charlene bought her Volvo SUV, she decided to hang on to her old white Accord rather than trade it in. It would be a great first car for Jesse, if Jesse ever bothered to get her driver's license.

It was easy to picture: Fred, with the house to himself for a few days, poking around, finding the Accord, digging for its keys in the kitchen junk drawer. . . .

But when I shouldered into the garage, there sat the car, dusty and buried in junk.

"So he got a ride when he left," Charlene said. "Who from?"

As we crossed the basement, I remembered Charlene's booze, Fred's first day here. My stomach sank. I froze.

"What?" she said.

I stepped to the shelf where I'd stashed the booze, pulled away painting supplies.

Fred had taken it all. Every bottle.

I leaned on the wall and explained it to Charlene.

She put her head in her hands.

Ninety minutes later, Randall and I eased past a carved-wood sign that said ALTA VISTA INN. Beneath it hung two smaller signs: OFF-SEASON RATES and WEDDINGS WELCOME.

"Must have nice views up there," Randall said, craning his neck to look at the huge brown Victorian. To get here we'd taken a hard right off Main Street, not far from Mechanic Street. Then we'd spooled slowly upward on back roads for a mile and a half. The Alta

Vista Inn sat on what had to be the highest lot for miles, centered in a three-acre clearing.

"Probably started out as an industrialist's house," Randall said as I pointed my truck back toward town. "Back when this town was something."

"Weird place for a city reporter to live," I said. "Unless . . ."

He looked at me.

"Unless she was working there, and a bed came with the job."

"Why would a gal like her change sheets at a B and B?"

"First, it kept her close to Tander Phigg," I said. "Also, she was black."

"So?"

I swept an arm at the main street. "Town like this, can you think of a better place for a black girl to fit in?"

Randall tapped an index finger to his cheek. "Sad but true," he finally said. "So what's her deal? Did Patty Marx get laid off, then move up here to stalk poor Tander Phigg?"

I shrugged. "Stalking him, or maybe stalking his money."

He thought a few seconds. "She didn't strike me that way."

I shrugged again. "First order of business, let's see what we can learn from the inn."

I backtracked out of town to an off-brand gas station specializing in diesel for a freight company next door. Drove past the station, swung into the freight-company lot.

Randall said, "You can't just pull up to the pay phone?"

"Security cams. Learned about them the hard way."

I fished under Randall's side of the bench seat, came up with a blue baseball cap that said FLATOUT in orange letters, passed it to him. "Pull it low. And, ah, try to sound black."

"The indignity of it all." He closed the door and jogged to the gas station pay phone. As I watched him trot, I shook my head: You'd never guess he had a strap-on foot.

He was back in three minutes. "Nice lady," he said, stuffing the cap beneath the seat. "She used to work in the financial district in Boston, hubby was a lawyer, they both took buyouts, wouldn't trade this life for anything."

"You got all that in three minutes?"

"Well, there wasn't much she could tell me about Patty Marx," he said. "Patty replied to an ad around Thanksgiving. Ski season was coming up, so they hired her more or less over the phone. She did nice work, maid and breakfast service. Never spoke except for small talk. The lady just about dropped the phone when I told her Marx used to be a *Globe* reporter. She kept to herself, hung out with her boyfriend on Mondays, which were her only days off during ski season. A few weeks ago she was just plain gone one morning. They're holding her last paycheck. The lady and her husband figured Patty got itchy when warm weather hit and took off. Happens all the time, she said."

I said, "Boyfriend?"

"You're good at picking out key concepts, aren't you?" Randall smiled. "Yeah, her boyfriend. Polite redheaded kid named Josh."

"Try again," I said, moving into the fast lane to blow past a semi. I looked at the speedometer. Ninety-three. We'd been moving that fast or close to it for three hours, would make Enosburg Falls in twenty minutes.

Randall punched in a number, listened, shook his head. Then again. "Straight to voice mail, Ollie and Josh both."

Soft rain fell as I left Route 89 and started the final eastbound run. We were quiet, talked out; we'd kicked around ideas for the first two and a half hours of the drive.

There was a lot we didn't know. We *did* know, though, that if Patty Marx was palling around with Josh Whipple, we needed to take a good hard look at both of them.

I cut onto Ollie's mother's street, spotted her house, pulled in behind an Oldsmobile Intrigue.

It was nearly seven, so we made long shadows as we walked the bluestone path and up four steps to the deep porch. I didn't like the vibe, the quiet. I noticed I was taking short breaths through my mouth, like a kid who's scared the bogeyman will hear his breathing.

I knew before I knocked that nobody would answer.

Tried anyway—heavy raps, doorbell, polite shouting. Randall had disappeared to walk a lap around the house.

The picture window in the living room had a smaller window on each side, and they were open. I was looking both ways, wondering if the neighbors were nosy, when Randall's voice carried from around back. "Shit!"

I heard him run toward me. "Shit shit shit," he said, taking the porch steps at two bounds. He took one look at the open windows, moved a rocking chair, kicked out a screen with his titanium ankle, and stepped through. Five seconds later I heard the front door's dead bolt slide, opened the door, walked inside. Randall was already in the kitchen.

It stank.

I followed Randall through a small dining room and toward the back of the house.

It was the type of kitchen that would make yuppies think twice about buying the place. Twelve by twelve, thirty-year-old fridge and oven, small window looking over the backyard, Formica countertops the color of pus, tired linoleum floor.

On that floor lay a woman who was old and dead, her head near the fridge. She was on her back. She wore white tennis shoes and a peach sweat suit. An apron that said *SOUPS ON* in script lay at her side, as if she'd been drying her hands on it when she died.

No, that wasn't it: I saw she'd been strangled with an apron string. Her neck was paper white up to the string, which had bitten so deep you could barely see it against her flesh. Above the apron string, her face was purple going on black and her eyes were bugged out like something in a cartoon. The white of her left eye was red where she must have popped a blood vessel.

On the Formica were two plates, with two slices of bread and a handful of Wise potato chips per plate. Next to the plates stood an open jar of pickles, a jar of mayonnaise. Next to the mayo were two plastic deli bags.

It wasn't the dead woman that stank. It was the cold cuts.

She'd been strangled while she made sandwiches for Josh and Ollie.

Standing next to me, Randall said, "Jesus Christ." Then he backed into the dining room. I heard him breathing, trying for control, trying not to puke.

"Don't touch anything," I said. "And breathe through your mouth."

"Jesus Christ." He dropped to one knee.

I touched his shoulder as I stepped past. "You okay?"

"I don't . . . I don't know. An old *lady*."

"Go to the front porch and breathe."

"Where are *you* going?"

I didn't answer, walked upstairs. Before I made the landing I heard Randall following.

The hall was tiny. I looked at four closed doors. Opened the one to my right. Technically it was a third bedroom, I guessed, but the woman had obviously used it as storage space. I closed the door. Dead ahead, I knew, was the house's only bathroom. Behind my left shoulder would be the master, most likely, with the killer mountain view.

So I opened the fourth door—the one that led, I was guessing, to Ollie's childhood bedroom.

"Oh hell," I said.

"Jesus Christ," Randall said.

Ollie was hanging from a frosted-glass light fixture.

There was one window at the gabled end of the room. It was shut. The room was stifling. And Ollie had shit himself while he died.

The stench reached out and took hold of you.

I stepped in. Randall stayed where he was. I put my hands in my pockets to make sure I didn't touch anything, and I breathed through my mouth.

Twin beds, boy-size. Both were made up but in a sloppy way—a guy way. So Ollie and Josh had been using the room while they stayed here.

Beneath Ollie's dangling legs—his right knee was still puffy and bandaged and he'd kicked off one Doc Martens—lay a tipped-over boy-size chair that matched the beds. Standing on the chair, or maybe the nearby desk, someone had stuck Ollie's head through a noose, then watched him die. Maybe Ollie kicked the chair himself. Maybe the killer slapped it over, trying to make the scene look like another suicide.

Any doubt about whether Ollie'd killed himself flew away when I took a closer look at the noose.

A necktie. Blue with little tennis racquets.

"Oh hell," I said. "I liked him."

Randall had pulled his shirt to cover his nose and mouth. He looked as pale as me.

I was puzzled. No cheesy light fixture would hold two-hundred-plus-pound Ollie. Using my feet only, I righted the chair and stepped up. I flinched at the stench even though I was breathing through my mouth. Tried not to look at Ollie's face, purple going on black, just like his mother's. I saw how they'd done it: The light fixture had been loosened and slid aside a few inches, and the necktie was knotted around a stout beam in the attic above.

I turned. "Whoever killed him put a lot of thought into this." I sounded funny, realized I was still holding my nose.

Randall's eyes were bigger than I'd ever seen them. He tapped his wristwatch, said nothing.

I nodded. We spilled down the stairs and out to the truck, gulping clean air the instant we got outside. The sun had dropped behind the mountains, and the temperature had dropped ten degrees. As I backed from the driveway I craned my neck in both directions. The houses I could see looked dead quiet.

———

We worked down Route 89 in the dark. We said nothing for a long time. I was thinking about Randall's reaction when he saw Ollie's mother. Finally I said, "Your old man once told me you weren't in Iraq long before you got blown up."

"Three weeks," he said, half laughing, "and thank you for putting it in such charming fashion."

"I never said I was charming," I said. "Three weeks. So I guess you didn't see a lot of . . . war."

"I know where you're going," Randall said. "You're right. My wound came on my second patrol, my first urban patrol. Before that I played a lot of Ping-Pong and drank a lot of ice-cold water. Inured to purple-faced corpses I'm not."

"What's 'inured'?"

"Never mind."

We were quiet some more.

We stopped in Ascutney, fueled the truck, took a leak. "What do you think?" I said when we got on the highway again.

Randall knew what I meant. "Here's what they want the cops to think," he said, looking straight ahead. "Ollie snaps. He already killed Tander Phigg over some damn thing, a claim that somebody owed somebody thirty-five hundred bucks. Maybe he figures the heroin deal is catching up with him, or maybe his business is deeper in the red than we know. Somehow his mother triggers him. In a twist even a made-for-TV movie would reject as hokey, he strangles her with an apron string. Then he realizes what he's done, trudges upstairs to his boyhood room, and hangs himself."

"So the New Hampshire Staties' party line that Phigg killed himself is blown up."

"The police couldn't be faulted for thinking that way before, but they need a new theory. I suspect they'll find the neckties used on Phigg and Ollie are knotted exactly the same way."

"It all hangs together."

"I should pardon the pun."

I said, "Huh?" Then I got it. I didn't smile. "Before, you said here's what *they* want the cops to think. Who's 'they'?"

"Montreal and his guy," he said. "Obviously."

"What about Josh Whipple? What about Patty Marx?"

"You said Ollie could fight like a tiger. Can you see Josh and Patty hoisting him into that noose?"

"Not conscious."

"Montreal is your man," he said. "Try this: Montreal's working his heroin deal with Ollie. Life is good. But along comes nosy, obnoxious Tander Phigg, whose Mercedes is nothing more than busywork to make Motorenwerks look legit. He pushes, he pesters, he figures things out. Montreal gets wind of this—through Ollie or Josh or God knows who. And Montreal is a serious man. He takes out Phigg, thinks that over a few days, decides he'd better take out Ollie for safety's sake. Ollie's mom is collateral damage."

"That's good as far as it goes," I said after a while. "But what about Josh? What about Patty Marx? And my take on Montreal is he was sniffing after Phigg's money. How's that fit?"

"Hell," Randall said.

Quiet.

I thought and thought, felt Randall doing the same. Part of the reason I liked him was he didn't have to fill the air with palaver every second.

After a while I dug through my wallet, found the card I wanted, dialed.

McCord picked up. "Sax," he said.

"You got any pull in Vermont?"

" 'Bout as much as I got in Nebraska. Why?"

"You must know some guys."

"Maybe a few. Why?"

"I can point you to a murder-suicide in Vermont," I said. "Or maybe a double homicide."

I pictured McCord pulling over in his Charger, taking a pen from his shirt pocket. "Where are you?"

"This Vermont mess is tangled up with the Tander Phigg thing in Rourke. Once they get a load of it, your detectives will have to admit he didn't kill himself."

"Where are you?"

"The favor I'm asking," I said, "can you leave me out of it?"

"No." He didn't even hesitate.

"Okay then," I said. "Vermont's a small state. Shouldn't take long to find the bodies."

I drove three-tenths of a mile before he said, "I'll try."

"That's fair."

"They'll get to you sooner or later, but I won't say your name in my first phone call. Best I can do."

"Enosburg Falls," I said, and told him the street address.

McCord clicked off.

I called Charlene, asked about Fred. No news. She'd called the Shrewsbury cops again, then the staties. They'd promised to keep an eye out for him.

Yeah, right.

I clicked off, let my mind go where it wanted. It had been a long day.

After a while I said, more to myself than to Randall, "Going to be a bitch to get that car now."

"*What?*"

"I was thinking about Phigg's Mercedes. Going to be hard to lay my hands on it once the state cops poke around at Motorenwerk."

"If you have any sense at all," Randall said, "you'll forget about the goddamn car."

I said nothing.

"You *do* have that much common sense, don't you?"

"This all started when Phigg asked me to fetch his car. Can't just drop it now."

When Randall finally spoke, he kept an artificial calm. "Let's work through this," he said. "A few minutes ago, the Vermont State Police found the bodies of Ollie and his mom. I'm going to take a flier and guess they don't get a lot of double strangulations in the Maple State, so it's going to be big *fucking* news."

"They call it the Green Mountain State, I'm pretty sure."

"Shut up," Randall said. "If you and I are very lucky, and if your pal McCord is very kind to us, we won't get arrested. On the other hand, maybe we will. Regardless, there'll be a mob of police prowling around Motorenwerk pretty damn soon. Agreed?"

"Okay."

"Once they start prowling, they *will* find heroin, or traces thereof. Oh, and I haven't even touched on the hanging of Tander Phigg, which your pal McCord is going to bring up because he thought all along it was homicide rather than suicide."

I said nothing.

"Let's review, shall we?" Randall said. "Three citizens strangled. Two of the deaths were supposed to look like suicides, while the third is a sweet old granny. One of the dead guys was an heir to a noted Massachusetts manufacturing family, but he had an illegitimate black daughter and he died broke. The other ran an innocent-looking auto-repair shop *that was a front for an international heroin-smuggling ring*." He looked over at me. "Gee, you think a case like that will get any publicity?"

We were quiet maybe two miles.

Randall said, "Motorenwerk is going to be sealed tight as a drum for a long time, my friend."

"I said I'd get a Barnburner's car back. I'll get it back."

"You've done some good here, amigo. Good work for little in the way of thanks."

"Who killed Tander Phigg?" I said. "Who took his money? I've done jack shit."

Randall said nothing until we hit the Massachusetts border. When he spoke, his voice was even lower and slower than it had been before. "Trey Phigg buying that house is the worst thing that could have happened to you."

"Why?"

"Because he bailed you out of a stupid mistake. He prevented you from learning a lesson."

"What lesson? Don't fix up old houses?"

"Don't play stupid!" He shouted it, jackknifing. Then he settled himself with deep breaths, calmed himself again. "Pissing into the wind. Pretending things are black and white when you know better. Pouring energy into lost causes to forget about everything you could be working on. *Should* be working on."

I said nothing. I hit our off-ramp faster than I needed to. The F-150's front tires squalled. When I lifted my foot from the throttle, the back end got light and tried to come around.

But I fought it. I saved it.

When I dropped Randall off, neither of us said a word.

CHAPTER TWENTY-ONE

In Framingham, Kieu and Tuan were asleep. I gave Trey a fast rundown on what Randall and I had found. Probably should've been gentler about it—when I got to the dead bodies in Vermont, his face drained and he went very quiet. I'd overloaded him.

I did a Google News search for Enosburg Falls. There was a four-paragraph story: Two dead bodies, idyllic town near the Canadian border, names being withheld, Vermont State Police investigating.

The twenty-four-hour news station that covered all of New England didn't have much more. A reporter who looked fifteen years old stood out front of Ollie's mother's house. The reporter walked around and made lots of hand motions, working hard to sell a story he had no facts on. He did say unconfirmed reports had it a possible murder-suicide. Enosburg Falls hadn't seen a murder since 1923.

I leaned in, ignored the reporter, watched behind him. Every light in the house was on. Crown Vics were everywhere. Three big guys in dark Windbreakers stood on the front porch. Probably state detectives taking a cigarette break, holding the smokes low while the TV camera rolled.

The reporter promised more details and tossed it back to the anchor.

"Shit," I said.

Trey said, "What?"

"One of those Crown Vics had a New Hampshire cop plate. That means Vermont called New Hampshire already. So they're going to take a hard look at your father's death. Hell, they're going to take a hard look at *you*."

"It's going to be a mess, isn't it?"

"I was you, I'd hide that seventy-five K in something safer than a trash bag."

Trey faced me and clasped his hands together the way he did sometimes. The move seemed formal, maybe something he picked up in Vietnam. "Conway," he said, "did Montreal murder my father?"

"I believe he did."

"Is he going to pay?"

"Yes."

He swallowed, and I noticed for the first time how big his Adam's apple was. "Will there be extradition, trials, dog-and-pony shows?"

"No."

Trey looked at me awhile. Then he rose and left the room.

I understood. I've been through it with Barnburners a hundred times. They need to be rescued from the jackpots they get into, but they don't appreciate it the way you might think. Everybody knows that without spiders, the world would be overrun by insects. But that doesn't make people love spiders.

I get it. I live with it. Sometimes, I guess, I wish it didn't work that way.

But wishing is pretty low on my to-do list.

Restless, I killed the TV and took off. Driving west, I thought about the cops reopening Tander Phigg's death. Thought about Patty Marx, Josh Whipple, Montreal, heroin, suicide that wasn't suicide.

Trey Phigg had said more than once he wanted to know more

about his old man. "Careful what you wish for, kid," I said out loud in the dashboard glow.

That reminded me of a call I wanted to make. It was really too late for this call, but . . . hell, I'd wake her if I needed to.

"Roper residence," she said when she picked up, pronouncing *residence* carefully. "This is Myna Roper; how may I help you?"

I said my name, asked if she remembered me.

"Of *course* I remember you," Myna said, and I pictured her standing erect, pissed at the question. "You were here two days ago."

"Want to talk to you about a couple of things. Have the police called about your daughter?"

"Why would they?"

I thought about giving it to her straight. Decided not to. "Miz Roper, there's a chance Diana is involved with a man who's gone on kind of a crime spree up here."

"*What?*"

"She calls herself Patty Marx, did you know that? She's a reporter, or was."

"I knew," Myna said, so softly I barely heard.

"Wish you'd told me."

"It's . . . embarrassing. The child rejects the mother's name. Embarrassing, Mister Sax. Who is this crime-spree man she's involved with?"

"I don't know for a fact she's dating him, and even if she is, she may not know everything he's up to." I thought Patty Marx was in it up to her eyeballs, but saying so would hurt my chances.

"What exactly do you mean by 'crime spree,' Mister Sax?" *Crime shpree*. "That's quite a broad term."

"The police are wondering if Tander Phigg's suicide was really a suicide."

"Oh my God!" I heard air go out of her, pictured her sitting hard on the sofa.

"Look," I said, "none of this is fact. I'm guessing, and even if my worst guesses are true, nobody knows how your daughter fits in. But you're going to get a call or a visit soon. The police will have questions about Patty."

"I don't have anything to tell them! I told you everything there is the other night."

"So tell it to *them*. Tell it all. Don't hold back, don't try to guess what they're after. Just tell it."

There was a long pause. Ice cubes clinked.

"You said you wanted to talk about two things," Myna said. "I certainly hope you didn't save the worst for last."

"I want to tell you about Tander Phigg's son."

And I did. I told her about Trey Phigg—his curiosity about his father's five good years, a fight that chased him to Vietnam, a young family, the way he came home to make peace with his father and found him dead.

She listened hard. No ice clinked.

By the time I finished, I was idling in Charlene's driveway. Myna was hooked. She jumped when I finally asked the favor. I started to ask if I could help with travel arrangements, but she interrupted me.

"Believe it or not," Myna Roper said, "we have the same Internet down here that you have up there." Click.

Charlene was sound asleep. I closed her bedroom door, went back downstairs, and flipped the news on, but they were just rerunning the report I'd seen already. I muted the volume and lay with my hands behind my head.

Vermont and New Hampshire state cops, working together. With the Enosburg Falls killings hitting the news, the New Hampshire detectives who hadn't listened to McCord about Phigg's death would look like idiots. No, worse: They'd look like lazy assholes who'd blown a chance to stop two killings. They ought to be embarrassed, but if I knew anything about cops, they'd be pissed at the world instead.

They were going to come after me, Trey, and maybe Josh with everything they had.

When they saw my record they were going to drool.

I was on parole for manslaughter two. I'd been seen with Tander Phigg the day before he died, and it was me who called in his body. I was a known associate of Ollie and Josh. Solid canvassing would show I'd driven them right to Ollie's mom's house.

Shit.

I pulled my cell, hesitated, dialed McCord.

He picked up and said my name. In the background I heard the Red Sox radio announcers. "Pretty late for a ball game," I said. "They on the west coast?"

"Seattle."

I took a guess and said, "You're sitting at the side of I-Ninety-three waiting for a drunk to go by."

"Or a speeder."

"So you figured out the Phigg thing first, but you're stuck working graveyard anyway? No promotion? No apologies from the detectives? No employee-of-the-month award?"

He either laughed or said, "Unh."

We said nothing while the Red Sox screwed up a hit and run. Then McCord said, "Nobody likes the guy tells them they screwed up."

"And they *did* screw up. Royally."

"What do you want, Sax?"

"I didn't do it."

He knew what I meant. "Which one?"

"Any of them."

"I hear they're looking at the son," he said. "They'll want to interview him again."

"He didn't do it either. I'll vouch for him."

"I had a look at your record. Not sure how much weight your voucher carries." He stifled a yawn. "Anyway, you'll get a chance to tell it to the detectives tomorrow. Two-state task force with an assist from the FBI."

"Jesus."

"They love a task force, especially when they're embarrassed."

We were quiet.

McCord said, "You understand I need to tell my boss about this call?"

"Sure," I said. "About that task force. No help from Canada yet?"

"What do you mean?" His voice was different, like he'd straightened up.

I realized he didn't know yet about Montreal. Most likely none of the cops knew. I said, "Have you guys taken a good look through Dufresne's garage yet?"

"Not sure. Why?"

I told McCord about the heroin runs, the Montreal connection, the guys from the black Escalade who'd creamed Ollie's knee.

McCord said nothing. I heard a keyboard as he took notes on his cruiser's laptop.

Finally I said, "That's some good stuff, huh?"

McCord was quiet.

"You tell the detectives all that," I said, "and maybe they ease off me and Trey Phigg. Plus you look good."

"Maybe." McCord clicked off.

The next morning, cereal-bowl clinks woke me. As I realized I'd fallen asleep on the couch, I craned my neck and saw Charlene doing something new—humming and dancing a box step in the kitchen while she ate her raisin bran.

She didn't know I was awake, so I held still and watched and listened. After a minute I figured out the tune: "I Feel Pretty." Morning sun lit the edges of her blond hair. She wore work clothes: black pencil skirt, pearl-gray blouse.

It was nice watching her while she didn't know she was being watched.

When she danced her cereal bowl over to the sink, I said, "You *look* pretty."

She jumped six inches, turned, put hands on hips. "How long, Conway Sax?"

"Couple minutes."

Charlene tried for a mad face but couldn't hold it, smiled, held her arms out like a TV spokesmodel. "The empty-nester life," she said, "is the life for me."

Then she ran into the family room—the tight skirt making for choppy steps—and plopped herself on top of me, straddling. Had to wiggle the skirt real high to make it.

I said, "Wow."

Charlene laughed and wriggled and put her hands on my chest. "No 'Where's my homework?' No three-day pout because somebody didn't get her way. Freedom!" She did the spokesmodel flare again and slowed her wriggle, gave it some purpose, moved her hands to the waist of my jeans.

"Got a stiff neck," I said.

"And then some," she said, giggling. When I tried to sit up to kiss her, she flat-handed my chest. "Stay right there, dragon breath."

I don't know how she got her panty hose off without climbing from me.

But she did.

After, Charlene was all business and bustle. A bathroom cleanup, fresh panty hose, check the makeup, ready to split. She glanced at the TV, which was tuned again to the New England news station, as she crossed the room. Said she wanted to hear more about the Vermont deaths, but it'd have to wait. She leaned down to peck my temple.

I grabbed her wrist. "What about Fred?"

Her eyes went hard for an instant—she hates being interrupted while on a mission, and she was on a mission to get to the office—but then she softened and sat. "I did everything I could think of," she said. "I drove around two hours last night looking for him. I called the Shrewsbury police and the state police *again*. I even e-mailed the gal who runs the town blog, sent her a cell-phone picture of Fred that Sophie took. I said Fred may be wandering around, implying he has Alzheimer's."

"Did you call Vicky Lin at Cider Hill?"

"I did," she said, brushing nonexistent hair from my forehead.

"And?"

"And she said it happens more often than not." Charlene kissed my forehead as she stood. "I'm sorry, Conway. Doctor Lin said this happens almost every time."

CHAPTER TWENTY-TWO

It was time to deal with Montreal. That meant driving to Rourke and acting like a worm on a fishhook.

I spent the ride thinking about Fred, wondering what pushed him out of Charlene's place. He tried to drink himself to death for thirty years or more. I wasn't sure I'd ever heard of such a hard case sobering up the way he had. I wouldn't have believed it but for Vicky Lin's tests.

So you stop using, cold turkey. You get through the worst of it, find yourself a cushy setup—Charlene's home, her money, a pair of adoring females—and hit the streets again?

I sighed. Knew it could happen, had seen it a hundred times. There's nothing rational about a man who drinks that long.

Once Fred cleared Charlene's neighborhood, he could blend in. The main drag was less than a mile from her house, and from there it was ten minutes to Worcester. In that city, bums lugging trash bags are a dime a dozen. And there's a hell of a rail yard to boot. My father could be rocking his way to Vermont, Florida, you name it.

"Jesus, Fred," I said out loud.

I was still playing around with ideas when I rolled into Rourke. My best guess put Montreal near Motorenwerk, eyeballing the place.

He thought there was a big pile of money inside the shop. I thought he was right.

As I neared Mechanic Street, I put on my left turn signal. There was no traffic coming the other way but I hesitated anyway, stutter-stepping the F-150 like a man trying to make up his mind. I canceled the turn signal, weaved back to my lane, and cruised toward Jut Road. I kept an eye on my mirror, wondering if he'd take the bait.

Montreal made it too easy. Maybe he was stupid. More likely he'd grown cocky and bored sitting around in a nothing town, waiting. I hadn't even cleared Rourke's three-block downtown when the black Escalade snorted out of Mechanic Street, squatted under acceleration, and came after me.

I might have smiled, McCord style, at my rearview mirror. The only drawback I could see to my plan was that I'd have to take a beating to make Montreal buy it.

I've taken beatings before.

I led them out of town. Montreal was behind the wheel of the Escalade. He tailgated me, trying to scare me half to death. I made a big show of noticing him, checking my mirrors again and again, trying to look nervous.

When we hit Jut Road, I pulled in like a man who'd run out of options.

As we parked, Montreal jammed his truck against my rear bumper. We all climbed from our vehicles. Montreal's lounge-lizard look was going strong: He wore another shimmery suit that looked gray or olive drab, depending on how the sun hit it, and his pompadour was tall.

He snapped his fingers like a gangster in a black-and-white movie. His muscle man, wearing a black T-shirt that advertised a gym I'd never heard of, moved in.

I gulped and made a *let's-all-take-it-easy* gesture with both hands. "Plenty for everyone," I said, just as muscle man punched me in the stomach.

I flopped against my truck and doubled up—and felt happy. I'd guessed muscle man didn't know how to fight, and the punch proved me right. For starters, I'd seen it coming two yards away. Had tensed my abs, barely felt it. Could have sidestepped if I'd wanted to, and he would've broken his hand on my door. And despite the big windup, the punch was all arm. He hadn't set his feet, hadn't started by torquing his thigh.

He probably worked as a bouncer and thought he was pretty tough because he could slam a drunk's head off an alley wall.

Thinking all this, I dropped to a knee. Muscle man got set to hit me in the face with a downward-slanting left that might have actually done damage, but I said, "Okayokayokay," and Montreal snapped his fingers again.

"First, a correction. There's *not* plenty here for everybody," he said. *Zere's.* "What is here is mine, and you will take me to it or my man will put you in the river and stand on you awhile, eh?"

I hoped I looked like a beaten man, holding my arm against my ribs as I stood. I jerked a thumb behind me at the shack. "You were close," I said. "When you bought a hammer and bashed up the walls inside."

"How close?"

"I'll show you," I said, and winced my way down the slope to the river.

Ten minutes later I knocked the last peg from its hole and slipped out of the way as the false floor swung down. It wasn't a hard job once you knew what you were looking for. There was nothing there, of course, and so I went into act two of my sell job—cursing, begging, swearing to God it was all supposed to be here. "Those goddamn—"

"Yes? Goddamn who?" Montreal said.

I looked at my boots, which were in six inches of water, and said nothing.

Montreal snapped his fingers again. You could tell he liked the move.

Muscle man grabbed the back of my shirt and kicked my feet out from under me, dumping me in the ice-cold Souhegan facedown, my nose grinding coarse sand. As promised, he kept one boot on my back as I flopped and struggled.

I'd been ready and had gulped a deep breath on my way down. But instinct is instinct, and after thirty seconds I didn't need to play-act my thrashing. He kept me under another thirty seconds. By the time he lifted his boot and I thrust my head from the water, I had a lungful of river. I gagged and retched on hands and knees.

Muscle man stood not two feet from me, his crotch level with my head, his arms folded, his pride obvious. I wanted to show him the truth about street fighting; it'd be so easy to reach out and twist his nut sack until he passed out. I doubted I could actually tear his balls off, not through his jeans. But I could try my damnedest.

But this was working. I fought back the urge and instead crawled ashore, coughing up water, making *I-surrender* gestures.

Montreal stepped over and toed my side. His knees popped when he crouched. He spoke gently. "You don't need to die here today in a cold river, Conway Sax. Who took the money from this place?"

"They'll kill me."

"*He* will kill you first."

"You don't get it," I said. "These are bad hombres. Survivalists, mercenaries."

Montreal sighed, stood, snapped. "Two minutes this time."

"No!" I said as muscle man stepped toward me. "Okay. I'll take you there. They live a couple towns over."

"You will indeed take us there," Montreal said. "You will also provide an address and a map. In case we get separated."

"If I give you the address, what's to keep you—him—from killing me right now?"

"If you *don't* give it," he said, "what is to keep him from standing on your back for two minutes, thirty seconds?"

I tried to look like I'd had it. Stood, sloshed over to my truck, pulled a pen and a map of New England from the glove box. Spread the map on my hood.

I managed to not crack a smile as I told them precisely how to get to the Beet Brothers' compound.

Fifteen minutes later we neared the place, the Escalade a car length off my bumper. I sat in a puddle and wondered how many times I had to get dunked in the Souhegan.

My directions had been perfect: We'd found our way over to Route 123, had paralleled railroad tracks, and now you could see the Beet Brothers' mailbox, cemented into a stack of old truck wheels to keep snowplows and vandals from knocking it over.

Time for me to make my move and hope. I put my turn signal on, began to swing into the dirt road—then straightened the wheel and gassed the F-150. The truck's six-cylinder engine didn't have a lot of juice, but I worked it through the gears as fast as I could, watching my mirror the whole time.

The Escalade had lurched to an awkward, angled stop when I took off. Now Montreal and his muscle man had a choice. They could hope I'd led them to the right place but had then panicked and rabbited. Or they could use their horsepower to chase me down, then beat on me until they got another address.

I liked my odds. Dealers were used to seeing people roll over for them, and they were used to people who panicked when the heat was on. Plus, after sitting around doing nothing for a week, they felt ready for action.

Wrong. They didn't want any part of Beet Brothers–style action. But by the time they figured that out, it'd be too late.

Before I disappeared around a gentle left-hand bend, I saw the Escalade cut down the Beets' dirt road. For maybe five seconds I felt bad for Montreal and his muscle man. They were dime-a-dozen crooks like a thousand other guys I'd known.

Then I thought about heroin, the things I'd seen junkies do. Thought about Ollie Dufresne, who survived the French Foreign Legion so he could be hung like a side of beef in his boyhood room. About his mom, a widow lady making turkey sandwiches in her own kitchen when muscle man wrapped apron strings around her neck.

But mostly I thought about Tander Phigg, Jr. Born in his father's shadow, tried to step out, didn't quite make it. Chased his only son away, hid inside a bottle of Scotch, climbed out, got greedy or stupid, lived in a shack while he watched his dream house rot, wound up hanging from a pipe stub.

There were plenty of people to feel for here. Montreal wasn't one of them.

The Beets' compound disappeared in my mirror. I headed south.

On the drive I shivered and played guessing games about Fred. I wondered how he'd walked out of Charlene's neighborhood without causing neighbors to call the cops, wondered where he'd go. Without really deciding to go there, I found myself aimed at Purgatory Chasm. By ten I was parked there, facing roughly east, squinting against the sun. Had the place to myself for thirty seconds. Then a big black Toyota Sequoia parked and spilled three little blond kids and a nanny driver. The nanny tried to round up the kids, but she didn't have a prayer— the two boys and a girl were all under six, and they scattered.

Soon they were all out of sight. Things went quiet. I rolled down both windows of my truck and pushed away Fred thoughts.

They were replaced by thoughts of Montreal. I'd done state time for manslaughter two after I shot someone who was trying to shoot me, but the calculated, indirect way I'd just handled Montreal and muscle man didn't sit right.

Tough shit. Barnburner sacrifice, like the time I'd spent at Mass. Correctional Institute, Cedar Junction, on the manslaughter.

After a while I locked the F-150, walked to an area with picnic tables, chose one in full sunshine, and sat drying. In my peripheral vision I saw a nothingburger car—dirty beige, Altima, Taurus, whatever—parked on the other side of the Sequoia.

The nanny had dumped a big cloth bag of toys and snacks on a picnic table. I noticed one of the blond boys and the girl were sticking close to the nanny as she walked laps around the picnic area calling for Jeffrey, saying it *Heff-ray*.

The sun was nice.

Wheels turned as I tried to tie off loose ends. Josh Whipple, Phigg's blown fortune, his hidden stash.

Patty Marx. I thought about our farm-stand meeting and realized she was the best kind of bullshitter, the kind that vibes *hey-I'm-giving-you-the-lowdown* straightforwardness. People like that know the soft sell works best when they're lying.

Patty Marx, Diana Marx, D.P.R. Marx. She was hiding her name and a lot more—meeting with Phigg the day before he died, living a couple miles from Jut Road, apparently dating Josh Whipple.

Patty and Josh? Working Phigg like a speed bag?

While I thought it through, the nanny's perimeter walk gained urgency, her calls for Heff-ray grew louder. The daughter, who was the youngest, picked up on the nanny's fear, squatted, and covered her eyes with her hands, whimpering some. The nanny peered down into the chasm itself, pulled her cell, made calls. I wondered why she didn't just walk down the chasm. It's not an easy climb, but people do it with kids. Then I saw she wore stiletto-heeled sandals. Stupid.

I sighed. Looked like I was volunteer-by-default to find the missing blond son. Dollars to donuts he was less than thirty feet away behind one of the big rocks.

As I began to rise, a hand on my shoulder pressed me back to the picnic-table bench. Behind me Josh Whipple said, "Where's the fucking money?"

CHAPTER TWENTY-THREE

Where the hell had he come from? Had he followed me?

"Money's not your problem," I said, turning. He looked awful. Blue-white face. Black bags beneath eye sockets deeper than I remembered. Crimson Windbreaker with a lump in the right pocket, the lump pointing my way like a joke, like when a junkie uses a finger in his pocket to hold up a convenience store.

He followed my gaze, wiggled the lump. "Found it underneath your passenger seat," he said, jerking a thumb at my truck. "I believe it belonged to Ollie originally, right?"

Shit.

I needed to gut this thing out. "I say again, money is not your problem," I said. "Every cop in Vermont and New Hampshire is looking for you. *That's* your problem."

The nanny approached, probably pissed that the big strong men hadn't yet offered to find Heff-ray. But before she could say anything, Josh shot her a look that stopped her in her tracks. As she retreated to the edge of the chasm I stood.

Josh said, "Where's the rest of the fucking money, Sax?"

"What money?"

"Don't play dumb. Tander Phigg's hidey-hole money."

I wondered what he meant by *rest*. Said nothing.

"Did you help him stash it in that pump-house floor?" he said. "Hell of a hiding place. Took me two days to find it, even though I knew it was *somewhere* in that shack. Hell, I figured out it had to be in the floor somewhere, but it still took me three hours to figure out how the bottom swung away."

I said, "Tell me about the money."

"What about it?"

"I thought playing dumb was over," I said. "He lived in a shack. He was broke. He picked up returnable cans in ditches. How the hell did he have seventy-five grand stashed?"

"That was for Ollie, for services rendered," Josh said. "Where's the *big* pile?"

"*What* big pile?"

He looked at me for damn near thirty seconds, saying nothing. Both blond kids were crying now. Behind me, the nanny sounded desperate.

"Tander Phigg wanted out," Josh said.

"What's out? Out of what?"

"When his daughter showed up," he said—did he stumble over *daughter*, or did I imagine that?—"he couldn't believe his luck. She was the link to his happy younger days, blah blah blah. They came up with a plan to cash out, disappear to Canada, and be happy *artistes* forever and ever, or some such bullshit."

Click. "So Phigg was converting everything to cash," I said.

"And Ollie was using his drug-stashing expertise to get them over the border. The seventy-five K was his fee."

"Why didn't he take the fee up front?"

"He didn't have much leverage," Josh said. "Phigg showed up at the shop and said he knew about Ollie's other trade. Phigg called the shots after that."

I thought for a minute. "What was the big deal about Canada? Phigg had enough dough to move anywhere he wanted in the States.

There was no need to cash everything in, smuggle it, all that non-sense."

"He liked the idea of fucking the IRS," Josh said. "He hated everything about taxes. Ollie once said Phigg was one of these half-smart guys who let the tax tail wag the fiscal dog."

He was right about that, when I thought about it. Phigg never missed a chance to talk about the death tax especially, about the feds helping themselves to half of everything his father had built.

Above us in the parking lot, I thought I heard wide tires on gravel. I needed to keep Josh talking a minute or two longer. I said, "Did Phigg know you were banging his daughter?"

His face went tight. "No more than he knew I'm going to gut-shoot you."

"Why not hang me? Plenty of stout trees around."

"Let's take a hike down there," he said, gesturing toward the chasm trail.

"The problem with a weak link," I said, making no move to turn, "is that it *stays* weak. Think Patty Marx will be any stronger for you than she was for Phigg?"

Gears spun in Josh's head. He licked his lips, made twitchy moves with his gun hand. I was scanning the horizon behind him. Nothing yet—maybe I'd imagined those tires on gravel, or maybe they'd belonged to a sightseer who'd rolled past.

Time to press. "If she was here right now," I said, "you could treat her like a loose end. But she's not here. She's picking up her mother at the airport. I know because I put the whole thing together."

"She's hip-deep in it," he said. But I felt his doubt; I'd killed his momentum.

"Of course she is," I said. "But when she's in a little room with three cops, and those cops are dying to talk with you, and Patty's looking at life no parole, do you think she'll *admit* she's hip-deep in it?"

Josh said nothing, licked his lips again.

"Or will she be a brave journalist who was kidnapped by Josh Whipple and dragged along on his two-state crime spree?"

His face was now the color of peed-on newspaper. "Turn and walk or I'll do it right in front of the brats, I swear I will."

I barely heard him. I was waving my arm and hollering by then, having finally spotted two park police. "This guy here!" I said, pointing at Josh, gesturing. "This guy thinks he saw Jeffrey! Hurry!"

It took Josh a couple seconds to realize what was going on. When he did, he looked at me in a way that made my neck hairs stand up. Then he pulled his hand from his Windbreaker, zipped shut the pocket, and played along. He wasn't crazy enough to shoot two cops, a nanny, and a couple of blond kids.

"Right back there, yes!" he said, bouncing on the balls of his feet as the cops, a man and a woman, both short and squat, scrambled toward us. "No, to your left, way down there."

I wanted to turn him in—until I saw the park police carried no side arms. If I forced Josh to make a choice, maybe he *would* start shooting.

While he gave the cops the runaround, with the nanny and the two kids barking useless advice, I quietly walked toward my truck.

But Josh had one more arrow in his quiver. "Take care, Conway!" he hollered, making sure both cops turned and looked at me. I had no choice but to make a friendly wave and say I'd talk to him later.

Josh cupped his hands. "I'll tell Fred you said hello!"

I stood. Couldn't move. My wet boots felt like concrete.

But the park police must have called another unit—a forest-green Ford Expedition pulled into the parking lot with its blue lights strobing.

So I brushed the window Josh had busted from the F-150's bench seat, climbed in, and drove out, flipping through new ideas. Josh plus Fred? Truth, or a bullshit bluff by Josh?

I called Randall. He picked up on half a ring. I said, "Guess who just about shot me with the little Browning I took away from Ollie?"

"Josh Whipple." No hesitation. He wasn't guessing.

"How'd you know?"

"I got an earful this morning from Patty Marx," he said. "You need to hear it."

I checked my watch. "She ought to be heading for Logan to meet her mother's plane."

"When she dropped this bomb on me I persuaded her to come to my place and sent a car service instead," he said. "Now I don't want to let her out of my sight. And oh by the way, why the *hell* are you pulling Myna Roper into this circus?"

"I, ah, I thought it would be good for her to tell Trey about his father. About his five happy years."

Long pause. I could picture Randall pinching the bridge of his nose, the way he does. Finally he said, "Priority-wise, that strikes me as pretty low on the totem pole, Conway."

I said nothing. Randall matched me.

"Let's meet at the farm stand in Berlin," I said. "Patty knows it. Bring her, but leave Myna in Framingham to talk with Trey."

"Okay, Mister Fix-It." Randall sighed. "See you there."

"Get an extra fork for me."

"Things are happening *rápidamente* now, eh?"

"Bet your sweet ass," I said, and clicked off.

When I got there, Randall and Patty faced each other across a picnic table in the sun. They sipped bottled water and stared at each other and ignored the apple pie sitting between them. The day's heat had spooled up, feeling more like August than June. Good. I sat next to Randall but with my back to the table and Patty, soaking up sun and heat.

I said. "Montreal's out."

"Meaning?" Randall said.

"Meaning out. That's all you need to know."

He shook his head, rose, walked to the stand.

I kept my face to the sun and said, "So what do you have to tell me that's so important?"

Patty waited a beat. "Maybe it's important enough for you to look at me while I say it."

"Maybe you should convince me you're not a fucking liar who helped Josh Whipple kill Ollie Dufresne and his mother."

"What?" She hissed it.

Now I did turn. I talked fast, ticked points off on my fingers, watched her reaction. "You met with Tander Phigg the day before he hanged himself. You haven't been with *The Globe* for a good six months. You were working as a maid in a goddamn B and B right in Rourke, I could just about throw a football from there to Phigg's shack. On your day off at the B and B, you ran around with your boyfriend, Josh Whipple."

Her mouth had dropped progressively as I said it. She clicked her teeth shut and shot death-ray eyes at me.

"These are all things you either lied about or left out of your story," I said, putting my back to Patty again and laying my elbows on the table. "So until you convince me otherwise, the big question here is whether I give you to the cops or Whipple. I was you, I'd be hoping for the cops."

"*Ass*hole!"

Randall came back with another bottle of water, read the vibe at a glance. "Don't let me interrupt," he said.

"Nothing here to interrupt," Patty said.

"I was just telling Patty," I said, nodding thanks for the water, "that unless we decide to help her out, fifteen, twenty years at MCI Framingham is the *best* thing that can happen to her."

"Conway," Randall said.

"The *worst* thing," I said, "is Josh Whipple. He took a pretty good run at killing me just now. And he said you and him are like *this*, Patty. Friends, lovers, partners."

"Conway," Randall said.

But I had a head of steam now. "I told Josh he made a mistake letting you out of his sight, Patty. And you know what? He knew I was right. So maybe I'll call him, hand you over, let him do what he needs to do."

"Conway!"

I finally noticed Randall was squeezing my bicep, hard. "You should hear what she has to say," he said.

I breathed myself calm. "Sorry. My father is missing and people keep trying to kill me."

We were quiet awhile. Then Patty looked at Randall. "Shall I tell him what I told you?"

He nodded.

Patty took a long drink from her water bottle, screwed its cap tight, placed both forearms flat on the table, and looked me in the eye. "Bobby Marx started fucking me when I was nine years old," she said.

CHAPTER TWENTY-FOUR

I said nothing, watched her eyes instead. I decided I believed her, knew Randall did, too.

Finally I said, "So he knew you weren't his. Your mother was fuzzy on that."

"Of *course* he knew. He used to tell me that. After. While we were cuddling." A tear rolled from her left eye. She made no move to touch it. "He was big on cuddling after, and he was big on reminding me I wasn't his biological daughter. Because that made it all right, you see?"

"Did your mother know?"

"She didn't know because she didn't want to know. After a while she hazed out with the booze, and then she didn't know much of anything."

I pushed the uneaten pie aside. "When did it end?"

"Halloween night when I was seventeen. He drove into a pond trying to avoid a pack of trick-or-treaters. He drowned." She barked a laugh. "They said he was a hero."

I glanced at Randall. His eyes showed me nothing.

"Can you blame me for wondering who my true father was?" Patty said.

"When the rape started," I said, "you stopped having friends. You found something to focus on. You fixed on the who's-my-father question and became an information seeker. To your mother, maybe your guidance counselor, it looked like obsession. To you it was a way to control something."

"You've heard my story?"

"I hear a lot of stories."

Patty began to shake, a little at first, then harder, tears flowing now. "Are you so *jaded*? Is my story so *common*?"

I took both her wrists. "Your story is yours," I said. "Your story is like nobody else's."

Then Patty Marx slipped her hands from mine, set her elbows on the table, covered her eyes, and cried a long while. Randall, who'd been hovering at the end of the table, sat next to her and set a big hand on her back.

I went to the stand, grabbed a handful of napkins, and brought them to our table. Patty used them to wipe her eyes and blow her nose. She looked from Randall to me and tried to laugh. "Sorry about the girly-girl nonsense. I haven't done that since college."

I said, "By the time Bobby Marx died, you were set to go to . . . Clemson, was it?"

She nodded, then told it. Talked about college, her career, moving from newspaper to newspaper, climbing the ladder. She kept her eyes on the table while she spoke, tracing the wood grain with a blood-red fingernail.

I knew the story already but heard her out, letting her tell it her way. By the time she got to the part about working for *The Globe,* the shade had worked around to our table.

"You met Phigg a year and a half ago when you wrote the story about dying cities," I said, as it all clicked into place. "You knew by then he was your father."

She hesitated, then nodded.

"Was the whole story a setup? A pretext to meet him?"

"Yes."

"You hit him with it. You told the poor guy he was your father."

"Yes." She whispered it.

"How'd he react?"

"He sat on a log and said it couldn't be true."

"You convinced him."

"I told him some things about my mother that would be difficult for a stranger to learn," she said. "To seal the deal, I showed him a photo."

"A photo he took back in the New York days."

"Yes."

"Of your mother."

"Yes."

"And?"

"He cried," she said. "He said he should have been with me the whole time. He wanted to know everything about my life and my mother's."

"Did you tell him about Bobby Marx?"

"God, no. Why would I?" But I'd seen the hitch in her fingernail tracing before she answered. Huh.

We sat quiet awhile.

"Talk about Josh Whipple," Randall finally said, and turned to me. "This is key."

"I met Josh while I was researching my father."

"Researching him?" Randall said. "Before, you called it stalking."

"I was joking, for Christ's sake." She fake-laughed and touched Randall's arm, then looked at me. "During my research, my stalking"—she rolled her eyes—"I followed Tander to Motorenwerk, where he shot the breeze for a good long time. It piqued my curiosity. Who spends forty-five minutes at a garage when they're not having a car fixed?"

"He was having a car restored," I said.

"Of course, but I didn't know that. So when Josh took his lunch break, I managed to stumble into him and start a conversation."

"You pumped him for info."

"Josh was . . . an opportunist." Randall and I glanced at each other, read each other's minds: *He wasn't the only one.* "He smelled money at Motorenwerk," she said, "and he wanted a slice. I could respect that."

"You started seeing him."

"He was intimidated by me, a black woman nearly old enough to be his mother, but I got him past that. I was the third black person he ever spoke with in his life. Yes, the *third*. He remembered precisely."

I said, "When did you realize Josh was something other than a garden-variety country bumpkin?"

"Once he got past the 'aw shucks' stuff, I saw he was a lot smarter than he let on. And he never talked about his upbringing."

"So?"

"I talked about *mine*," she said. "Including the Bobby Marx part. Josh and I spent a lot of time staring up at ceilings, side by side, do you see? I opened up to this kid, unloaded all this baggage, and he gave me nothing in return."

"You got curious," I said. "You *researched* him." Same way she'd researched Phigg.

Her skin was darker than Randall's, but I saw her blush.

"You bet I did. And got my money's worth."

I waited.

"Only child, raised by his mother, never knew his father," Patty said. She was leaning in now, elbows on the table. The storyteller side of her had taken over, and she knew she had a doozy going. "So the mother died when Josh was nine. Fell down the basement stairs, broke her neck. Josh bounced over to an aunt and uncle in White River Junction. They had two girls. One night, their propane tank exploded.

Aunt, uncle, and girls, all dead. Josh was at a middle-school basketball game. He was twelve."

"Holy shit," I said. "Is this going where I think it's going?"

Patty raised an index finger to shush me. "The only other family was a grandmother near Utica. So Josh bounced *there*. The morning of his seventeenth birthday, he called the cops and said he was worried about granny, she'd locked herself in her room."

She paused to sip water, extending a pinky. She'd chosen the right line of work. I was holding my breath, knowing what came next, dying to hear it anyway. Patty knew that, relished it.

"So the cops showed up and broke through the door. Which Josh could easily have done himself, by the way." She screwed the cap on her water. "*Apparently,* Granny had tied one end of a pair of pantyhose around her neck, then the other around her iron bed's headboard. Then she'd just rolled off the side."

"Apparently," I said.

We all went quiet.

Three sets of killings. But the first one came when Josh Whipple was nine. Who suspects a nine-year-old? And the others were spread across a couple of states, in rural counties.

"The nearest anybody came to tying it all together," Patty said, guessing my thoughts, "was a feature story in a little Vermont paper. 'The Tragic Life of Joshua Whipple,' orphaned at nine, et cetera. Whoever wrote the piece was a sap. Had all the pieces laid out in front of him, but couldn't get past the Josh-as-victim angle. By then he was homeless, panhandling and riding the rails. He said after the article ran, some social-services do-gooders tracked him down and set him up for mechanic training. He eventually wound up working for Ollie."

We were quiet awhile.

"You think?" Randall finally said to me. "Nine years old?"

"What do *you* think?" I said to Patty.

She shrugged. "In light of recent events."

A semi Jake-braked past on Route 62, trimming speed as he neared Berlin's tiny downtown. I needed to press, needed to throw Patty Marx off balance. When the noise died I said, "So when were you and Phigg going to cross the border?"

Her double blink told me I'd nailed her. Randall straightened, too: This was new to him.

"I told you Josh tried to kill me not two hours ago," I said. "Guess I forgot to tell you we had time to chat. So I know Phigg was cashing out to run to Canada with you, devoted daughter. Live the artsy-fartsy life forever and ever."

"Complete and utter bullshit," she said.

"Like hell," I said. "I got you. I can read it in your eyes. But it's not enough. It doesn't fit."

"Do tell."

"You sold him the idea, didn't you?" I was figuring it out as I went along. "You wouldn't last six months carving ducks in a freezing cabin, any jackass can see that. You got Phigg to convert everything to cash because you were going to separate him from it, and sooner rather than later."

Patty Marx said nothing, looked hate-rays at me instead. I knew I'd scored. But there was another piece, a keystone that held it all together—and I couldn't find it. So we had a stare-down.

Finally Randall cleared his throat. "Shall we turn to practical matters? Patty, you know what's prudent and right."

"Turn state's evidence."

He nodded.

"I wasn't consulted and I wasn't present," she said. "Can we be absolutely clear on that? As far as I know, the Dufresne tragedy was a murder-suicide, even though . . ." She trailed off.

"Even though?" Randall said.

Patty locked eyes with him, and for the first time in ten minutes I saw no trace of journalist bullshit or legal-beagle bullshit. "Josh was in such a fine mood when he got back from Vermont," she said. "He chuckled to himself and sort of skipped around. When the news broke about Ollie and his mother, Josh explained how something like that might, just *might*, have happened." She swallowed, obviously scared even now as she recalled it. "The way he talked . . . the *detail*, for God's sake . . . things became pretty clear."

He took her hand in his. We sat quietly.

"So you weren't an accessory before the fact," Randall finally said. "All the more reason to hop over to the good guys' side. The sooner the better."

"I know that's the smart move," she said, patting his hand. "Still . . ." She looked at me, evaluating, and I knew what she was thinking.

Money changes people.

"Big picture!" Randall said, knuckle-rapping the table. "You are involved, in several senses of the word, with a man who kills anybody who looks at him crossways. No sum of money will improve your lot if he hangs you with your own panty hose."

Patty cut her eyes from him to me to him, still trying to see her way around to a big payday. Jesus, money makes people stupid.

I sighed, pulled my cell. "One button dials Josh," I said. "If you don't promise to dime him out, here's what'll happen. I'll punch you in the face while Randall takes your keys. I'll tell Josh exactly where you are. Randall and I will drive away, leave you here on foot. How long will it take Josh to find you?"

Patty touched her right jeans pocket.

Randall held up a set of car keys. "You left them in the ignition." He smiled. "That wasn't smart."

"Congratulations," I said. "Now I don't have to punch you in the face."

"Fucking assholes," she said, but her eyes clicked acceptance and she rose, arched her back, stretched. She'd tried her best, had played every card. She'd lost the trick, and she knew it. But she was still in the game.

What an operator. You could almost like her.

Almost.

"What are you going to do about Josh?" she said after a while.

I thought about Montreal and muscle man, the death sentence I'd laid on them. Was I prepared to take out Josh Whipple the same way? What if I was wrong again? My eyes met Randall's. He was thinking the same thing. "I want to give Trey a heads-up and find my father," I said. "Let the cops take care of Josh."

We headed for Framingham. The all-news radio station said state cops and FBI had swarmed "Motorworks"—they screw everything up—in Rourke, New Hampshire. An FBI spokeswoman confirmed the search had to do with the deaths of garage owner Oliver Dufresne and his mother. FBI wouldn't say more, wouldn't comment on why drug-sniffing dogs were part of the show.

I thought about calling the Framingham cops or the staties but couldn't see how I'd do it without getting hauled in myself. Got an idea, texted McCord: *Tell MA cops look 4 josh whipple, beige altima/taurus, sutton area, last seen purg chasm*

I hoped McCord got something good out of this mess. But had a feeling he wouldn't.

When we pulled up at my house, Trey's rented Dodge wasn't in the driveway. Inside, Kieu pidgined that he was gone and that Myna Roper was napping in a bedroom. Kieu tried to explain where Trey was, but I couldn't understand. About the time we both got good and frustrated, she rubbed her belly and pointed at me with a question on her face. I nodded like crazy. She got a bunch of stuff from the fridge and started making a batch of the shrimp-and-noodles thing I loved.

Randall helped Kieu cook. Patty Marx, who according to Randall hadn't said a word on the ride down, wanted her laptop. I said no goddamn way, and took her cell to boot. "So the deal is I'm a virtual prisoner?" she said.

"Yes," I said.

I motioned Tuan to follow me to the second-floor apartment. I had propped the door open so the cats had the run of the house, but I suspected they mostly stayed upstairs. Both cats had been smacked around some before I got them and were stranger-wary.

I freshened their food and water, cleaned their box. Tuan said something in Vietnamese that ended in a question. After a few tries I figured he wanted to know the cats' names. "This one's Dale," I said. "Dale Earnhardt Senior. Died February 18, 2001, at Daytona." I pointed toward the food dish. "That's Davey over there. Davey Allison died July 13, 1993, in a helicopter wreck. I beat him a couple times in Busch races. He was about my age."

Then Kieu barked something up the stairs and Tuan pulled my sleeve.

I said, "Food ready?" Rubbed my belly.

Tuan smiled and nodded and buzzed downstairs before I could stand.

Kieu had piled a serving platter with shrimp and noodles. We all dug in.

We were mostly finished when Trey stepped in the kitchen door. He must have kicked off his sneakers on the deck, because he stood in damp white socks and the lower six inches of his pant legs were wet.

After introducing Patty, I motioned Trey out to the deck. "Where you been?" I said, closing the kitchen door behind me.

"You advised me to stash the money."

"I was thinking about a safe-deposit box," I said, looking at his wet pant legs.

"I thought of a better place. No key required."

"Safe?"

"Safer than safe," he said, then laughed. "Safe *as* a safe."

"You want to tell me where?"

"What's the old saying? Three can keep a secret as long as two are dead."

"Come *on*, Trey."

"I need to clean up," he said, and stepped inside.

Randall and I drank coffee on the deck. Soon Trey stepped from the kitchen in fresh clothes, his hair wet. Instead of pulling up a chair he just squatted, the backs of his thighs pressed tight to his calves. He folded his arms across his knees and said, "What's going on?"

"You know Josh Whipple, the kid I told you about from Motoren-werk?" I said. "If Patty Marx is right, he's a flat-out psycho. Got started killing his mother when he was nine years old."

"Mother of God."

"Killed aunts, uncles, cousins, grannies," I said. "It was him killed your father, Ollie Dufresne, and Ollie's mom."

Trey worked his mouth. After a while he said, "What about the police, Conway?"

"They're looking for him. I hope they get him soon. But he knows about your father's stash, and he wants it."

"He can have every penny if he'll let us alone," Trey said.

I was proud of him. There aren't a lot of people can kiss seventy-five grand good-bye, especially once they've got it spent in their heads. "Wish it were that simple," I said. "But there's more dough. A lot more."

"Where?"

"Wish I knew." I had an idea, but wanted to keep it to myself.

"Tactically speaking," Randall said, "the primary question is whether Josh can find us."

I shook my head. "Thought about that. The house is still in my friend's name, and Josh never heard of him. Takes a year or more for the records to transfer and the databases to catch up."

"So this is a safe base of operations," Randall said.

I nodded.

"I know you well enough to guess what happens next," he said. Trey watched our conversation like a tennis match.

"So tell me," I said.

"We're going to take a run at Josh."

"*I'm* going to. I need you to keep an eye on things down here."

"But we just agreed this is a safe house."

"Belt and suspenders."

Randall smiled with one corner of his mouth. "When you find Monsieur Whipple, what are your, ah, intentions?"

"Give him to the cops."

"Really?"

"Really. I don't go looking for . . . for the things I run into."

"You do manage to find them, though."

"Yes," I said. "I do."

"Ever wonder why?"

"No."

"Yours is but to do or die," Randall said, and snorted a laugh. I didn't bother to ask what the hell he meant.

CHAPTER TWENTY-FIVE

Inside the house, I worked my cell. Called Charlene. No word on Fred. I hemmed and tap-danced, then finally asked her to stay away from her house, to come to Framingham after work instead.

"Why in God's name would I do that?"

Shit. "One of the players in this Tander Phigg thing is bad news," I said.

"So?"

"So he might come looking for me."

"He might show up on *my* doorstep looking for *you*?"

"He busted into my truck today. Your address is on the registration."

"And that," she said, "is how things go when Conway Sax is in your life."

I said nothing.

"*Jesus*, Conway!" Click.

Waiting. I'm better at it than I used to be. Prison does that.

Long evening. To pass time I prowled the yard, picking up construction scrap. Cell in one pocket, cordless home phone in another, hoping for word on Josh.

On Fred.

Looking down, I started to round the corner into the backyard . . . and heard a voice that stopped me.

Myna Roper. With all hell breaking loose, I'd forgotten about her. I slowed, stuck my head around the corner, looked at the deck.

She sat next to Trey on folding chairs. She was talking, he was listening. Spread across their laps was an oversize three-ring binder. Myna would point at something in the binder, talk about it, look at it a few seconds, flip the page. Next time the page flipped, I saw a black-and-white photo.

Myna was showing Trey his father's five happy years.

In her trailer, she'd pointed at Tander's stunning picture of her and claimed it was the only memento she saved from back then.

It was a lie.

I was glad.

I smiled, backed away, and walked softly to the front porch.

The next morning I headed north before dawn. I was dying to get in touch with McCord, see what the Motorenwerk task force had turned up, but with things as hot as they were, it couldn't be good for him to have cell contact with me.

McCord was thinking the same way. As I worked north on Route 495, a text buzzed in from a strange number: *Know who this is?*

Smart. He'd bought an el cheapo prepaid cell. I texted back: *U drive a charger. Mwerks search?*

H yes, $ no

Thoro?

They tore it apart

Thx

Use this #

Duh

So the task force had found heroin traces in Ollie's garage, but no big pile of money.

Huh.

So why did I still think Phigg's Mercedes was the key? Why'd I think I could find what thirty cops with Sawzalls had missed?

Because I knew the pride Ollie had taken in stashing drugs. Because I knew Phigg's obsession with the car.

Because the suicide mission, the stupid odds, the brass-balls attack is what you live for.

Okay, that, too.

I drove and I thought, trying to click pieces in place.

Patty Marx showed up a year and a half ago, did the tender reunion bit with Tander Phigg, and sold him a horseshit vision of the two of them in Canada. Phigg bought it and started cashing out.

At some point, I still believed—despite the thirty cops tearing apart Motorenwerk and coming up dry—Phigg had Ollie hide the money in the Mercedes. He'd somehow figured out Ollie's drug connection. The knowledge had to be his leverage, and it explained why Phigg and Ollie hated each other from the get-go. Phigg made the deal worth Ollie's while with seventy-five thousand untraceable—but kept the whip hand by paying only on delivery.

I played with ideas. Josh hadn't been working at the shop for long, so the Mercedes could have been all buttoned up and buried under a car cover by the time he hit the scene. Then maybe he got a whiff of the deal via Phigg's big mouth. It was easy to picture Phigg bullshitting around at Motorenwerk, saying golly he was broke but not really, wink wink. It was the type of thing he'd do. And smart-as-a-whip Josh, acting dumb and doing oil changes, wouldn't miss a word.

You could build a scene where Phigg owed Ollie the seventy-five grand from the pump house—stash one—but was holding back for some reason, and couldn't get his Mercedes—stash two—until he paid up. Mexican standoff.

And you could picture Josh getting nosy, antsy—two big wads of money so close he could nearly touch them.

You could picture him forcing the issue. It felt right.

But something wouldn't click. I sighed. The more I chased it, the greasier it would be. Had to wait until it came to me. So I headed for Motorenwerk.

But had a stop to make first.

I slowed when I saw the mailbox embedded in the steel rims, pulled slowly down the dirt road to minimize bumps and dust. The sun was just rising behind me, and as I rolled into the Beets' clearing I noticed that for the first time, the goddamn dog behind the main house wasn't howling and going nuts.

I looked to my left.

Black Escalade, Quebec plates. All four tires and wheels were off, the SUV sitting on half-assed jack stands of cinder blocks and wood. Best of all, the rear portion of the roof had been hacksawed off to turn the thing into a huge four-door pickup truck.

For all I knew, the dog out back wasn't howling because he'd finally been fed a decent meal.

I backed out. Didn't feel as bad as I'd thought I would.

Heroin.

As I passed Dot's Place in Rourke, a block and a half from Mechanic Street, the thing I'd forgotten, the piece that prevented everything from clicking into place, hit me. It hit hard, the way those things always do. Hard enough so that I pulled over in front of a real-estate storefront with yellowing poster board in its window, the poster board covered with edges-curling snapshots of homes that would never sell.

I called my house. Waited, three rings, glanced at my Seiko, not yet seven o'clock, four rings, come on, don't let it go to voice mail. . . .

"Yes?"

"Trey?"

"Yes."

"It's Conway. Get Patty Marx. Hurry."

She'd slept on the family room couch, basically our prisoner though nobody said so, Randall and I nervous over what she'd do if we sent her away. It took Trey forty-five seconds to wake her and get her to the phone, me staring at my watch, clicking possibilities.

" 'Lo," she finally said.

"You researched Josh Whipple," I said. "The Utica killing happened when he was seventeen, and next thing you told us a Vermont newspaper profiled him."

"The tragic orphan. Right. So?"

"Where in Vermont?"

"What do you mean?"

"What paper? What town?"

"Jesus, I don't know. Want me to look it up?"

"Yes."

I waited some more as the laptop was fired up, the folder and Word document found, the link followed. What had Josh said at Purgatory Chasm? *I'll tell Fred you said hello!* I'd assumed it was bullshit talk, that Josh had somehow learned Fred was missing and was shooting me a little *fuck-you-very-much* look.

Could it have been more than that? As I listened to Patty walk back to the phone, my belly prepped me for the worst, the way it always does.

"Brattleboro Reformer," she said.

It was the town I didn't want to hear. But knew I would.

"Brattleboro Reformer," she said again. "Got it? You there?"

"Have Trey put Randall on."

"You're welcome," Patty said. I heard grousing.

Trey got back on the line. "Isn't Randall with you, Conway?" he said.

"What?"

"He left shortly after you did. He said he was backing you up. I assumed you had arranged it."

Jesus Christ, that was a bad move. If I was right, and my belly told me I was, Fred was with Josh—and could lead him right to the house. And Josh had every reason to believe there was at least seventy-five grand there.

"Listen up, Trey," I said, keeping my voice calm. I needed him steady. "Wake everybody *now* and get the hell out of that house."

"But—"

"Now, Trey. Pile in cars, pajamas and all, and drive to a police station, okay? Wait for me to call with an all clear. *Now.*"

Spun my truck around, buried the throttle, dialed Randall. "I know you followed me," I said when he picked up. "Bad move. Worry about it later. Right now, let's make tracks for Framingham."

"Why?"

"Josh can find my house."

"How?"

I looked at my speedometer. Eighty-six and climbing.

"How, Conway?"

"I think Fred's working with him."

"Oh, Jeez—"

I clicked off and drove.

Brattleboro Fucking Vermont. A hippy-dippy town, bums welcome. Hell, in the summer the whole town common turned into a big homeless camp, Panhandling Central.

Fred spent summers there for fifteen years at least. Somewhere along the way, he must have met Josh Whipple. Must have spewed hate about his son, the big NASCAR driver who never did a god-damn thing for him. The son who didn't even offer him a lift when they saw each other at a toll booth.

Before Fred took off, Charlene had heard those mystery phone calls.

When he took off, we assumed he'd gone on a bender.

Maybe he had.

But maybe he'd visited Josh and pitched revenge.

I prayed I wasn't too late.

But knew I was.

CHAPTER TWENTY-SIX

Forty minutes later in Framingham, I stepped from my truck into a nightmare, the kind where you run and run through hip-deep mud. I knew right away Trey hadn't cleared the house in time. Why the hell not? He should've had time.

I had to park thirty yards up the street because an ambulance and three Framingham Police Crown Vics clogged my driveway. One cop squatted behind his open door, service automatic in one hand, microphone in the other. He looked fourteen years old. He was scared shitless. I ran past him, turned up the driveway, saw Trey's rented Dodge blocked in by the ambulance.

Nightmare sound track, the three types of sirens you hear at these things: cops, ambulance, and coming up the road a Framingham Fire Department truck, blatting looky-loos aside. They always send a fire truck, and nobody ever knows why.

There was something else in the sound track. Something buried in the mix, something I couldn't ID yet.

"The fuck outta the way!" It was an EMT, pulling the crash cart from the ambulance. I let him pass, then followed him across the brand-new deck and into the kitchen. He left the crash cart on the deck. On the kitchen floor, another EMT was working on something that looked like a bloody pile of bath towels.

It wasn't bath towels. It was Kieu Phigg, all hundred pounds of her. Barefoot, cotton pants, cotton top the color of an unripened banana, straight dark hair.

There wasn't much of a face left. There was blood and pulp and one eye that may or may not be aware of what was going on.

As both EMTs worked on Kieu, I finally ID'd the buried part of the nightmare sound track. Trey Phigg stood in the doorway leading to the stairs and living room. He pressed his hands to his head, a fist-ful of hair in each. His eyes were perfect circles. His mouth, too.

He was screaming.

Not screaming anything in particular. No words. He was making a howl that went on and on, and each time he ran out of wind he took a deep breath and screamed again. There was no comprehension in his eyes. He didn't recognize me. He just screamed and tried to pull his hair out.

Trey would have to wait. I stepped past him and turned to go up-stairs. But I heard heavy footsteps and a cop-belt rattle, heard a voice say, "Upstairs clear."

I was lucky. It was Matt Bogardis clomping down the stairs, clip-ping his radio mic to his shirt pocket. I've known Matt a long time, since before he got on the cops. He said, "What the hell, Conway?"

"It's my house."

"I know. What the hell?"

"I don't know. My cats okay up there?"

"Didn't see 'em; must be hiding," he said, and took a left into the kitchen. "Stick around, okay?"

I said nothing. Walked into the living room as Matt and one of the EMTs tried to calm Trey.

And there he was. He was so still, so quiet, a couple cops might have walked past without noticing him for all I knew.

Tuan Phigg.

He sat on the floor a few feet from the TV, watching a blue puppet try to pogo-stick.

In the kitchen, Trey's scream wound down. When the last one died he switched to something else: He said, "Ow." Like he'd bumped his knee on a table. Then he said it again. "Ow." His voice was hoarse: He'd screamed his throat raw. "Ow," over and over.

Tuan stared, sitting cross-legged, rocking a little at the waist.

I knelt. I stroked his hair. I said his name.

He eye-locked the TV.

I picked him up. He didn't resist, but as I carried him out he stared at the TV until he couldn't see it.

A voice said, "Who the fuck are you?" As I turned to face the voice I heard fumbling, then *"Freeze!"*

It was another cop, stepping from the smaller first-floor bedroom. Like the guy out front, he looked very young. "Got one out here, Matt!" he hollered, his gun shaking. "Release the child! *Release the child,* motherfucker!"

They watch cop movies, cop TV shows. They think it's how they're supposed to talk.

Matt Bogardis stepped through the doorway. "Settle down," he said to the other cop. "He's the home owner. He's okay."

I watched the other cop's Adam's apple bob as he gulped, relieved. He nodded toward the bedroom he'd just left. "Get an EMT in there," he said to Matt. "Got another vic, an old lady."

Jesus. I'd forgotten about Myna. And where the hell was Patty?

While Matt hollered for an EMT and stepped into the bedroom, I went to the kitchen, making sure my body blocked Tuan's view of his mother. Trey sat in a kitchen chair, an untouched glass of water on the table in front of him. Two EMTs worked on Kieu, not giving up, but the way her face looked . . . there couldn't be a lot of urgency anymore.

"Trey," I said. "You don't need to be in here. Come to the living room."

Nothing. He stared dead ahead. I saw dots of blood at his temples where he'd torn his hair.

"Trey," I said, rocking his shoulder with one arm, blocking Tuan's view as the boy squirmed.

Nothing.

I got pissed. "Trey Phigg!" I punched his right bicep—harder than I meant to. "Be a man!"

The way I said it made the EMT turn to look at me. "Easy, bro."

"His kid needs him!"

The EMT made an *okay-okay-back-off* gesture and turned away.

Trey Phigg stood. I passed him Tuan. "Your boy needs you," I said. "Get him out of this room."

As Trey took Tuan, I made sure his eyes registered what was going on. Good: The thousand-yard stare was fading. Trey was coming back.

I hustled into the small bedroom. It was crowded: Myna Roper on the twin bed, the EMT working over her, both cops watching. But one whiff and one glance told me everything I needed to know.

"She just passed out," I said. "Drunk."

"It's not even nine," Matt said.

I pointed at the bourbon and vermouth that topped the press-wood dresser in the corner.

"I think he's right, fellas," the EMT said as Myna began to snuffle and blink.

In the living room, Trey sat on the sofa. Tuan faced him, legs spraddled, and played with his father's shirt buttons and spoke soft Vietnamese.

I said, "What happened? Why didn't you clear everybody out?"

"I tried," he said. "Tuan slipped out the front door while I was shaking Miz Roper. You've seen how quick he is. He was three houses down by the time I got outside. Then he spotted a cat in the bushes, and that was that: I had to chase him down. But I swear we weren't gone ten minutes."

"Then what happened?"

"Coming back up the driveway, I heard a noise like somebody beating a rug. I joked with Tuan that mommy was overcleaning again. She can never relax, you know?"

I nodded. Needed info *now,* but I had to let Trey tell it his way.

"I heard a man's voice and I knew something was wrong," he said. "The voice kept saying '*Where? Where? Where?*' And then I'd hear that rug-beating noise. So I picked up the pace. And then I heard . . ." Trey paused for a deep breath and shook on the inhale, holding Tuan close to his chest. The boy wrapped his arms around his daddy's neck. "You know the sound a Ping-Pong ball makes when you hit it and it breaks?"

I went to one knee. "Was it Josh Whipple?"

"I'll never forget that sound. I don't know what this Josh looks like."

"Younger than you, redhead, slim."

Trey nodded and held his son. In a few seconds he began to cry. I rose, got set to leave. From the bedroom I heard Myna. She sounded pissed. She said she'd just been resting her eyes, was an old woman allowed to *do* that anymore, and what in the good Lord's name were all those sirens for? Myna's voice made me wonder again where Patty was. I hadn't noticed her Jetta outside, but I hadn't been looking for it.

I turned back to Trey. "When you came in, Josh was still here?"

He nodded.

"Why didn't he start pounding on *you?*"

"I told him where I hid the money," Trey said, staring at nothing. "If Tuan hadn't run out the door . . . if I'd grabbed him a little faster . . ."

"Where's the money?"

"Right where we found it."

"What?"

"The false floor, the shack in New Hampshire," he said. "I

thought since the shack had already been searched . . ." His voice trailed ". . . I thought that was very clever of me."

As I left, stepping around the EMTs while they put Kieu on a backboard, I heard Trey in the living room. "Very clever of me," he said over and over.

Matt Bogardis had told me to stick around. He'd said it as a cop, not as a pal. But I needed to go. I angled, ducked, cut through backyards. It worked: By the time I made the street, I'd cleared the perimeter set up by the cops.

As I neared my truck I saw Randall had parked up at the mouth of the street, knowing that if he drove inside the perimeter they wouldn't let him out. That was smart, I thought. *Very clever,* Trey had said.

Yeah. Me and Randall, clever as hell. Now Josh was gone, Patty was probably with him, they were flying toward the seventy-five grand, and Kieu Phigg was dead or close to it.

Very clever.

I backed toward Randall and saw he hadn't parked after all: His father's wagon was at a crazy angle. And its hood was buckled. Huh.

Closer. Now I saw why: Randall had rammed a car trying to leave the street.

A Jetta.

"Hot damn," I said out loud, putting the F-150 in neutral and hopping out.

Patty Marx sat in her driver's seat, looking dazed. The car's left front corner was destroyed. Randall stood next to the car holding its keys. "I was up here blocking the street," he said, "and I watched her sweet-talk a cop and roll past the perimeter. It seemed like a good idea to halt further progress."

"It was," I said, grabbing the Jetta's door handle. It didn't budge.

"Crunched shut in the wreck," Randall said, and nodded toward my house. "How bad?"

"I think Kieu's dead." I looked around as I spoke. Spotted a rusty old wheel near a curb, stepped to it, hefted it.

"Dear Lord," Randall was saying. "Conway, I . . . I thought trailing you was the smart play."

"Very clever," I said. "Lot of that going around."

Then I heaved the steel wheel at the driver's window, not much caring if it went through and wrecked Patty Marx's face. It didn't, but it shattered the safety glass nicely. I elbowed most of the glass out, reached across Patty, undid her seat belt, grabbed her jeans jacket with both hands, hauled her out the window.

She screamed. Down the street, a cop turned. He gave us a long look, spoke into his shoulder mic, and began walking our way. With his right hand on his holster.

"Stay here," I said to Randall. "Deal with the cops, Trey, the hospital." I walked Patty Marx to my truck.

I didn't know what I expected to find at Jut Road, other than an empty space where seventy-five grand used to be. But I didn't know what the hell else to do either. Called McCord's real cell—not the prepaid one—got voice mail, said the staties should head for Rourke and look for Josh Whipple.

I aimed north and tried to muster adrenaline. Felt empty, heavy, slow on my feet. I thought about Fred telling Josh how to find my house. Thought about Patty Marx, playing both ends against the middle and then some. Betrayal all around.

"How'd you work it with Phigg?" I said after a while.

"Fuck you." She twisted the rearview mirror to look at her face. Made a tutting sound, pulled Kleenex from her jacket pocket, began dabbing at air-bag dust and tiny glass shards.

"How'd you work it?"

Long pause. "I explained it in straightforward fashion," she finally said, still wiping. "I told him Bobby Marx laid hands on me four hundred and three times. That was a stone-cold fact. I kept a tally on the flyleaf of my Bible. The figure I had in mind was a thousand dollars a pop."

"Straight blackmail?"

"That's the way I planned it. But the jackass went and fell in love with me." That last part hung for a split second too long before she said, "As an estranged daughter, of course, and a link to his oh-so-happy past."

"And the Canada plan fell out of that."

"I needed a tool to convince him to liquidate everything."

"I can't believe he went for that," I said. "He wasn't a dumb guy."

"Around me he was."

It didn't hang together. I had that heavy feeling again, knowledge bearing down. "What was the stick?"

"Hmm?"

"The carrot was a chance to help his daughter who'd had a helluva rough break," I said. "But what was the stick?"

Nothing. I glanced at Patty as we neared the exit for Route 119. And I knew. And my heart hurt.

We played chicken, neither wanting to say it.

The game lasted 2.3 miles. I lost. "You fucked him," I said.

Nothing.

"Deny it," I said. "I'm begging you."

Patty Marx said nothing.

My heart hurt.

"Please deny it."

She folded her arms.

"You slept with Tander Phigg," I said. "*Then* you told him he was your father."

"I didn't kill him," she said so quickly I barely made it out.

"You must have helped."

"No no no! Josh knocked him out, then lifted him by himself. He's ridiculously strong."

I thought back to the first day I saw Josh. He'd carried a tire and wheel under each arm like they were spare pillows.

"The cops never said anything about Phigg being knocked out." But I knew they weren't looking for anything like that, were content with their path-of-least-resistance suicide theory.

"Josh knew how to half fill kids' balloons with sand," Patty said, "and tunk people on the head, knock them out with minimal damage. He bragged about it."

"A sap," I said, nodding. "Old school." It fit. It worked. But then I thought of something. "Did he hit *me* in the head, that day at Motorenwerk?" I fingered the lump. "Because that was no dainty minimal-damage shot. Busted me open."

"It was him," she said, "and that one wasn't *supposed* to be dainty. He thought he could scare you off."

We rolled north in silence.

After maybe ten minutes Patty said, "I won't cop to that. Not in public. I'll dime out Josh all day long, but if you mention . . . what you just said about Tander and me, I'll deny it. And I'll sell the denial very, very well."

I said nothing. Everything felt so heavy.

"What do you say to that?" Patty said.

"You won't have to dime out Josh."

I felt her looking at me. "You are a very serious man," she finally said.

"I assume Josh and Fred met in Brattleboro?"

She nodded. "That's what Josh said. After his granny died in Utica—after he killed her, as we now suppose—he took his shitty little inheritance and bummed around a few years. Wound up broke in Vermont."

"So? What was the connection?"

"When I told Josh that Tander was meeting one Conway Sax for breakfast, Josh looked like he'd won the lottery. He said he had a lever for you."

"How'd he make the connection between my father and me?" I said. "I hadn't seen Fred but once in fifteen years."

"Apparently you were all he talked about with the homeless set," she said. "His son, the big-deal NASCAR driver."

CHAPTER TWENTY-SEVEN

He talked that way about me?" I said.

"I guess he did."

We were quiet awhile.

"What was the pitch?" I said. "What did Josh promise Fred?"

"The usual, I would guess," she said, rubbing thumb to fingers.

But that wasn't it. I didn't bother to tell her. I thought about watching a light turn green, about driving away from Fast Freddy Sax with a blank IOU in my hand.

Handing me to Josh on a silver platter must have meant more to Fred than any payday. It hurt my insides to think about it, but there it was.

You try to tamp down your hopes. You prep yourself for disappointment.

Hope fights through anyway. Hope that Josh's crappy old Audi would croak on the way here. Hope that a heads-up cop had pulled him over. Hope that he couldn't swing loose the false floor by himself, that I'd catch him tangled in rope, vulnerable.

We eased down Jut Road and saw right away the hidey-hole had been opened. It dangled amid a mess of climbing rope.

"Hell," I said. Climbed from my truck, looked down at tire tracks made by an all-wheel-drive car—Josh's Audi.

He was long gone.

But hope fights through. I walked to the edge of the slope, looked over the half-assed sling he'd rigged. Slipped down the steep muck barely under control, got one work boot wet. Looked up.

Gone gone gone. The money and Josh both.

"Well?" Patty said.

"Gone." I had my hands in my back pockets, was looking at the river.

"What do you think he'll do?" she said, shouting. "Make a border run?"

"Safer to stay in the States. Ditch his car, make it to a bus station, he can be invisible in eighteen hours."

"Still," she said, shouting again over the Souhegan's rush, "I bet it's tempting to head for Canada when you're this far north."

If she hadn't kept hollering like that, babbling in a way that was unusual for her, he would have pulled it off. The river noise and woods thrum was plenty of cover.

But half a beat after the second time Patty shouted, I realized she was making noise to cover for Josh. I spun, threw myself against the steep bank, and looked up. As I did I heard a sound like two one-by-twos slapping together, then a flat *plint* as a bullet hit water.

There was Josh Whipple, Ollie's P35 in his hand, surprised he hadn't just killed me. I could understand the surprise: He was braced on one knee and had fired from eight feet away with a nice downward angle.

The moment of the adrenaline spurt is a lot like what happens in racing: Even though your world, your life, hinges on the next three seconds, an additional branch of perception opens up and you take in more data than people think possible. After a race at Thompson

Speedway in Connecticut, one driver commented that on the third lap, a squirrel had tried to cross the track in turn three. I told him that was no squirrel, that was a chipmunk, and it was the *fourth* lap. Another driver overheard and asked if we were both blind, it was a *family* of chipmunks, and two of them made it, but he squished the papa with his left front tire.

So: The work boots dig in, splayed out duck style, chopping through muck for traction. Josh is above me and to my left, but instead of charging straight at him I crab to my right. This forces Josh to swing the P35 to his left, across his body, making for a tougher shot. I remember the gun's been modified to fire heavier-than-stock .40 S&W loads, which give it hellacious stopping power but make it hard to fire accurately.

There's that second round, fired as I make the top of the slope. As I hoped, Josh has swung the P35 too far—this one whangs past my right shoulder as I turn to charge him. Next to his leg puddles a white trash bag, kitchen-size, its plastic drawstring tied in a nice bow. That's the seventy-five grand: I watched Trey bag it up, watched him tie the bow. Next to the bag stands Patty Marx, and I would swear in a court of law she is ignoring the semiautomatic pistol three feet from her ear, the two men trying their hardest to kill each other. She only has eyes for the sack of money.

I scrabble at Josh's shins, low low low, mostly because I slip as I charge, but it's a good move because his third shot whangs over my left shoulder. I hear it, and the *zzzzz* sound squirts more adrenaline, and I feel clever—*very clever,* the phrase of the day—for staying so low, and I take one last chopping step and angle upward, meaning to hit Josh with what football players call a form tackle, squared up, wrapping my arms around his torso.

And Josh, stepping back, off balance, panicking for the first time I've seen, flinches and grimaces and shoots me in the stomach.

———

Before I hit the water, arms locked around Josh as planned, I had time to feel like a jackass. Why hadn't I checked the shack before scrambling down to the river? Had Patty somehow warned him we were coming? Or had he decided on his own to stash his car and take me out right then? Any way you sliced it, I'd been stupid to not glance in the shack.

Then we slid into the river and the cold stole my wind. Josh ended up on top of me. My head settled into the muck. I stared through clear water at the sky.

Josh kneed me in the balls. When I coiled up out of instinct, he stood, hesitated. I wondered if he was getting set to shoot me, then figured he couldn't find the gun. I took a weak kick at his legs. Nothing. He jumped in the air and landed on me with both feet.

That was when the gunshot shock wore off and my right side, maybe two inches above my pants pocket, began to hurt worse than anything I'd ever felt. A warm trickle front and back told me the bullet had gone through and through.

The warm trickle.

The icy water.

The stomped balls.

I almost gave up.

Almost.

Instead: Josh bent over, reaching for my throat with both hands. I waited until he was fully committed, saw the hard smile in his eyes, kicked *him* in the balls. He twitched at the last instant or I would've had him. As it was, he fell next to me and rested on hands and knees.

I didn't know what to do, but I needed to get the hell away from there. I half stood, facing the shore, and as Josh rose with a good-size rock in his right hand, I used what was left of my leg strength to flop away into the Souhegan.

He dove after me, wrapped his arms. I grabbed a lungful of air as Josh dragged me under, my belly facing the sky. I reached for the pier that ought to be behind me. My fingertips brushed it, slipped away, grabbed, missed. Josh was bear-hugging us both to the bottom. He hadn't been shot, and he was young, and he was going to hold his breath until I passed out.

There—fingertips on the pier again. I got my hands around it and began to climb, climb. I felt Josh loosen his arms to adjust his crushing grip. Before he could, I wrapped my legs around his torso, scissors style. He tried to move his arms, couldn't, thrashed and panicked.

And then my face was above water, my arms clamped around the pier. I breathed, breathed, had never known air to have an actual *taste* like this.

And all pain, all wounds, all bleeding, all cold were pushed from my mind as I squeezed Josh Whipple underwater with my legs, using every muscle, holding him under the Souhegan a full five minutes after I knew he was dead.

CHAPTER TWENTY-EIGHT

Exactly three weeks later, on a Saturday morning, I stood in front of a roll-up door on Mechanic Street, put two fingers in my mouth, cranked off a whistle. The pit bull sounded off. The Mexican looked through a small window, stared for ten seconds, vanished. In another ten seconds he stepped from the shop's front door, kicking at the pit bull to keep it inside.

"The fuck you want?"

"You remember me?"

"Who's gonna forget you? You all over the news."

"I need to do some work in there," I said, jerking a thumb at Motorenwerk. "Cops ever roll by these days?"

"Hardly ever. Things pretty much back to normal."

"Anybody swings past, I could use a heads-up."

"I got work of my own."

"Pay you a grand to sit out here in your favorite chair and call me if a cruiser comes by."

"You got shot, uh?"

I nodded.

"Save your grand," he said, sitting and waving a hand. "This could be entertaining."

We pulled our cells. I set mine so he had a unique ring tone: If a cop came by, the Mexican would speed-dial me and I wouldn't even have to pick up.

They said McCord found me on the riverbank with Josh's dead body still between my thighs. I'd either been unwilling to let go of him or, more likely they said, unable—muscles spasmed, locked up. It made for a hell of a picture: me dog-paddling in from the pier, using my arms only, with a leg-lock on Josh Whipple.

I nearly bled to death and I nearly froze to death. When the New Hampshire State Police tried to shuffle me into some podunk hospital, Charlene and a half dozen lawyers she could afford laid a near-death experience on *them,* and so I wound up in Mass. General getting the best care in the world.

I'd suffered the easiest wound you can get north of your ass, my surgeon told me proudly: low on my right side, through and through, no vital organs pierced, an abductor muscle "molested" (the surgeon's word).

Easy wound or not, that molested muscle hurt like hell as I crossed Mechanic Street, scoping out Motorenwerk. The shop had that *Twilight Zone* look that businesses get after they go out of business but before their guts are auctioned off.

The same squadron of lawyers that terrorized the New Hampshire Staties made sure I never spent so much as an hour in a cop shop, even when I was healthy enough. By then, Josh Whipple's thirteen-year murder spree was the biggest story in the country. People wanted me to write a book. People wanted me to do a reality show. Network news shows sent fruit baskets.

I had the fruit baskets forwarded to Diana Patience Roper. She'd changed her name again: Patty Marx was dead, long live Diana. The Massachusetts Staties grabbed her three hours after she took the trash bag full of money and stole my truck. When it was time for her phone call, she buzzed a producer she knew at a tabloid TV show and sketched out her story.

Her memoirs come out in October. The other day, Sophie saw her on the cover of *Us* magazine.

An embarrassed cop is a hardworking cop. Two weeks too late, the geniuses on the Josh Whipple task force confirmed what no-longer-Patty had told me: Phigg and Ollie each had very minor bruising on the backs of their heads where Josh had sapped them before hoisting them into necktie nooses.

I hadn't noticed the skylights in Motorenwerk's roof until now. Standing in the shop, with the unlockable window closed behind me, I was grateful for them—plenty of morning light.

As McCord had warned me, the cops had torn the hell out of the place. It was one thing to be thorough, but a lot of what I saw was plain mean. Window glass stomped, boxes of subassemblies swept to the floor. Like that. The work of bored, mean assholes.

They'd sliced the interior from Phigg's Mercedes, and they'd removed, drained, and cut open the fuel tank. I thought about the pride Ollie had shown when he talked about his work. To him, stashing drugs in cars was no different than doing a faithful restoration. The idea was to cover up your work once you'd *done* your work. It reminded me of the old Westerns, where the last thing a guy did to cover his tracks was walk backward wiggling a handful of brush in the dirt.

With a droplight in my hand, I lay flat on my back—my wound had hurt like hell when I'd swung under—and stared up at the car's underside. "Shit," I said out loud. If this was anything other than a quarter-century-old Mercedes that had spent most of its life on New England's winter-salted roads, Ollie Dufresne was a genius. No wonder the cops had focused on the interior.

I'd worked on this car myself, so I knew all its finicky, ahead-of-their-time systems looked just the way they should. The brake lines, the stupidly complex air-ride suspension, the steering rack, the fuel line—I'd replaced them all at least once, and they'd been untouched since. I saw nothing that looked like fresh paint, nothing that looked smooth or shiny when it ought to be rough or corroded.

The fuel line. Silver with light corrosion, quarter inch in diameter, attached to the left-side stiffening rib with stout brackets.

Why was I looking at a fuel line?

Like virtually all modern cars, the Mercedes had a unit body. That meant there was no traditional frame; the entire body served as the frame. Unit-body cars usually have two hollow rails running length-wise down their undersides. Civilians look at these rails and call them a frame, but they're not. They're just stiffening ribs.

And they're hollow.

They make a convenient place to hide the plumbing that runs from the front of a car to the back.

Like the fuel line.

I remembered like hell, wriggling on my back, looking up. Five, six years back, a fitting on Phigg's fuel line had cracked. It made a help of a mess and stink because the fuel line ran through the stiffening rib. Typical pain-in-the-ass German overengineering.

But I was positive: The fuel line had run through the rib. So why was I looking at a fuel line on the *outside* of that rib?

I wished for my reading glasses, crawled back and forth, ignored the worsening pain in my side. Finally I found what used to be the hole where the line disappeared into the rib. The hole had been filled, painted, and distressed perfectly. The setup was disguised so well I wouldn't have found it in a million years if I hadn't replaced the line myself.

Ollie *was* a genius.

I slid out from under and turned on the shop's air compressor, a good Ingersoll Rand unit. Jesus, it was loud. I winced at the hammering noise. But this was Mechanic Street, where there was nothing unusual about a compressor on a Saturday. I hoped. I hooked a plasma cutter to the air hose.

Three minutes later, I had safety goggles on and the business end of the cutter—it looked like the spray nozzle you screw on the end of a garden hose—was burning a twenty-seven-thousand-degree hole in the car's stiffening ribs. It took five minutes to cut a notch at each end of each rib, plus one neat line lengthwise.

I killed the plasma cutter and the air compressor, took a deep breath in the silence. I found a cat's-paw pry bar hanging above a tool bench, dove under the Mercedes again. Got the cat's paw deep into the line I'd just cut, levered. The steel gave way easier than I'd figured, moved a good half inch.

And showed me thick plastic.

I slid forward eighteen inches, pried again. Then again, then once more. Then I worked my way back, watching the gap spread. After a couple more trips from the rear of the rib to the front, metal fatigue took over and I just pushed the rib back. It was packed with plastic-wrapped packs.

Of money.

I knew at a glance they'd been wrapped by whomever had wrapped the money in Phigg's false floor. The plastic was industrial strength, and from the density, I guessed they'd sucked the air from each brick using one of those food-storage systems. Each brick was the length and width of a dollar bill and about three inches thick—the perfect thickness for the car's stiffening ribs.

I cat's-pawed seven bricks from the left rib, then went to work on the right, trying not to think about how much money I was dealing with. Finished up, shoved the money bricks out from under, climbed out, stood, tossed the goggles on a bench. I'd been here nearly two hours. Instinct screamed *Get the hell out*. I ignored it. The cops had never paid as much attention to Motorenwerk as they should've, and I could keep it that way if I did minor cleanup.

I crawled under the Mercedes one last time and bent the stiffening ribs to their original positions. Found a push broom, swept away metal dust and the crud that had fallen from the ribs. Put all the tools away, looked around. The place looked about the same as when I'd come in. Not one person in a hundred would notice I'd been here.

McCord would notice. But he wouldn't be coming by. He quit. Had dropped by the hospital to tell me.

"Why are you leaving the staties?" I'd said. "No good deed goes unpunished?"

"Something like that."

"What will you do?"

"Think I'll head up to Alaska. Walk the coast."

That was how he put it. Not hike, not backpack. He was going to walk the goddamn coast of Alaska.

"That's a lot of coast, isn't it?"

"That's okay," McCord said. "Got a good pair of boots." His joke must have tickled him, because he smiled a full quarter inch.

I looked around the garage, found a canvas tool bag that swallowed the fourteen money bricks. I started to leave, thought things through, stopped. Grabbed an X-ACTO knife, sliced through one brick's plastic, thumbed the brick. "Holy shit," I said out loud.

Like the bills in the other stash, these were old and beat up—laundered. But there were no fives, tens, or twenties here. Strictly fifties and hundreds.

"Holy shit," I said again.

Thinking about the Mexican outside, I pulled four grand and stuck it in my jeans pocket. Used red shop towels to cover the money, then grabbed a few decent power tools and filled the bag the rest of the way.

I smiled. To honest thieves, stolen tools are mother's milk. They might as well be cash.

I waddled across the street toward the Mexican, my side stinging.

The Mexican peered in the bag, spotted an air gun, a torque wrench, a new set of metric sockets, a few other things I'd grabbed.

Slow smile as he looked up. "Candy from a fucking baby, uh?"

I took the four grand from my pocket, pressed it into his hand. "You and me," I said. "Honest thieves."

"Just another day on Mechanic Street," he said, and waved a slow hand and walked through the door of his shop.

I never saw him again.

So I had a bag of money for Trey Phigg. That was something. Kieu had been a lot closer to death than I was. An eye socket that needed to be rebuilt nearly from scratch was the least of her injuries. Trey's health-insurance status was beyond sketchy. Charlene had been footing the bills. She didn't mind, but Trey did. Whatever was in the bag would make a dent.

That was about all the enthusiasm I could put together. I'd been driving around a lot, enough so Charlene worried. She wanted me to see a shrink. The closest I came was a visit to Vicky Lin, the doc at Cider Hill.

"This is more common than not," she'd said in her office. "I wish I could tell you otherwise."

"He was sober when he showed up here," I said. "That's the part I can't get around. Forty years shitfaced, then he sobered up like *that* for a couple of weeks. And now he's worse than ever."

She looked at her blotter and played with the indentation on her ring finger. When she caught me noticing, she stopped. "It seems Fred had a mission in mind when he got sober."

"To fuck me over."

"Revenge," she said, nodding. "It's powerful. Has Fred . . . approached you? Physically or by phone?"

"No. People see him around, they call me. Cops pick him up, but it's always a different town, and they never ID him till it's too late."

We sat. I'd only been out of the hospital two days, so I was sort of twisted in my chair to ease my wound.

"You've been through quite a bit," she finally said.

"Not as much as Fred." I winced to my feet and left.

Before Vicky's office door even closed, I wished I'd said more.

After that meet with Vicky, I'd driven out to Purgatory Chasm. It was where I wound up most days.

Every day, truth be told.

Today: not busy at all, dog-day heat keeping people away. One or two families out for a weekend activity, a few more serious hikers.

I tried to float, tried to let the bag of money cheer me up, tried not to think about Fred.

My cell rang. Charlene's home number, probably Sophie calling. She was worried as hell about me.

I didn't pick up.

I floated away. I dreamed of Minnesota. I never remember what happens in my dreams, but I do remember the overall vibe. If it's a good vibe, it was a Minnesota dream.

My eyes blinked, then snapped wide.

Jesus Christ.

My father stood not thirty yards away, right at the head of the main trail. He'd spotted me and frozen.

We stared each other down.

He'd aged twenty years in three weeks. Sunken cheeks, gray skin, a bum's no-color Windbreaker.

In his right hand he held a cardboard six-pack of Rolling Rock.

I knew it! my head screamed. *I knew he'd come here!*

I climbed from my truck like he was a deer I didn't want to scare.

I said his name, stepped toward him.

"That's close enough," he said.

"Past is past, Fred. Want to come home? Want to come to Charlene's?"

"That cocksucker Josh tricked me," Fred said. "Said we'd squeeze some money out of you, that was all."

"That's all over, Fred. Josh is out of the picture." I eased forward a few steps while I spoke. I was close enough to see Fred's eyes flashing from sanity to somewhere else and back.

"*I said that's close enough!*" He held up his six-pack to ward me off.

"You haven't cracked that sixer yet, have you?" I said. "So you're sober today. Why not keep it that way?"

My father's eyes flashed sane/not sane, back and forth. He took my offer seriously. "I *am* sober, ain't I?" he said. "Technically. Today."

"Hell yes you are."

"It's a good day to be sober."

"Hell yes it is," I said, and relaxed just a little as he lowered the six-pack.

So I was caught flat-footed when he took off down Purgatory Chasm. He disappeared from my view. I sprinted to the head of the trail, my side stinging.

Dear God, he was beautiful, just as he'd been thirty years ago. In the time I'd taken to run twenty yards on flat ground, he had mountain-goated forty through boulders. I caught a flash of green: Fred had pulled one Rolling Rock from the carton and tossed it over his shoulder like a grenade. It exploded on a rock. A mother holding her son's hand farther down the trail said, "Hey."

I hesitated half a beat. Then I took off.

It came back instantly, completely. That fully alive feeling, making twenty decisions every second—and yet no decisions at all, just running the rocks, floating, gravity my ally.

Fred was flying. What he was doing would be hard for the best athlete in the world. It was impossible for a healthy man in his seventies. For a lifelong drunk who could barely climb a flight of stairs, it was unreal. It was destiny.

I was closing on him. Another beer grenade exploded twenty-five yards ahead. Then a third, twenty yards ahead. I felt a rip in my side, felt the warmth of blood, didn't even consider slowing.

Fred tossed the rest of his six-pack in the air. While he put on his final burst of suicide speed, I had to duck flying beers. As I regained my balance and slowed, I saw new motion ahead and looked up.

Fred was flying, truly flying, ten yards ahead.

He'd lost his balance, pinwheeled along for a few strides, and taken one last leap. I saw him in full swan-dive position—back arched, arms out, wrists and fingers curled like an orchestra conductor's.

Then he augured five yards straight down to a rock the size of a grand piano.

The sound when he hit was sharp and dull at the same time, like helicopter rotors.

Somebody said, "Oh my God."

Somebody else said, "Nine-one-one. *Nine-one-one!*"

I slowed, came to a clumsy, boot-slapping halt.

I made my way to Fred, holding my bloody side, sucking air.

He was absolutely still.

I rolled him over.

Blood burbled where his right eye had been. His nose was smashed. His forehead was concave.

He was awake. He was aware.

I got an arm around his neck. "It's okay, Fred," I said. "They're calling nine-one-one."

He tried to say something. A tooth blew from his mouth and hung by a flesh-thread.

"Don't try to talk," I said.

But he shook his head. Stubborn. "Payfoo," he said.

Painful? "I bet it is."

More head shaking. *"Payfoo,"* he said, and pantomimed writing something.

Then I understood.

I used my left hand to pull my wallet. Opened it, plucked the slip he'd given me at the intersection that day. The one that said *IOU*.

"Paid in full, Pop." I let him see me crumple the paper and flip it over my shoulder.

My father smiled and closed his eyes and died.

I ignored the little knot of people who told me not to move him. I lifted Fast Freddy Sax, feeling my side rip wide open. Before I began the climb I took a breath, steadied myself. I had a long way to go. Couldn't afford to slip.

I carried my father up the hill.

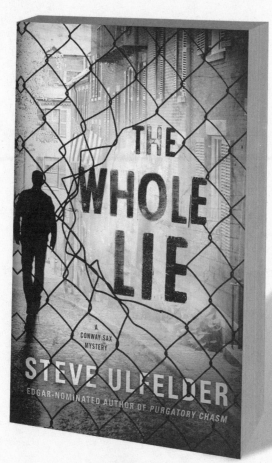